CODE OF SUBMISSION

'Room service? You ordered breakfast for eight o'clock, Mr Dexter.' A dark-skinned young man with short, almost cropped curly black hair was standing in the doorway. He smiled at Nathan, revealing brilliant white teeth.

'Thank you,' said Nathan, indicating that the Moroccan lad should place his tray on the coffee table. As he did so, Nathan noticed the long heavy shadow swinging beneath the white pantaloons of his traditional garb. The lack of underwear revealed everything, and Nathan was intrigued to see that there was an impressive erection growing within the silk folds of the pantaloons.

'Is there anything else, Mr Dexter?' the boy asked politely, but the unspoken question hung in the air.

CODE OF SUBMISSION

Paul C. Alexander

First published in Great Britain in 1998 by
Idol
an imprint of Virgin Publishing Ltd
Thames Wharf Studios,
Rainville Road, London W6 9HT

ISBN 0 352 33272 7

Cover photograph by Colin Clarke Photography

Typeset by SetSystems Ltd, Saffron Walden, Essex
Printed and bound in Great Britain by
Mackays of Chatham PLC

The Terrence Higgins Trust ♡

SAFER SEX GUIDELINES

These books are sexual fantasies – in real life, everyone needs to think about safe sex.

While there have been major advances in the drug treatments for people with HIV and AIDS, there is still no cure for AIDS or a vaccine against HIV. Safe sex is still the only way of being sure of avoiding HIV sexually.

HIV can only be transmitted through blood, come and vaginal fluids (but no other body fluids) passing from one person (with HIV) into another person's bloodstream. It cannot get through healthy, undamaged skin. The only real risk of HIV is through anal sex without a condom – this accounts for almost all HIV transmissions between men.

Being safe
Even if you don't come inside someone, there is still a risk to both partners from blood (tiny cuts in the arse) and pre-come. Using strong condoms and water-based lubricant greatly reduces the risk of HIV. However, condoms can break or slip off, so:

* Make sure that condoms are stored away from hot or damp places.
* Check the expiry date – condoms have a limited life.
* Gently squeeze the air out of the tip.
* Check the condom is put on the right way up and unroll it down the erect cock.
* Use plenty of water-based lubricant (lube), up the arse and on the condom.
* While fucking, check occasionally to see the condom is still in one piece (you could also add more lube).
* When you withdraw, hold the condom tight to your cock as you pull out.

* Never re-use a condom or use the same condom with more than one person.
* If you're not used to condoms you might practise putting them on.
* Sex toys like dildos and plugs are safe. But if you're sharing them use a new condom each time or wash the toys well.

For the safest sex, make sure you use the strongest condoms, such as Durex Ultra Strong, Mates Super Strong, HT Specials and Rubberstuffers packs. Condoms are free in many STD (Sexually Transmitted Disease) clinics (sometimes called GUM clinics) and from many gay bars. It's also essential to use lots of water-based lube such as KY, Wet Stuff, Slik or Liquid Silk. Never use come as a lubricant.

Oral sex
Compared with fucking, sucking someone's cock is far safer. Swallowing come does not necessarily mean that HIV gets absorbed into the bloodstream. While a tiny fraction of cases of HIV infection have been linked to sucking, we know the risk is minimal. But certain factors increase the risk:
* Letting someone come in your mouth
* Throat infections such as gonorrhoea
* If you have cuts, sores or infections in your mouth and throat

So what is safe?
There are so many things you can do which are absolutely safe: wanking each other; rubbing your cocks against one another; kissing, sucking and licking all over the body; rimming – to name but a few.

If you're finding safe sex difficult, call a helpline or speak to someone you feel you can trust for support. The Terrence Higgins Trust Helpline, which is open from noon to 10pm every day, can be reached on 0171 242 1010.

Or, if you're in the United States, you can ring the Center for Disease Control toll free on 1 800 458 5231.

Prologue

James's thick veined cock was almost painfully stiff, his sensitive helmet rubbing against the carpet and sending shivers of base pleasure through him. All he wanted to do was grab it in his hand and pump it until the long-denied release consumed him, wank himself until the forbidden orgasm could take him over. He wanted to see his come shooting over his stomach, mingling with the thick hairs; he wanted to feel the pleasure flooding through him, out of him.

But that was something his master would not allow.

To touch himself, to wank himself, to do anything without his master's specific instructions, would be to invite the severest of punishments: those were the rules that governed him. So he continued to squat there on the carpet in silence, impatiently waiting at his master's feet, the thick leather and metal collar tight around his neck. But the collar wasn't necessary to ensure his obedience: take it off and he would feel the same. The obedience, the loyalty . . . that came from inside.

Trying not to attract his master's attention or displeasure, James glanced round at the full-length mirror on one wall of his master's room, just beside the overloaded bookcase. In the

1

reflection, he was able to see both himself and his master, and that sight alone was almost enough to bring him off.

His master was sitting on the sofa, watching some documentary on the TV and seemingly paying James just the slightest of notice. One hand was holding a cigarette; the other was loosely around the leather strap of James's leash – the leash which was attached to his collar.

James was in his favourite position, the one that he always liked: on his knees in front of his master, a dog-bowl full of beer in front of him. But even drinking from that was forbidden until his master gave him permission. Here, in his master's house, free will was not an option. The only way was obedience.

As he waited for his master to pay him attention, James examined himself in the reflection and, not for the first time, was struck by the curious contradiction this image embodied. James was a large man in his mid-twenties, thick-set and muscular, with heavily tattooed arms, a thickly haired chest, and closely cropped hair – he was well aware that he was an imposing, if not downright frightening, figure; that was part of the reason why he was the unofficial leader of his group of mates down the pub, the 'alpha male', someone had said. James wasn't sure about that – psychology wasn't all that big down the Mile End Road – but he knew that he commanded respect from the others. But his appearance was only part of the reason.

As far as his drinking buddies were concerned, James was as straight as they were: he had a girlfriend, eyed up the birds with the best of them, and liked nothing better than giving a girl a good shagging. Just like them. No, more than them. He was the one they looked up to, the one that had a fucking big cock and knew what to do with it, the one that the others came to for advice, for support.

In many ways, he was their hero – all that they could want in a mate. How would they react if they knew that he spent every Wednesday night in a house in Bayswater, tied up like a

2

dog at his master's feet? What would they say if they found out that he liked to feel another man's cock inside him, and liked to take another man's cock in his mouth and suck it until the come hit the back of his throat, and then swallow it and get off on the hot, salty taste? They'd go ballistic, that was obvious: they'd call him a filthy poof; they'd kick the shit out of him. His status as hero, as leader of their little tribe, would be gone – he'd become nothing ... no, less than nothing. They wouldn't understand how big James Simonson, who had spent much of his youth with his mates, bashing up queers on Hampstead Heath, needed the domination that his master provided, needed someone bigger, better in his life. They wouldn't be able to get their heads around the fact that he needed this release – that it was only that which allowed him to dominate them in turn.

Without his weekly dose of submission to his master, James Simonson would be nothing, just another bloke spending his cash getting pissed down the pub of a weekend. He knew he wasn't queer: he didn't *love* men. He just liked the physical act of being with another man, the feeling of another man. What was wrong with that? It was only the logical next step from the ... the male bonding, that's what they called it, that he and his mates indulged in down the pub, wasn't it?

Besides, he knew that Kenny and Dave often sat and watched porn movies together, especially after a few pints and a few joints; he knew that they sat there, eyes riveted to the writhing bodies on the screen, their cocks held tightly in their hands. Who was to say that they were getting off on the pussy? For all James knew, it was the sight of those big cocks, gushing come, that turned them on. James knew that they somehow managed to come at the same time, and he felt sure that they carefully watched each other as the thick gouts of come shot from the ends of their cocks. Who knew what else they did when James wasn't around? Perhaps their curiosity, their need, got the better of them; perhaps they experimented, sliding their

3

cocks, greased with spit and pre-come, into one another's arse. Perhaps they even liked it, like James did. What was so different between that and what James did with his master every Wednesday night?

James suppressed a sigh. Who was he kidding? He came here because he needed his master, he needed the satisfaction that only another man could give him.

That was the moment when his master looked down at him and smiled, stroking James's broad back and nodding towards the dog-bowl. There was genuine affection in the gesture, but not in a queer way: this was something different, James assured himself, even as the physical contact made his cock twitch with excitement, made his balls tighten. His master had remembered him, remembered that he was sitting there, waiting for instructions, waiting to be told what to do.

'You've been a good boy this evening, James,' his master said softly. 'I think you can have another drink now.'

As James leant forward and put his mouth over the rim of the bowl, sucking up a mouthful of cold beer, he thought back over the previous month, to that time over Christmas when his master had gone missing. For two months James had been without his weekly sessions, and all of his mates had quickly noticed his change in behaviour – it had been almost impossible for him to hide his need. The most important part of him had been taken away, and James just didn't know how to handle it.

At first, it had just been little things: he had become snappier, more bad-tempered, biting his mates' heads off. But as time had gone on, it had got much worse. He had become aggressive, angry, until he didn't know how to calm himself down. He had tried everything he could think of, but it didn't really help: okay, so the physical relief had been easy to arrange. Fucking his girlfriend at night, and hanging around the toilets down Soho at weekends, giving and receiving the odd blow-job. For a time, a short time, that had seemed to help. But then the instant pleasure went away, to be replaced by that longing, that need.

Every time he gave his girlfriend a shag, every time he had someone in the toilets, he knew that it wasn't the same as his time with his master, and, denied his release, he had continued to become more and more moody, more and more angry. He could see that his mates were growing away from him: ironically, as he became more macho, he was really frightening them, as if their own masculinity was nothing more than a clever act, a set of masks that they never took off in public. They appreciated, needed, his strength, but only when it was controllable. When he started to lose that control, that was when they were forced to confront their own insecurities. That was when they started to back off.

When the realisation hit him, he was terrified. Slowly but surely, he was losing control of the group . . . and the worst thing was, even though he knew what the problem was, there was absolutely nothing that he could do about it. Not without his master. He even started to consider getting another master, but something inside him told him that that was disloyal. He only had one master, and if his master didn't want him he didn't deserve another. That was when he had walked away from his friends, walked away from his girlfriend. He had been at breaking point.

When the phone call came, he could hardly believe it. His master had phoned him up. He had been away on business, he explained, and hadn't been able to tell anyone, even his loyal puppy dog. But he was back now, and wanted to know: did James want to continue their regular meetings?

His master's tone had been nonchalant, as if his absence had meant nothing, just another business trip. But to James, hearing his master's voice had been the happiest moment of his life. He had a purpose again; he had a reason!

Even though it hadn't been a Wednesday, James had been at his master's house within the hour, and in the collar, his leash in his master's hands, only minutes later. The sex that followed had been the best sex that James had ever had, feeling his master's cock inside him, grinding away, then his master's mouth around his own dick, sucking him, drinking his come . . .

Now everything was back to normal. His girlfriend had accepted him back, and now thought he was playing pool with his mates. His mates, glad that the old James had returned, thought he was spending an obligatory night in with his girlfriend, but James knew he was with the one man who was closer to him than any woman could be. Not that James loved his master – at least, not like James loved his girlfriend. James loved his master like a dog loves its master: his master commanded total and utter respect. He deserved it, and James didn't want to do anything to let him down. It was more than his life was worth.

Suddenly, with a tightness in his stomach, he realised that he had been clumsy, and had spilt some of the beer: there was a small wet patch on the carpet where it had dribbled from his mouth. Nor did it escape his master's notice – but then nothing ever did.

'Bad boy!' he yelled, and slapped James across his naked arse. It hurt, but James didn't mind the physical pain. He had let his master down, and he was now going to be punished. His erection began to subside as he prepared to face his master's anger. But, deep down, he knew that that was what he wanted. To be punished, to be treated like the piece of shit that he was.

There was a sharp pull on the chain, yanking his head backwards. 'Turn round!' his master bellowed, and James did as he was told, swivelling round on his knees until he was kneeling at his master's feet, his master's cock just inches away from his mouth. He looked up at his master's face, and was terrified to see the anger in his eyes, the blond, bearded face regarding James with disdain – no, with contempt. Seeing that look, knowing how worthless he was . . . he felt his erection starting to rise once again.

'You've been a very, very bad dog, haven't you, boy?' his master snapped, standing up. As he did so, he yanked the leash again, pulling James's face into his groin, tantalising him with the musky smell of man and fresh sweat, before letting the leash go slack and pushing him away.

James looked up at him and considered the man who, for the duration of these sessions, was the most important person in his life: his master. No, who was he kidding? His master was the most important man in his life.

His master was dressed as he always dressed for their sessions: nothing but a full body harness over his well-muscled body, leather straps across the smooth solid chest, highlighting the two tit-rings. Another leather strap went down to his groin, ending in a metal cock ring which surrounded a thick, eight-inch cock and big balls. James longed to take each of those balls in his mouth and play with them, before releasing them and sliding his lips over the glistening helmet and veined shaft of his master's dick. But that was not something he could do without permission, and he knew that that wouldn't be granted: he had misbehaved, and now he had to be punished. Perhaps when he had been suitably punished, sex would follow. But not always. It depended on whether his master forgave him or not.

'Your master isn't at all happy with you. And you know what happens when you've been a bad boy, don't you?' His master's voice was low, threatening.

James nodded, knowing that he was not allowed to speak. Unless permitted, the only sounds he was ever allowed to make during his Wednesday nights were growls, just like the dog his master treated him as.

'You worthless piece of shit!' His master slapped him hard around the face, once, then again, leaving James's cheek stinging. But he couldn't touch it, couldn't rub it: he just had to wait for the pain to go away.

'I don't know why I put up with you – perhaps I should get

rid of you and get a new dog.' His master gave an evil smile. 'There are plenty of other people who would love to be my little dog, my little puppy, my little slave, you know.'

What? James hoped that his eyes and face reflected his fear. To be abandoned by his master? Thrown out like . . . well, like a dog? James didn't know whether he would be able to cope with that. Not again. He depended on his Wednesday nights, depended on the release that they provided him with. Without his master, James would be nothing. Less than nothing.

He tried to express his feelings in his face, hoping and praying that his master didn't mean it, was just trying to frighten him. At the same time, he felt his erection begin to stir even more. The knowledge that he depended on his master was the ultimate excitement for James; the knowledge that big, rough James Simonson, cropped, tattooed thug, needed another man to tell him what to do was almost overwhelming. His cock was almost bursting for release, and he prayed that it would come soon.

Suddenly, his master's face softened, and James hoped that his master was going to take pity on him. 'Perhaps I've been a bit harsh to my dog,' he said softly, stroking James's cropped head, then his cheeks, gently running his fingers over the sore redness that his slaps had caused. 'I know that my dog means well, but he can be a bad boy at times, can't he?'

James nodded, and let out a low growl. He'd been a bad dog, and bad dogs needed to be disciplined. Bad dogs needed to be taught who was the master.

'All right, I'll forgive you. If you're a good puppy and suck Daddy's cock.' Another sharp tug on the chain. 'A good suck, though, dog: Daddy wants his puppy to drink every last drop of his come.'

Daddy? That was the term that his master used when he was feeling especially affectionate towards James, and James smiled: he hadn't expected that. He'd expected more punishment, more abuse, followed by his master fucking the arse off him, ignoring his cries of pain as he forced his cock into James's tight arse. James hadn't expected his master to allow him to suck him off, to drink his come.

Just as James leant forward, his master grabbed him by the throat and forced James's face in his groin. 'But if I don't enjoy this, boy, this will be your last time here. Do you understand?'

James swallowed hard. It was a test. A test of how good he was, whether he was good enough to be his master's . . . no, his *daddy's* best dog. And James wasn't about to let his master, his daddy, down.

Edging slightly forward on his knees, James ran his tongue over his master's balls, savouring the man-smell that assaulted his nose, the smell of sweat and piss that he couldn't get enough of. Then he took the left ball in his mouth and sucked it hard, squeezing it, licking it, in the way that he knew his master liked. He got the desired reaction: his master gasped in pleasure, and that made James happy. If his master was happy, James was happy. His hard-on became even stiffer, threatening to burst of its own accord, but James knew that that couldn't happen.

He moved on to the next ball and sucked it, while his hands caressed his master's firm thighs and their covering of short blond hair. What he really wanted to do was take his master's cock, but he knew that his master would be angry if he hurried: he loved having his balls sucked, and James would do anything to please his master.

As he massaged each ball in his mouth, running his tongue over the hair-covered sacs, he tried to ignore his own cock and balls, which were stiffer than he could remember, the cock ring that constrained them making them more sensitive than ever. The cock ring had been his idea: he had never worn one before, and had asked his master if he could have one of his own, just to see what it felt like. His master had punished him for being so forward, but, at the next session, had provided James with one. Now James wore it every time he saw his master, and he loved the way it made his cock really, really sensitive, making every touch of it almost unbearable. He also liked the way it made it bigger: although James's dick was a proud eight inches, the blood that the cock ring forced into it made it thicker, redder, made the veins stand out more. Just like his master's.

Leaving his master's balls, he ran his tongue up the thick shaft until he reached the helmet. His master's helmet was already wet with pre-come, and James drank it greedily, his tongue probing the leaking dick-slit in search of more. Then he sank on to it, taking first the helmet, then the shaft into his mouth. He forced as much of it in as he could before pulling back until only the helmet was covered; then he slid his mouth all the way along once more. The way that his master was gasping, he could tell that he was doing a good job. He was being a good boy.

Before he could continue, his master pushed him away with both hands on his shoulders. James looked up expectantly, not quite sure what he was supposed to do next.

'That was very good. You're being a good boy for your daddy, aren't you?'

James nodded mutely. He had pleased his master!

'Now Daddy wants you to be an even better boy. Turn round.'

James knew what was coming next. Part of him was frightened, but part of him wanted it desperately. Not just wanted, but needed. Without saying a word, he turned round so that his back — and, more importantly, his arse — was facing his master, his hands supporting him so that he was crouched on the floor. Like a dog. Like the dog that he was.

Glancing into the mirror, James could see his master ripping open a packet of condoms, before rolling the latex over his stiff red cock. James watched as his master squirted lubricant over his dick, and then smeared it around his arsehole and up his arse.

'Now you're going to make Daddy very happy, aren't you?'

James nodded, nodded like the dog that he knew he was,

and waited to feel his master enter him. It wasn't a long wait: seconds later, he felt the familiar pain as his master forced his dick into his ring. But that pain, that humiliation of being penetrated, was all part of what James truly enjoyed. His master's hands were pressing down on his shoulders, ensuring his obedience, ensuring his submission; James gasped as his master's fingers squeezed into his flesh as his cock was squeezed into James's arse. Just as the pain almost became too much for James, it stopped, replaced by the warm feeling of completeness: his master was inside him, the helmet of his cock just stroking that spot inside his arse that made him feel so good.

His master massaged his shoulders. 'Good boy. Just the way I like it. My cock, right inside that tight straight arsehole of yours. It's how you like it as well, isn't it, boy?'

James nodded mutely, afraid to open his mouth in case he cried out, either in pleasure or in pain – he didn't know which. Then he felt his master partially withdraw his cock, felt the thick hardness pulling itself out of his arse, before slamming it back inside him without caring whether it hurt or not. But why should he care? James was his.

His master's balls slapped into his arse as his master's cock entered him fully once again, the hairy sac hitting against his cheeks as his master built up his rhythm, sliding his cock in and out of James's eager ring, the helmet touching that spot, making James gasp.

James found himself pushing backwards, urging his master to enter him, forcing him to take James like the slave he was. As he took more of his master, he was desperate to grab his own cock, to relieve the pressure that was building up there, but that was impossible: he was dependent upon his master for any pleasure he would experience, dependent on the sensations that were forming inside his arse as his master's cock battered at his prostate, pushing him closer and closer.

Suddenly he felt his master's hands moving from his shoulders; seconds later, he felt the sharp pressure of fingers reaching through his thick chest hair and squeezing both of his nipples tightly, squeezing and tugging at them. But oddly, the pain didn't hurt: if anything, it made him more excited, sent even more blood to his already swollen dick. James knew that he was very close to coming, whether he touched his cock or not. And his master's heavy panting and hot breath on the back of his neck meant that he was very close as well.

Just as he thought he would shoot regardless, James felt his master's hand slide down his furred chest, down his muscled stomach, and then grasp his cock firmly. Unable to hold out any more, he tumbled over the edge and started to come, distantly hearing his master groan with pleasure. Then he felt his master's cock throb inside him, depositing his come inside James's arse, the final pressure on his prostate. It was James's turn: as he let out a deep yell, thick white spunk shot from his dick, landing heavily on the carpet in front of him. Exhausted, he bowed his head and knelt in silence. Soon he would know whether his master considered his performance to be satisfactory or not.

'Good boy,' said his master quietly. But there was something in the tone of his voice, something which suggested that his mind was far away from the flat in Bayswater, far away from their Wednesday-night sessions. His next words – words which made James's stomach tighten – confirmed it.

'I'm afraid we're going to have to call it a night, James.'

James was so taken aback that he actually turned round and faced his master; under other circumstances that would have brought him some severe discipline. But not this time. James's master even looked preoccupied – he wasn't even looking at him. It was early – only nine o'clock. Normally, James wouldn't have left till midnight at least. What was going on? Something told James that he didn't want to know the answer.

As James rapidly undid the collar and put on his sweatshirt and jeans, he knew that his master's business was nothing to do with him. That was part of the arrangement: their other lives – James hesitated to call them real lives, since his evenings in Bayswater were real to him, far more real than a night in front of the TV with his girlfriend – their other lives were kept firmly outside of the flat. But he couldn't help himself.

'Is . . . is everything all right?' he asked.

His master looked at him and smiled softly. 'Actually, no. I'm afraid I'm going to have to leave the country for a while.'

James felt his stomach knot. His suspicions had been correct. Not again, he thought with dread. I don't think I could face being without him again.

His master must have read his expression. He stepped over to him and placed a hand on his shoulder. 'It won't be like last time, James. I'd like you to come with me. In fact –' He walked over to the desk that stood against the wall and pulled out a package from one of the drawers. He handed the package to James.

'In fact, I'd rather been counting on it.'

James opened the padded envelope and extracted two small folders.

Plane tickets. Unable to understand what he was looking at, he read the names on the tickets – tickets for Gran Canaria, flying out the following week.

'James Simonson,' he muttered under his breath. He looked up. 'This ticket's for me?' he asked.

His master, pulling on a white towelling dressing gown, smiled. 'Of course. I want you to come with me.' Before James could protest, he held up his hand. 'I realise that you have things to sort out, but that won't be a problem. Your boss at the factory owes me one, so I've arranged the time off. And I'm sure you can persuade that girlfriend of yours why it's so important for you to be away for a while, can't you?'

Even as he nodded mutely, James's thoughts were whirling. From a Wednesday night's distraction from his mates and girlfriend, it had turned into something unbelievable. As he pulled on his jacket, he handed the tickets back to his master, his eyes idly glancing over the name on the other ticket.

His master's real name, the name that James would never dare use.

Adrian Delancey.

For James Simonson, it was the beginning of something that he would live to regret.

If he was lucky.

One

_____

Morning hit Nathan Dexter like a bucket of cold water, the brilliant sunshine bursting through the window and making him blink in confusion as he was forced to wake up. But what sunshine? What window? He knew one thing was for sure: it wasn't the weak sunshine of a February England; nor was it the window of his bedroom in his Docklands house. Definitely not.

For a moment he was confused. Then it came to him, blearily, barely breaking through the hangover that saturated his brain: the sunshine and the warmth were typical . . . if you were in Marrakesh. But what was he doing in Morocco? He tried to remember, but his thoughts were hazy and confused – proof that he must have had a very good evening the night before. With more than a little difficulty, he pulled himself upright in the soft, comfortable bed – too soft, too comfortable – and looked around, trying to work out why he wasn't where he should have been.

The room was lavishly furnished; indeed, it was more of a suite than a room, with a raised area for the enormous bed, a large lounge with sofa, chairs and coffee table, and an ornate

15

archway which Nathan vaguely remembered led into the bathroom. The style of decoration was faintly Arabic in nature, with crenellated marble walls and an exotically patterned marble floor, leading to a set of glass patio doors which opened onto a vista of palm trees and distant, snow-capped mountains. All in all, Nathan appeared to be in the lap of luxury. But why Morocco?

Then Nathan remembered why he was in Marrakesh.

He was on Elective business.

He still found it difficult to take it all in: having spent most of the previous year attempting to uncover the truth behind the Elective, the faceless organisation of gay people which wielded tremendous power across the entire world, his life had inadvertently but inevitably collided with that of the shadowy figure in charge of the British branch of the Elective: Adrian Delancey, the Comptroller.

The common link between the two of them had been Scott James, Nathan's new boyfriend. Unbeknown to Nathan, Scott had had a weekly sexual appointment with Delancey, and the Comptroller had exploited that in an attempt to destroy Nathan and prevent his investigation.

Delancey might have succeeded: indeed, with the power of the Elective behind him − power that included some of the richest and most powerful people on the planet − how could he have failed? But Delancey hadn't reckoned with his own deputy, Marco Cappiello, who had reasons of his own for bringing Delancey down. Together, Nathan and Marco had managed to smash the Comptroller's twisted scheme to kidnap leathermen from the gay scene and sell them into slavery. The cost had been high for all of them: Nathan had nearly lost Scott for ever, he had almost been killed, but they had finally won the day. The slaves were free, and Delancey had lost his control over the Elective.

However, that hadn't been the end of the matter. The ultimate power behind the Elective, the shadowy Director, had appointed Marco the new British Comptroller, while Nathan had been made his deputy. Together, they had been charged with clearing the Elective of the corruption that Adrian Delancey had infected it with. Delancey may have been gone, but his handiwork – and possibly his allies – still remained, hidden away in the dark corners of the Elective. And, since the Elective covered the entire world, there were quite a few of those corners to be found.

That had been December: two months ago, although it seemed like only yesterday. There had been so much to do: the January which followed had been hectic, as Marco and Nathan sat down and examined the entire structure of the Elective in detail, trying to work out where they should go. After a month of paperwork, the answer was clear: despite Delancey's fall from grace, there were definitely parts of the Elective which needed to be investigated. And that investigation would fall to Nathan and Marco. Although the Director suspected he knew all of the areas that Delancey's dark touch had corrupted, he couldn't be certain: that was why he needed Nathan's skills as an investigative reporter to assist Marco.

Not that the two of them were alone in their mission: Nathan's boyfriend, Scott, and Marco's boyfriend, Leigh, were also part of it. To say that the Elective was a hierarchical organisation was an understatement. Titles meant everything, so Scott and Leigh had been appointed Adjutants of the Elective: an archaic term, but one which offered them, like Nathan and Marco, access to the Comptroller's dark secrets, the cancer that he had introduced into an organisation that had been set up to help gay people across the world – not to enslave them.

And that was why Nathan was in Morocco: his researches suggested that the Moroccan branch of the Elective had been tainted by its erstwhile British Comptroller. Meanwhile, Marco and Leigh were in Las Vegas, at the request of Greg, the local Comptroller. That left Scott to kick his heels in London:

Nathan felt rotten about leaving him back in the house in Docklands, but he was still a student, and in his final year. Despite the excitement offered by the Elective, they both agreed that he should finish his degree. Of course, that all sounded very noble, but it didn't help much when Marco, Leigh and Nathan were off on their travels, and Scott was having to put up with the English weather. Still, there would be enough time – and money – for travelling once this situation had been resolved.

To be honest, though, there was another reason why Nathan wanted Scott to stay in Britain: a personal reason. Adrian Delancey's punishment for his crimes had been to become the very last victim of the slavery ring which he himself had created, a penalty which had resulted in being sent to Morocco himself as the unwilling slave of two strict leathermen. Although it was very unlikely that Nathan would see Delancey – his incarceration wasn't in Marrakesh but in Tangiers – part of him hoped that he would: that bastard had tried to manipulate him through the most hurtful route possible. Delancey had tried to deter Nathan from his investigations into the Elective by using Scott, and as far as Nathan was concerned that was a crime beyond imagining. Nathan detested Delancey with a red-hot hatred that almost consumed him, and the thought of punching that bastard in the face was quite a tempting one. And if that eventuality occurred, he wanted Scott to be as far away as possible.

But that was the past, he reminded himself, as he tried to acclimatise himself to the decidedly non-February warmth of Morocco and drag himself out of bed. He and Scott had come to terms with what had happened: indeed, it had strengthened their feelings for each other. True, it had changed the parameters of their relationship, but now it offered them exactly what they wanted: both were free to enjoy themselves with other people, but both knew that there was the solid core of their love for one another to return to. Scott and Nathan lived for

18

the present and the future, both too aware of how fragile it could be, but also aware of how much they loved one another.

Yawning, Nathan finally found the energy to drag himself out of the comfortable soft bed – still too comfortable, still too soft – and walked over to the window, catching sight of himself in the dressing-table mirror as he did so. At thirty-three, he was still in reasonable shape, although the good living that his new position in the Elective had brought him meant that he was beginning to develop a bit of a stomach. Although he had moaned about it, and had vocally decided that he would have to take advantage of one of the Elective's chain of exclusive gyms when he finally got back to the UK, Scott had admitted, just before Nathan had flown out, that he found Nathan cuddly. Nathan had thrown a bit of a strop at what he had considered a back-handed compliment, but he still smiled at the memory.

Standing in front of the huge mirror, he stretched and, with a touch of vanity, admired himself. He was about five feet ten, with cropped hair, a goatee beard, and an impressively hairy chest. He liked to think that he was still quite good-looking; that was what Scott said to him, and that was the opinion that counted. Who was he to disagree with his boyfriend?

There was a sudden knock on the door, and Nathan grabbed the black towelling bath-robe from the sofa, where it had been thrown the night before. He couldn't remember whether it had been he who had thrown it or one of his guests. He had the vaguest of recollections that it had been quite a night. Pulling himself into the dressing gown, he hauled himself over to the door and opened it slightly.

'Room service? You ordered breakfast for eight o'clock, Mr Dexter.' A short, dark-skinned young man with short, almost cropped curly black hair was standing in the doorway, a tray laden with food held out in front of him. He smiled at Nathan, revealing brilliant white teeth.

'Come in,' said Nathan, ushering the boy into the room.

Nathan estimated that he was in his late teens, a few years younger than Scott. But unlike Scott, with his broad shoulders and muscular chest, the Moroccan was slim and boyish, his body dressed in traditional Moroccan garb: a white silk shirt, white silk trousers, and an embroidered red and gold waistcoat.

'Thank you,' said Nathan, indicating that the boy should place the tray on the low table in front of the sofa. As the boy did so, Nathan noticed the long heavy shadow swinging beneath the white pantaloons. The lack of underwear revealed everything . . . and Nathan was intrigued to see that there was an impressive erection growing within the silk folds of the pantaloons: Nathan guessed that the boy was definitely well-endowed. Even with his hangover, the glimpse of that cock made Nathan desperate to see more, to do more.

'Is there anything else, Mr Dexter?' the boy asked politely, but the unspoken question hung in the air.

Nathan couldn't help smiling. The boy may not have been his type, but the thought of seeing that dick, of sucking that dick, was difficult to resist. He could feel his own erection beginning to grow beneath the towelling of his dressing gown, and knew that the boy would be unable to help seeing it pressing at the fabric. Indeed, the boy looked down at the intruder and grinned.

Without a word, the boy pushed the door shut, and came over to Nathan. Reaching out, he pulled the belt, undoing the knot and allowing the robe to fall open. Nathan's dick was hard now, eight inches of thick, uncut prick, standing almost vertical against the thick hairs of his stomach.

The boy fell to his knees and looked up at Nathan with an expression of longing. Nathan knew that this was all part of the service, but it didn't matter. Suddenly, he was as randy as hell, and wanted nothing more than the young Moroccan's mouth around his cock.

Leaning forward, the boy started to lick the sensitive skin between Nathan's legs. Nathan gasped at the sensation as the boy's tongue passed up and along the sides of his balls, licking the covering of black hairs. Reaching his balls, the boy took one in his mouth and sucked it, exerting firm yet wonderful pressure. At the same time, Nathan placed his hands on the boy's shoulders and gently pulled off his tunic, throwing it onto the sofa.

The boy went from one ball to the other and back again; as he did so, Nathan could see that his earlier suspicions about the boy's cock were confirmed: the boy was crouching, which caused the fly of his pantaloons to gape open. This showed off his cock in all of its dusky glory: it must have been at least eight or nine inches long, although it wasn't particularly thick, apart from the circumcised helmet, a large, dark-red mushroom that glistened in the morning light.

Nathan's attention sprang back to his own dick as he felt the boy's tongue sliding up his shaft with darting movements. Seconds later, his length was engulfed by the warmth of the boy's mouth, as he swallowed as much of Nathan as he could. Nathan could feel his helmet tickling the back of the boy's throat before the boy pulled back so his lips were caressing the sensitive ring around his helmet, while his tongue was flicking Nathan's dick-slit.

Nathan felt his breathing quicken. Normally, he wouldn't come this soon, but the almost unreal environment of the hotel room and the view of the Morocco, coupled with the very different sexual partner who was on his knees in front of him, gave it all the semblance of a fantasy, a wet dream. But Nathan didn't want it to end yet: he still had some time to kill before his meeting, and this was exactly the way that he wanted to spend it. Gently, he urged the boy away and then pulled him to his feet.

With urgent fingers, he undid the three buttons that fastened the white shirt and pulled it off. The boy's body was lithe, with a nicely defined chest and stomach. A thin line of downy black hair travelled from his navel to his chest, where it grew into a soft covering over his nipples. As Nathan admired him, he undid the single button that held up the boy's pantaloons and let them fall to the floor, revealing his first clear view of the boy's cock.

Nathan had been right about the length and girth; what he hadn't seen were the two heavy balls, the sac almost invisible in a forest of dense black hair. Without hesitating, Nathan fell to his knees and returned the favour.

The balls smelt wonderful: that heady mixture of sweat and natural musk that always turned Nathan on. But there was another smell, almost indefinable: an exotic aroma of spices that amplified the unusual circumstances and made Nathan even more desperate. Nathan muzzled his face in the balls for a moment, drinking in their smell, before succumbing to temptation and taking as much of the boy's impressive dick into his mouth. For a second, he was afraid that he would choke: then he got used to the length and began to slide it in and out of his mouth, his tongue licking the helmet that was already wet with pre-come. As he did so, his fingers probed the hot furry crack of the boy's arse, seeking out his ring.

Finding his target, Nathan slid his finger inside, pleased to encounter little resistance. He pushed his finger in as far as he could, and then began to feel for the spot that would have the boy shooting down his throat. He found the tiny nut of his prostate and began to stroke it rhythmically: the results were immediate. The boy began to groan loudly, and he started to grind his thighs into Nathan's face, almost choking Nathan once more. Just as the boy began to tremble with pleasure, Nathan took his mouth away from his cock and wanked it, fast hard strokes that elicited another yell. Suddenly the boy came, and thick droplets of come sprayed all over Nathan: his face, the hair on his chest, his legs . . .

Drained, the boy slumped back and rested against the dresser. But only for a second: the boy knew that it would be bad manners to leave an unsatisfied guest, and this *was* all part of the service. Pulling Nathan to his feet, he resumed his exploration of Nathan's cock, his tongue sliding around Nathan's helmet and teasing it with gentle flicks, each one making Nathan gasp with the sensation. Nathan knew that he wasn't far off: as the boy stroked his thighs with one gentle yet firm hand, the other hand was rubbing his stomach and chest, the fingers entwining in the thick black hair.

Nathan couldn't hold out any longer: with a loud grunt of triumph, he shot his load into the boy's mouth, groaning with pleasure as he came. The boy swallowed every drop, his lips squeezing all they could from him until Nathan's cock was too sensitive for him to continue. Nathan pulled his still stiff dick from the boy's mouth and stepped backwards shakily. He smiled.

'That was brilliant,' he gasped. 'Thank you.'

The body nodded coyly. 'You are an honoured guest, Mr Dexter. If you ever need any more . . . favours from Kalil, simply ask room service.'

Sex on tap? I could get used to being on Elective business, Nathan thought with a smile. Then he remembered: business! He glanced at his watch, a foot away on the dresser, and realised that he was now in danger of being late. Reaching into his crumpled jeans – a further casualty of last night's revelry, he guessed – Nathan pulled out a hundred-franc note and pressed it into the grateful boy's hand.

As the boy left, Nathan headed off to the shower. It wouldn't do to be late for this meeting. Not given the circumstances.

Mike hurried along Poland Street, well aware that his shift behind the bar started at 7 p.m., and it was already 6.55 p.m. He'd only just got the job: the last thing he wanted to do was lose it. Not when he was getting so close.

Pushing open the wood-panelled door, he virtually fell into the bar. As he knew only too well, the Brave Trader was always busy at this time: although it was in the heart of Soho, the pub was more like a local than the other gay bars in the area, with people dropping in on their way home from work to meet up with their friends, rather than just on the lookout for a casual shag . . . although Mike knew that that was never far from many of the regulars' minds. There was a sense of community, a sense of belonging, that was tangible in the atmosphere of the Brave Trader. People knew one another, they looked after one another. And, most importantly to Mike, people trusted one another with their closest secrets – especially after a few drinks.

That community spirit was what drew people here, and that was why the pub was inevitably packed, whether it be straight after work or later in the evening. At this time, the majority of customers were in suits, having just finished work; in another two hours, it would start filling with clones and bears, all drinking side by side. But that was not to say that the Brave Trader was one communal love-in; far from it – even in the short period of time that Mike had been working there, he himself had been witness to two fights, one never-to-be-healed rift between former friends, and one near-glassing. In short, it was a microcosm of real life, almost like a television soap opera.

Mike smiled to himself at that description: perhaps he could do that one day, and write all the gossip and intrigue up as a book, a novel along the lines of Armistead Maupin's classic *Tales of the City* books. *Tales from the Brave Trader*, now there's a thought . . .

As he stood in the open doorway, trying to work out the best route to the back of the bar, Mike recognised quite a few of the after-work crowd: Peter and Sean, one of the nicest couples he had ever known; Simon and his latest boyfriend – he seemed to have a new one every five minutes, it seemed; Australian Michael; Paul and his friend Neil . . . But this wasn't the time for sightseeing or identifying familiar faces: he could do that when he was on the other side of the bar, being paid to look around. Glancing at the old-fashioned clock next to the bar, he saw that he was almost late, and he knew that Steve the landlord didn't like that. The Brave Trader had a reputation for friendliness and efficiency — it had to, or else the machinations and intrigue wouldn't have a stable base on which to operate — and late bar staff always threw a spanner in the works. Then again, pushing through the crowd wasn't that difficult for Mike — people tended to get out of your way when you were six foot five — but he still reached the Royal Enclosure with only moments to spare.

The Royal Enclosure was a small area between the bar and the kitchen, given its name due to the fact that only the time-honoured regulars of the Brave Trader of Queensland were tolerated there. Other people might accidentally stand there, unaware of the traditions that pervaded the Brave Trader, but the combined looks of the Royal Enclosure would inevitably be sufficient to make them move away. Little John, Suspenders Alex, Morgy, JT, Trolley John . . . the core of the Royal Enclosure was already there, large G&Ts, Fosters and glasses of Merlot already stacking up. The Brave Trader's unofficial royal court: a group of people who could make or break anyone in the pub. If that image was true — the Royal Enclosure as courtiers — it was time for Mike to make his apologies to the royal family itself.

Mike said his brief helloes to the Royal Enclosure and, ignoring the slew of friendly insults that were fired after him, walked into the kitchen to hang up his leather jacket and grab his key for the tills.

'Sorry I'm a bit late,' he muttered.

Steve and his assistant manager, Kevin, were bent over the office computer at the far end of the kitchen, clearly checking the tills. Mike knew that their new electronic till system was giving them more than a few headaches, and that it would have been a matter of a few moments' work for him to have sorted them out. But to do that would have been to blow his cover, and it was too soon to do that. Far too soon.

'Cutting it a bit fine, aren't you?' said Kevin in his Irish brogue. Kevin was quite short, with cropped black hair and a cropped black beard. And you didn't want to get on the wrong side of him: that was a lesson that Mike had learnt very early on. He was a nice bloke, but he didn't take any shit. The King's vizier, so to speak.

'Knock it off, Kev,' Steve chastised. 'He's only been here a week.' Mike smiled at this show of support as he hung his coat behind the office door.

If Kevin was the trusted adviser, Steve, the landlord of the Brave Trader of Queensland, was undoubtedly the king himself. He was about five foot eleven and slightly overweight, without being fat, with short dark hair, shot through with premature grey, and a short goatee beard. He was in his mid-thirties, and had stepped in to take over the Brave Trader after the previous landlord, Nigel, had taken another job up north. But here was another of the great mysteries of the Brave Trader: why had he gone up north? No one seemed to be absolutely certain, but there were enough rumours flying around, ranging from the absurd to the ridiculous. Did it have something to do with his brother? Questions, questions, questions – Mike just hoped that he would soon get some answers.

His reverie was interrupted by Kevin's lilting tones. 'Go on, then: key's hanging up; Ivy and Vera are on with you tonight,' he explained, before returning his attention to the computer. 'Have fun.'

As Mike attached the till key to his belt and walked out of the kitchen into the hurly-burly of the bar, he wondered, not for the first time, why he was working in a pub, even one as much fun as the Brave Trader. Surely there were easier ways of accomplishing what he had to do? It wasn't as if he needed the money: he had a regular job in computers that gave him more than enough money to lead a comfortable lifestyle. Then Mike thought about his brother, and what had happened to him, and knew why he was working at the Brave Trader.

He needed to know the truth. And the Brave Trader was as good a place as any for Mike to start.

Making his way through the Royal Enclosure and stepping behind the bar, he smiled at Ivy and Vera – Ian and Paul – and then noticed that Australian Michael was waiting to be served. Stepping over to him, Mike grinned. Time to forget Mike the computer whiz – time to become Mike the barman.

'Evening, Michael,' he said to the man who many people in the pub treated as a father-confessor. 'The usual?' Even as he served him, Mike's mind was racing: perhaps Michael knew the answer? He looked up from pouring the pint and scanned the faces in the crowd, some familiar, some not. Somewhere, somewhere in the Brave Trader, was the answer, the truth about his brother. And Mike would learn that truth – whatever it cost.

Two

Mike wiped the sweat off his forehead and glanced at the clock mounted on the pillar that separated the Royal Enclosure from the rest of the bar. Only a couple of minutes and the shift would be over. Then there would be about half an hour clearing up before he could go home, snatch a few hours' sleep, and then start his day job. He sighed: if he didn't get a lead on his brother soon, he would have to give up the bar job or risk losing his full-time career due to an inability to keep his eyes open at his desk.

'Can I have a pint of Fosters, please?' Mike looked up and saw a small man with glasses squashed up against the bar. He was about five seven or five eight, with short dark spiky hair and a well-kept moustache. Behind his steel-framed glasses, his eyes were blue and friendly. Mike hadn't served him before, and guessed that he had just come into the pub. But there was something about him that simply captivated Mike.

Mike grinned, and was pleased to get an equally warm grin in return. As he pulled the pint, he glanced at the man and realised that he was staring at him. Being so tired, it took Mike a couple of moments to realise that the man was actually interested in him.

'That'll be £2.19, please.' The man counted out the money and pressed it into Mike's hand, his fingers momentarily stroking his palm. Mike felt a shiver run through him, and grinned at the man, who he reckoned must be in his late twenties. But before he could say anything, Ivy rang the bell to indicate time; by the time Mike returned his attention to the bar, the man had vanished.

Oh well, he thought, you're not here to enjoy yourself, Mike: you've got a job to do. But he still tried to locate the man through the throng as he started to collect glasses. Sadly, he was nowhere to be seen. Clearly Mike really wasn't meant to enjoy himself.

By half past eleven, the pub was clear; the glasses had been washed and put away, the bar and tables had been cleaned and the rubbish had been put on the pavement. Another night at the Brave Trader was over, the Royal Enclosure was empty, and Mike was no closer to solving the mystery of his brother than he had been before starting the job. Perhaps he was wrong; perhaps the answer didn't lie in the Brave Trader; perhaps it was time to look elsewhere, like the Harness in Vauxhall, or the Courtyard over in East London.

Finally, finished, he said his goodnights to the other bar staff, grabbed his coat from the kitchen and walked out of the pub, shivering in the cold February night as he walked down Poland Street. As he passed the Korean restaurant at the top of the road, he glanced at his reflection: six feet five, good, solid build, gingery brown flat top, good-looking . . . how could that bloke not have been interested, he asked himself in amusement. Face it, Mike – tonight just wasn't your night.

'Excuse me?'

The voice was quiet, but in the silence of the winter evening Mike almost jumped out of his skin. He turned round and was very surprised – and very pleased – to see the man he had served earlier.

'Sorry, didn't mean to make you jump.' He smiled nervously. 'I was just wondering . . . do you fancy a coffee?'

Mike regained his composure. There was something really cute about this bloke, and, despite his tiredness, Mike suddenly felt very randy. And why not? Nothing was going to bring his brother back, and he was in very real danger of forgetting about real life altogether.

'I'd like that.' He just hoped that the man had a place of his own, preferably near by; Mike was currently lodging in a room in Forest Gate, and he knew from bitter experience that it might as well have been the back of beyond as far as most people were concerned.

His prayers were answered immediately. 'I only live a few minutes' walk away in Cambridge Circus. Is that okay?' And then, almost as an afterthought, he held out his hand. 'I'm Jason, by the way.'

The man's shyness really turned Mike on: he just wanted to cuddle him and reassure him. To begin with. He squeezed Jason's hand. 'Mike,' he replied. 'Mike . . . Mike Johns.' As much as he liked Jason, he had no intention of breaking his cover just yet. 'Shall we go?' he asked, guessing that Jason needed a bit of direction. With that the two of them started walking through the Soho night towards Cambridge Circus.

One of the first things that Mike had noticed after moving to London was that Soho was a creature of the night: during the day it was busy, with media types running around showing off their own self-importance, but only when it got dark did it really come alive, the buildings and streets taking on a reality all their own. Even this close to midnight, the narrow pavements were full of people spilling out of the pubs and bars, while the air was thick with the smells from the countless restaurants and music from the jazz clubs. There was something unreal about Soho: almost as if it existed outside of the normal rules of behaviour. Which was why Mike loved it.

As he and Jason strolled down Old Compton Street, they chatted idly about nothing in particular. Mike explained that he was working in the Brave Trader to earn a bit more money – a lie, but he wasn't going to spill everything to a complete stranger, however cute, was he? – while Jason told him that he was an accountant. He had recently split up with his boyfriend after about five years, and that was why he was a bit nervous: the London gay scene was a bit of a mystery to him. The more that Mike got to know the man, the more attracted he became to him.

You can't let anything distract you, came the chastising voice. *You can't let anything get in the way*. But Mike ignored it. His investigation into his brother's disappearance had virtually taken over his life, but that didn't mean that he had to sacrifice everything, did it? For as long as he could remember, he had always lived in his brother's shadow, always looking out for him, always getting him out of trouble. Okay, so it was a bit late for that now, but even his brother wouldn't have blamed him for having a bit of downtime. *Especially* his brother, he thought fondly.

They crossed Charing Cross Road and headed down Earlham Street, a tiny little road leading to Seven Dials, best known for its street market. Jason opened a heavy yellow door and ushered Mike inside.

Jason's flat was a couple of flights up, and Mike was annoyed to find that he was out of breath when he reached Jason's front door. Jason grinned nervously: he was panting as well. Mike hoped that they'd both get their strength back before too long.

The flat was small and quite minimalist: Jason explained that he had basically had to start again from scratch when he and his boyfriend had split up, and it certainly looked that way. The double bed took up virtually all of the available space in the small living area; the remaining floor space was covered with a ramshackle hi-fi – one of those systems made up by mixing and matching different units – and a large brown teddy bear. Minimalist but homely – just like its occupant, thought Mike.

At Jason's invitation, Mike sat down on the bed. Moments later, Jason sat next to him, handing him a can of beer.

'Are you okay?' asked Mike.

Jason shrugged. 'I'm a bit nervous. It's been a long time since I did this.'

Unless he took the initiative, they'd still be sitting there when dawn came. Mike gave Jason a reassuring smile, took Jason's can from his hand and placed both drinks on the floor. Then he leant closer to Jason, removed his glasses and kissed him on the lips. For a couple of seconds, there was resistance, but it didn't take long for Jason to respond: he placed his arm around Mike's shoulders and hugged him towards him tightly, while his tongue entwined with Mike's.

Mike placed his hand on Jason's thigh and began to stroke it, his hand moving further and further up Jason's leg. His other hand massaged Jason's shoulders, forcing the stress from them. Finally he pulled away slightly.

'How was that?'

Jason grinned. 'I think it's all coming back to me now,' he said, before reaching out and undoing the buttons of Mike's blue denim shirt. It didn't take him long to undo them all; in one swift movement, he pulled the shirt off, revealing Mike's solid body, a light dusting of reddy-brown hair covering the upper part of his chest. Without prompting, he leant over and started to chew on Mike's nipples: first the left one, then the right, then back again. Mike gasped: although it hurt, the pain was overridden with a thrill of sexual excitement that made his balls contract and forced his cock to grow within his jeans. As Jason continued to nibble his tits, Mike started to undo Jason's white cotton shirt. It didn't take very long: Mike urgently ripped the shirt off and was pleased with what he saw. Although

Jason wasn't muscular, he was quite chunky, with a line of dark hair climbing from a slightly furry stomach up to a hairy chest.

He pushed Jason back onto the bed, ensuring that the man's teeth were still clamped around his tit. Then he arranged himself over Jason so that he could return the compliment: his tongue licked both nipples, wetting the chest hair and whetting Jason's appetite for what was going to happen next. Without warning, he squeezed his teeth around Jason's left tit. He felt Jason's body stiffen, but whether it was with pain or pleasure, Mike neither knew nor cared. Jason was really getting him going, and Mike was just on the point of completely letting go.

He felt Jason's hands pulling at his belt, so he moved slightly to allow him to undo it. As Jason did so, Mike did the same, and it almost became a race to see who could do it first. As it turned out, it was a tie: simultaneously, they pulled one another's jeans down and off, throwing them into the crowded corner and saving the teddy bear from any further embarrassment.

Mike was wearing briefs, while Jason was wearing a pair of blue boxer shorts. Both of their erections were visible through the thin fabric. Mike knelt between Jason's legs and kissed him, before moving his mouth further and further down his body, his tongue tracing a line between his tits, down through his stomach, and then on to the cotton of the boxers. His tongue flicked at Jason's hard-on through the boxers, making it twitch as he did so. Then Mike grabbed the boxers and roughly pulled them down.

Jason's hard-on was about six inches long, uncircumcised and nicely fat; within seconds, Mike was crouching between Jason's thighs, that fat cock in his mouth. His hands reached out and found Jason's tits once again, and continued to squeeze them.

Jason's hands started to massage Mike's shoulders, kneading

the solid muscles. Then his hands slid down Mike's back, gently stroking him, relaxing him.

Mike continued to suck Jason's cock, his mouth sliding up and down the hot, fat flesh, in and out of his mouth, Jason's gasps of pleasure proof that Mike knew what he was doing. Mike suddenly stopped, and pushed Jason's legs into the air, letting his balls hang down and revealing his waiting arse. Mike took Jason's hairy ball-sac in his mouth, squeezing, sucking, and making Jason groan with the sensation. Then his mouth moved further down, his tongue drawing a trail from his balls, down and down until it found his ring. Mike licked at the thick hairs, revelling in the hot smells of man and sweat; one of his hands dropped down to his own cock, and he started to wank himself, pulling away at his hard dick as he pushed his tongue further and further into Jason's hot, hungry ring, tasting the taste of Jason, the dark, special taste of a man's arse that Mike found irresistible. Jason began to toss himself off as Mike's tongue bore into him, as Mike fucked him with his tongue.

Jason started to pant, his breaths short as he approached his climax. Mike redoubled his efforts, letting go of his own cock so he could force Jason's cheeks apart, so that he could push more of his tongue into him. His tongue pushed in and out, licking and tasting the hot hole, forcing Jason closer, closer . . .

With a rough yell, Jason came, come pumping from his fat cock, shooting all over his stomach, his chest, his face. Load after load – Mike was amazed to see how much Jason had come.

Letting Jason down onto the bed, he reached out; with one hand, he ran his fingers through one of the strands of come on Jason's stomach, scooping it up before putting it in his mouth. With the other hand, he began to wank himself again, squeezing his cock tightly, pulling at his cock, driving himself towards orgasm. With the taste of Jason's salty load in his mouth, that was enough to push him over the edge: with a grunt, he came.

Spunk shot from his cock, dropping onto Jason's dick and stomach, mingling with his own load.

Finally, he was drained, empty of come. He smiled at Jason. 'Cheers, I needed that.' And he had: his obsession with finding out the truth about his brother had begun to consume everything. It was time to get a bit of perspective, Mike decided. And perhaps Jason was the person to give him that perspective.

Jason nodded, clearly exhausted. 'So did I,' he said. Then he glanced at his watch. 'I don't like to rush you, Mike, but could you leave now? It's just that . . . well, my boyfriend will be home in about half an hour. We're trying to sort things out.'

Boyfriend. Typical. Just when he thought things were looking up, something like this had to happen.

Without saying a word, Mike started to get dressed.

Boyfriend, indeed. Just my luck.

Nathan closed the room door behind him and looked up and down the brown marble of the corridor, half-heartedly hoping that the room-service waiter might still be there. Then again, it wasn't as if he didn't know the room number, was it? Anyway, he was late for his meeting, and, since he was here on business, that just wouldn't do.

As Nathan navigated his way around the hotel – it was designed as an open square, almost like a fort surrounding a quadrangle of ornate gardens and swimming pools, with tall, minaret-like towers at each corner – he wondered why he had done it. It wasn't as if the waiter had even been his type: Nathan was renowned for his passion for rough straight-looking men – better still, rough, straight men. Skinheads, builders, rugby players . . . not really Moroccan youths, however well-endowed. Then again, Nathan had been incredibly randy after he'd woken up – so, what's new? he thought – and the outline beneath the boy's white pantaloons had definitely lived up to its promise.

With a faint grin of satisfaction on his face, Nathan made his way towards the correct stairwell, the one that would lead him straight to reception where his contact would be waiting for him. He just hoped that he had some good news for him: so far, all of the information that had come from the Elective's base in Marrakesh had been disappointing at best, and downright worrying at worst. That was why he had decided to come in person. The Moroccan branch of the Elective was obviously aware that it had a reputation to protect – the positively Bacchanalian orgy of the previous night, which Nathan was only just beginning to remember – but that was all window dressing to Nathan. It had been fun, but he needed to get to the heart of the matter. He needed to talk to Raul Aziz.

As he stepped into the gold and marble opulence of the hotel reception – part of him still felt guilty for staying in a place where the nightly room charge was bigger than his monthly mortgage – he spotted his contact sitting at one of the small occasional tables at the edge of the reception area, underneath the huge portrait of the crown prince of Morocco, and right next to the fountain.

'Raul,' he called out, recognising the man's dark, Arabic features from the photograph he had been given before setting off for Morocco. As he reached the table, he held out his hand which was grasped tightly and warmly.

'Mr Dexter,' said the other formally, standing up and grinning, showing a mouthful of brilliant white teeth – obviously a national trait. He was dressed in a similar, although far more expensive, version of the outfit worn by the waiter: a white silk shirt and pantaloons, and an exquisite black and silver tunic. 'Welcome to Morocco. Although . . .' Raul raised an eyebrow. 'Although my sources suggest that you were quite, ah, warmly welcomed at the little reception we laid on for you last night.' The grin grew even wider.

Nathan smiled, although he also felt a tinge of embarrassment. The young room-service waiter had not been his first taste of Morocco since flying into Marrakesh, and Raul obviously knew it: indeed, given Nathan's hazy memories of the party, he probably knew better than he himself did. He considered composing a cutting response – Nathan was a Deputy Comptroller of the Elective, and deserved a little respect – before remembering that Raul Aziz was his opposite number in Morocco.

Sitting down and trying to hide the embarrassed flush on his cheeks, Nathan nodded as Raul offered to pour him a small cup of the dark, strong coffee favoured by the Moroccans. 'What have you found out, Raul?'

Raul frowned. 'Nothing good, I'm afraid. That was why I couldn't attend the reception last night.' He stroked his forehead with his hands. 'I was still in Tangiers.'

Nathan felt a sudden twinge of disquiet. As far as he knew, as far as the Elective files he had seen had told him, all Elective activity was centred around Marrakesh.

'I wasn't aware that there were any problems in Tangier, Raul,' he said, wincing at the hot coffee. Even as he said the words, a faint yet disturbing thought began to germinate in his mind.

Raul whistled through his teeth. 'Nor was the Moroccan Board of the Elective until three days ago. While I was carrying out the review of procedures requested by yourself and Mr Cappiello, I discovered that there had been no communication from Messrs Kuster and Herrige for nearly a month.'

Kuster and Herrige . . . Why were those names familiar? Nathan racked his brain for a few moments. But when the realisation hit him he dropped the coffee cup to the floor with a crash, ignoring the spreading brown pool that grew over the mosaic and the attention that suddenly centred on him from around the reception area.

Erich Kuster and Dieter Herrige were a couple of well-respected leathermen of the old school, strict disciplinarians who could have walked straight out of a Tom of Finland drawing, according to Marco's description: both of them well over six feet tall and built like brick shithouses, and well known for their love of heavy S&M. Nathan had never met them, but he knew of them . . . oh, yes, he knew of them all right. They also happened to be the two leathermen who had been entrusted with the safekeeping of Adrian Delancey. If there was a problem . . .

'What's happened?' he demanded, well aware that he was raising his voice. 'Tell me!'

Raul held up a warning hand. 'I would advise you to keep your voice down, Mr Dexter. The business of the Elective is for our ears only.' He took a sip of coffee, ignoring Nathan's obvious impatience. Finally, he stared at Nathan, his deep brown eyes transfixing him.

'They are not at their home, Mr Dexter. Nor has anyone seen them for over a month. Whilst they are known to be frequent travellers, it is unusual for them to leave without informing their neighbours. This they did not do.' Raul sighed deeply. 'I visited their house on the outskirts of Tangier, but found it . . . less than clean and tidy.' Another sip of the coffee. 'In my opinion, something . . . something has happened to them. Something unpleasant.'

Although Nathan knew his next question was going to sound callous, with complete disregard for the two Germans, he couldn't help saying it. Too much depended upon it.

'What about Delancey?' he hissed.

Raul shrugged. 'There was no sign of him. None whatsoever. But logic dictates that he is the one responsible for their disappearance.'

Logic dictates? There was nothing logical about the situation. Nothing. Despite the midday warmth, Nathan shuddered. Adrian Delancey was free, free to practise his special brand of evil. So much for the power of the Elective. So much for keeping that bastard under lock and key for what he had done.

Nathan jumped to his feet. 'I have to return to London,

Raul. Immediately.' With Delancey at large, nobody was safe. 'This takes precedence over everything – the others need to be warned.'

'Of course, Mr Dexter: I shall have the private jet made ready as soon as possible. But what is the rush? Surely you can pass this information back to London from here?'

Of course he could: the Elective's communications network used encrypted phone and data links, so there was no danger of the information being leaked: that was the one way that the Elective could maintain its secrecy while influencing so much of the world. But Nathan wanted to get home as quickly as possible: he wanted to be with Scott. 'That's not the point, Raul. I have to get back to London because that's where Delancey will have gone – I'm sure of it. That's his power base, that's where he can cause the most damage.' And if I know Delancey, damage – revenge – will be uppermost in his mind. And I know who he blames for his downfall: me.

Nathan turned to leave, to return to his room and pack.

'But if you are here, and he is there, surely you are safe, Mr Dexter?' asked Raul.

'Safe?' Nathan laughed bitterly. 'Oh, *I'm* safe. But it's not me I'm worried about.'

Nathan knew Delancey. Knew the way that his twisted mind worked. I'll be the last on his list, he thought angrily. Before he finally has the balls to confront me, he'll work his way through everyone who's close to me. Marco, Leigh . . . and finally, the one person who is dearest to me above everyone: Scott.

The last time, Delancey had almost torn Nathan and Scott apart simply for the hell of it. Fuelled by hatred and revenge, who knew what he was capable of now?

Three

_____

The first thing that struck Marco Cappiello as he stepped out of the air-conditioned hotel on to the street was the almost solid wall of heat that greeted him. Marco wasn't a stranger to high temperatures – he had spent the first twenty-five years of his life in Melbourne – but this was different: a dry heat that caught at the back of his throat and dried the sweat almost before it had a chance to form. But a dry heat was only to be expected, if you were in the middle of a desert. Which was exactly where Las Vegas was.

Not that you would have known that you were in the middle of a desert: the desert in question was the Nevada Desert, and Marco was standing outside the enormous bronze lion's head that marked the entrance to the MGM Grand Hotel, Las Vegas. As far as he could see, hotels and casinos stretched into the distance, each of them offering the ultimate escape from reality: fantasy.

'This place is unbelievable!' came a voice from beside him. Leigh Robertson, Marco's boyfriend, was looking around with an expression of awe on his face. Leigh was in his late twenties; short and stocky, with cropped hair and an almost permanent impish grin on his face. He was currently wearing a pair of khaki shorts and a white T-shirt, showing off his solid legs and well-muscled body.

Marco laughed. 'I couldn't agree more. I've seen it in films, but to actually be here . . .' He trailed off, aware that, wherever he looked, there was something to stare at. Across the road – and what a road: it was more like a motorway that a road – was New York, New York, possibly the most incredible of the hotels in the city. The hotel itself was hidden behind a façade of scaled down New York landmarks, including the Statue of Liberty, and the guidebooks claimed that this theme was extended inside, with a miniature Times Square and Central Park to boot. Leigh had already shown an interest in visiting the hotel, mainly because he wanted to go on the roller coaster that was on the hotel roof, which afforded an excellent view of the Strip: the name given to the mile or so of the city that was lined with hotels and casinos – the view of Las Vegas made famous by countless films.

'Where do you fancy going first?' asked Marco. They did have some Elective business to attend to, but they weren't due to meet their contact, Greg, until much later that evening. They had the whole day to explore and unwind, and the whole of Las Vegas was their playground – especially given the Platinum American Express cards that the Elective had thoughtfully provided the two of them with. There was certainly enough to keep them entertained.

Leigh shrugged. 'I've never been here before, have I? Not all of us are seasoned world travellers. Before I met you, the furthest I'd been was Yorkshire.'

'When I was Deputy Comptroller, Leigh, it wasn't all business trips and posh lunches,' Marco said, laughing. 'If anything, they were thin on the ground. That bastard Delancey made sure that he was the one clocking up the air miles.' And doing the work, he thought bitterly. If only I'd known exactly what sort of work he was doing, I might have been able to stop him. But he had stopped him, eventually. Now it was time to make sure that it never happened again.

Leigh visibly shuddered, and Marco immediately regretted bringing that name up. 'Don't talk to me about Delancey. Not after what happened.' His voice was quiet but his tone was unmistakable: *you don't want to go there.* Marco instinctively put an affectionate arm around Leigh's shoulders to reassure him. Leigh had been one of the last victims of Delancey's perverted slave trade: seduced and drugged, before being shipped off and put in the tender ministrations of two German leathermen. Even though Delancey was part of the reason for their trip to Las Vegas, it wasn't fair to rub Leigh's nose in it.

Marco let go and put up his hands in mock surrender. 'I apologise. Just for that, you can choose where we go.'

Leigh looked up and down the Strip. Over breakfast, they had pored over the guidebooks, and had come up with a sightseeing list that would take them at least twice as long to complete as the time they had in the city.

'What about the Luxor for starters?' Leigh indicated the huge black glass pyramid to their left. At the front of it, almost standing guard, was an enormous stone Sphinx. 'That sounded good. Remember all that Egyptian stuff?'

'Okay.' Marco looked at his watch: it was nearly lunchtime, and the dry heat was playing hell with his throat. 'As long as I can stand you a beer.'

'It's a deal.' Together, they set off towards the Luxor, laughing and joking, without a care in the world.

High above them, in room 4001 of the MGM Grand, a man picked up a mobile phone, although he never took his eyes off the diminishing figures of Leigh and Marco.

'It looks like they're heading for the Luxor,' he said. 'Do you want me to follow them?'

Nathan Dexter was furious. Furious with the Elective, furious with the aeroplane, but, most of all, furious with himself. Since the flight to Marrakesh had been trouble-free, he had fully expected the return journey to be just as painless. *You're getting complacent, Nate*, came the little voice. *The Elective's made you soft in the middle.*

The thought of travelling back to London in one of the Elective's private jets had been so alluring, so decadent, that Nathan hadn't thought to ask how long it would take: all he could think of was Joan Collins in *Dynasty*, and that image just took over. Meanwhile, Raul had underestimated Nathan's urgency, simply assuming that, as one of the top people in the Elective, comfort came first.

The private jet didn't have enough fuel to make the journey to London in one stretch: it had to refuel at Munich. And that was where the problems had begun. For all of the Elective's power and influence, it was still prey to bad luck. And one of the plane's engines showing signs of wear was definitely bad luck. According to the pilot, there was no way that the plane could be made airborne before morning, and there were no scheduled flights back to the UK until the next day anyway.

There was only one option: Nathan would have to spend the night in Munich.

As his taxi raced down the autobahn towards the centre of the city, Nathan tried – and failed – to calm down. Under other circumstances, he would have been quite pleased: Munich was one of his favourite cities, and speaking fluent German was definitely a help. But tonight he wanted to be back in London, he wanted to be with Scott, protecting him, keeping him safe.

Thankfully, he had finally managed to contact Scott: after shouting at him for switching his mobile off, he had briefly explained the situation and told him to get out of the house for the night. Normally, he would have asked Marco to look after him, but Marco and Leigh were away in Las Vegas, and there weren't any other friends that he could turn to and feel secure; even Neil and Paul, his old university friends, had gone on holiday that morning. So he had decided on the only available option: he had told Scott to spend the night at the Brave Trader, and had arranged with Steve so that he could stay there. It all sounded very melodramatic, but Nathan's experiences with Adrian Delancey meant that no precaution was too excessive.

He looked out of the car window as the taxi reached the centre of town. One option would have been for him to stay in one of the airport hotels, miles from town, but Nathan always found those to be cold, soulless places full of cold, soulless people who stood silently around the hotel bar, unwilling or unable to engage in even the minimum amount of social intercourse. And, to be blunt, the chances of a shag in those places was virtually zero, although Nathan still harboured fond memories of a certain sales rep he had met in the bar of a hotel near Stuttgart. But Nathan wanted to be around people tonight, not nursing a drink while surrounded by shop-window dummies.

The taxi pulled up outside the Senator Hotel, one of Nathan's favourites. With his Platinum Amex, he could have stayed at the very best Munich had to offer, but the Senator was almost like a second home to him: one of his first business trips – in those far-off days before the Elective, before even becoming a freelance journalist, he had been a staff writer on a national magazine – had been three weeks in Munich, and he had stayed at the Senator. It had made such an impression that he always stayed there when he was in Munich, and tonight its homely charms were even more welcome.

He got out of the taxi and allowed the doorman to take his bags. 'Guten Abend, Herr Dexter,' he said politely.

'Guten Abend, Pieter,' Nathan replied, pleased at seeing his first friendly face. Pieter was part of the Senator's fixtures and fittings – and one hell of a fuck when he was off duty. Oh well, if Nathan didn't score tonight, there was now a contingency plan, he thought mischievously as he passed through the glass doors.

Stepping into the hotel foyer, he was unaware of the man standing on the opposite side of the road, speaking quietly into a mobile phone.

The Luxor had been magnificent: a totally extravagant tribute to Ancient Egypt, with huge Egyptian statues and relics, all laid out in the most over-the-top manner imaginable. Okay, so it was nothing like the real Egypt – even Leigh realised that; more like the Egypt that most Americans knew from Cecil B. DeMille films. But it was certainly a sight to behold.

After a quick drink in one of the casino's many bars – in Las Vegas, the hotels only existed as somewhere for the gamblers to stay when they weren't spending their money – he and Marco had made their way along the Strip, heading towards a particular bar where they were due to meet their contacts.

As they passed – or, more usually, popped into – each hotel on the way, Leigh become more and more amused at the shameless way that the hotels tried to outdo each other. Full-size galleons fighting pirate ships, re-creations of Ancient Rome, tamed white tigers . . . there didn't seem to be anything that the rival hotels wouldn't do to be top dog. His cynicism was firing on all cylinders, but Marco seemed totally enraptured by it all, especially once the drinks started flowing. As they sat outside the Mirage Hotel, waiting for the volcano to erupt – volcano, indeed! – Leigh looked at Marco affectionately. The Australian was a few inches taller than Leigh and a lot stockier, with short brown hair and a moustache. Thick brown fur covered his chest, both of his bare arms and the backs of his huge hands – hands which he definitely knew how to use. Normally he couldn't be parted from his leather biker's jacket, but the dry heat of Las Vegas had forced him to leave it in the hotel; he was wearing a white singlet and a pair of knee-length black shorts. And he looked downright sexy in them.

'What?'

'I was just thinking about all of this,' said Leigh.

Marco took a sip of his beer before replying, 'Then don't think. Just enjoy it.'

'It just doesn't seem real.'

'It isn't real – this is Las Vegas. About as far from reality as you can get.' As if to reinforce his point, the volcano chose that moment to erupt, fluorescent lava streaming down its rocky cone. 'I mean, you wouldn't get that down Oxford Street, would you?'

Leigh shook his head. 'I don't just mean Las Vegas. All of this: the Elective, the trips abroad . . . I just can't seem to get my head around it.'

Marco assumed a thoughtful expression. 'I know what you mean. I hadn't heard of the Elective when I first came to England. I had just graduated, and wanted to see a bit of the world before I became a banker, or an accountant, or something like that. Within a couple of weeks of arriving, I met this bloke . . .' His voice trailed off for a moment, and Leigh could guess why. Both Leigh and Marco had suffered at the hands of the Elective, but Marco had never gone into details. Until now, it seemed.

'Lawrence. Lawrence ran a club, or rather a series of clubs. He'd start one up, make it successful, get bored and start all over again. We met, fell in love, and I ended up moving in with him. Everything was fine for the first few months – until he set up a club that was so successful that it came to the attention of the Elective. They wanted the club, but Lawrence refused to submit to their demands. It wasn't the money – Lawrence was rich anyway, thanks to some dead millionaire relative – it was more the principle of the thing.' Marco took a deep swig from his beer bottle. 'That time, the Elective left it. The Comptroller at the time was a reasonable man, and decided that bullying Lawrence would be more trouble than it was worth. A couple of years later, the situation repeated itself:

Lawrence and I were running a club in Bermondsey, near where Scott and Nathan live. For once, Lawrence was enjoying the success, and wasn't planning to move for a while. It became a real draw for leathermen, clones and bears – the right music, the right atmosphere. It also came to the Elective's notice once again. And this time, the Comptroller wasn't so reasonable.'

'Delancey?'

Marco nodded. 'That bastard. He threatened Lawrence, he threatened me. Made us even more determined not to hand the club over to him. So Delancey had both of Lawrence's legs broken.'

'Just to get a club?' Leigh gasped.

'Just to get a club,' agreed Marco flatly. 'Seeing Lawrence in a wheelchair . . . well, I decided that the club wasn't worth that much.'

'But you're a fully paid-up member of the Elective now. How did that happen?'

'Lawrence and I left the club, but the Elective wasn't able to continue its success. The punters started leaving in droves, and Delancey was forced to come crawling to me to ask my help.'

'Surely you turned him down?' Leigh was briefly aware that, down the Strip, the galleons in front of Treasure Island had started firing on one another again, but he didn't let his concentration waver. Something told him that this was Marco's defining moment: the point in his life from which every subsequent decision stemmed.

'No. I accepted. But on one condition: he made me part of the Elective.'

'Why?' Leigh just didn't understand it. After what they'd done to his boyfriend, surely Marco would have wanted to get as far away as possible?

'Because I wanted to see how it worked. I wanted to change it, prevent it from ever hurting anyone like it had hurt Lawrence again. And if I wasn't able to change it, I wanted to tear the whole fucking thing apart. Delancey agreed – he had to, or the fiasco over the club would have been a very black mark on his record – and that's how I got in. Started at the bottom and discovered I was good at it. Managed to stop most of Delancey's excesses, thought I was doing something *right*. Lawrence didn't see it that way. He listened to my reasons, then threw me out and ended the relationship.' Marco finished his beer and thumped the bottle on the tabletop. 'Eventually, I found myself becoming Deputy Comptroller. You would have thought that that would have been sufficient to stop Delancey's kidnapping ring, but he was clever at this point: almost too clever. I just didn't see what was happening. I'm sorry.'

Leigh reached out and took his hand. 'It wasn't your fault. I'm here now, aren't I?'

'Anyway, at first, the Elective did seem like a dream come true: membership of the best clubs, international travel, the finest meals in the best restaurants . . . But you get used to it. It's like a broken tooth: for the first few days, you can't stop touching it with your tongue, but after that, you're used to it.'

Leigh had to say what was on his mind. If he couldn't talk to his own boyfriend, who could he talk to? 'I . . . I don't want to get used to it, Marco. I want my old life back. I just don't feel comfortable about accepting all of this for nothing. I wasn't brought up that way.' He threw his arms open. 'I'm a graphic designer, not a jet-setter. This just isn't me.'

Marco frowned. 'And you think it *is* me? My childhood in Melbourne was hardly a whirl of trips abroad and dining out, Leigh. This is as overwhelming for me as it is for you. But I see your point.' He frowned and squeezed Leigh's hand in his big, hairy paw. 'But why didn't you say anything earlier? You seemed fine when we were in Paris.'

Paris had been their first 'business' trip abroad, a long weekend in a hotel in the shadow of the Arc de Triomphe. 'That was different. I could convince myself that it was a one-off. But the more times we go away, the more uncomfortable I start feeling. And to be here –' he waved his hand around to encompass the whole of Las Vegas '– this is all so unreal that it just brought it home to me, I suppose.'

Marco stayed silent for a few moments, stroking his chin absent-mindedly – a sure sign that he was thinking about something. Finally he looked at Leigh with an decisive expression on his face.

'Nathan and I think that we'll have completed the audit for the Director in about two months' time. Once we've done it, I'll resign. Okay?'

'I'm not forcing you to give this up, Marco.' Leigh knew that the easiest way to destroy a relationship was to force the other partner to change against their will: it had happened to him more than once, from both sides. But he also knew that the excesses of the Elective would destroy their relationship just as surely. 'I know how much the Elective means to you –'

'Leigh, Leigh, Leigh . . . becoming part of the Elective was a means to an end, nothing more. I wanted to stop bastards like Delancey throwing their weight around; I wanted the Elective to give something back to the gay community – my God, that was what it was set up for! Delancey's gone, and the Elective's doing just that. My job's almost finished anyway. If you must know, I'd already decided to get out of it. But I was afraid to tell you, because I thought you'd be disappointed to give all of this up.'

Leigh laughed. 'You idiot! But what about Nathan? What will he do?'

'I half suspect that he wants to return to journalism. But then again, you know Nathan: just when you think you know him, he'll do something to surprise you.'

Nathan hadn't expected to be spending a night in a leather bar, so his suitcase was woefully lacking in that department: no leather trousers or chaps, no body harness . . . Thankfully, he still had his leather jacket and his DMs, so he wouldn't look entirely out of place when he walked through the door.

The Teddy Bar was down Hans Sachs Strasse, a ten-minute taxi journey from the Senator. From the outside, it didn't look much: a painted-out window and a door, the interior obscured by one of those horrid curtains made from plastic strips so favoured on the Continent. But inside was a very different matter.

Pushing his way through the curtain, Nathan was pleased to see that nothing had changed in the year since he had last been there. The décor was traditional: polished wood everywhere. In that respect, it could have been any bar anywhere: indeed, there were striking similarities between the Teddy Bar and the Brave Trader. What made the Teddy Bar distinctive was the same thing that gave it its name. It was full of bears. Every available surface was covered in teddy bears of every conceivable size, shape and colour; bears hung from the ceiling, bears sat in the corners . . . But this wasn't just an affectation: it was an indication of the nature of the clientele. The Teddy Bar catered for bears and their admirers – it was famous for it.

As Nathan entered the bar, everyone looked up. Since it was fairly early on a Tuesday night – 10 p.m. was early for the German gay scene – there were only about fifteen or so people in the bar, and Nathan recognised about half of them. But his first greeting was reserved for the mountain of fur behind the bar itself: Heinz – Daddy Bear, to his friends. Daddy was about six feet five, and built like a brick shithouse. He was the proud possessor of an incredibly bushy grey beard – and an equally impressive dick, if the rumours were to be believed. That was something that Nathan still had to experience first hand.

'Nathan!' he bellowed, extending a huge, paw-like hand. Nathan met his grip and tried not to wince at the pressure Daddy exerted. 'Why didn't you tell me you were coming?' he asked in German.

'Sorry, Daddy – didn't know myself until I arrived. Only here for the night, though,' he explained in fluent German.

'Never mind, never mind – it's good to see you. You're

50

looking well: must be that new man of yours.' With that he poured two glasses of schnapps. 'Love always brings out the best in you, Nathan.'

Nathan frowned, even as he threw the schnapps down his throat. How did Daddy know about Scott? It wasn't as if Nathan kept in touch with him, any more than the regular Christmas card. 'Which new man?' he asked innocently.

Daddy slammed the small glass of potent spirit down on the bar. 'One of your friends told me the other day. Told me that you'd recommended my bar as well, so you've earnt this beer,' he said, placing a huge stein of beer in front of Nathan.

Nathan picked up the stein – with not a little difficulty – and sipped it thoughtfully. He'd made no secret of the Teddy Bar among his circle of friends, so it wasn't beyond the bounds of possibility that one of them could have visited. Especially his friends in the Brave Trader, who could walk into a virtual German duplicate of their local and feel totally at home. But there was something nagging at him, something not quite right. Deciding that it wasn't important, he looked around the bar. The Teddy Bar was comforting and familiar – it was almost like a home from home. He nodded at a number of familiar faces, before recognising a very familiar face. Nathan sauntered over to the far side of the bar towards someone he knew very well. 'Hi, Kirk,' he said warmly.

Kirk was a bear in his mid-thirties, with short receding dark hair and a very close-cropped beard – almost no more than stubble. Tonight he was wearing a white T-shirt, a leather waistcoat and jeans, and looked just as shaggable as ever. Sadly, the knowledge that Kirk had a regular boyfriend, Wolfgang, made that impossible. Whereas Nathan and Scott were comfortable with each other having sex with other people, Nathan knew that Wolfgang's jealousy meant that Kirk was most definitely out of bounds. A pity.

'Nathan!' Kirk replied, a smile lighting up his face. Nathan realised that the usually easygoing Kirk had actually been looking quite down: there was a frown on his usually cheerful face. 'I saw you come in: you didn't call to say you were going to be in Munich.'

Nathan usually phoned Kirk to tell him if he was due in town, as part of his ongoing quest to sleep with him. Their mutual game of cat and mouse had been going on for about five years now: Nathan never managed to time it correctly so that he was in Munich when Kirk was between boyfriends. Kirk had even phoned him up once to tell him that he was single, only to find another boyfriend before Nathan could reach Germany.

'Sorry, Kirk – I didn't know myself until we landed here.' Nathan briefly explained the situation, taking care not to mention the Elective, before asking Kirk whether he was okay.

Kirk assumed an almost hound-dog expression. 'Sorry, Nathan, I'm a bit down tonight. Wolfgang and I split up last week, and I haven't taken it too well.'

'Oh. I'm sorry to hear that,' said Nathan, trying to make his words sound sincere. Wolfgang had been something special to Kirk, and theirs was a relationship that Nathan genuinely admired. That didn't stop his inner voice from having a go, though. You hypocritical bastard, he thought to himself, trying hard to stop himself grinning. It's just what you've always wanted: he's free!

Then again, Kirk didn't exactly look in the mood for some casual sex, and Nathan decided not to broach the subject: there might be other occasions, and he didn't want to spoil them by showing Kirk what an insensitive bastard he could be. Because of that, the next half an hour was spent in some of the most inane, inconsequential smalltalk it had ever been Nathan's misfortune to take part in, especially when Kirk's friend Jacob joined them and took the conversation to new depths of banality.

Finally, looking at his watch, Nathan explained that he was

leaving. Jacob showed the faintest trace of sensitivity and left, but Kirk suddenly seemed concerned.

'Where are you going?'

'Since I'm only here one night, I thought I'd slot in a quick drink in the Ochsengarten.' The Ochsengarten was Munich's equivalent to the Collective back in London: a dark, sleazy leather bar with lots of corners and a quite amazing back room. Nathan had spent many an enjoyable night in the Ochsengarten. Enjoyable and busy. And Nathan could see no reason why tonight should be any different.

'Do you want some company?' Kirk asked innocently. But there was something more than innocence lying behind those casual words: for the first time since they had met, Kirk was actually showing some signs of enthusiasm — and that wasn't something that Nathan was going to let pass. He gave Kirk a broad grin.

'That'd be great.' Saying his goodbyes to Daddy, Nathan couldn't help smiling. For the first time since Raul's revelation about Delancey, things actually seemed to be going Nathan's way. Part of him felt nervous — unsurprising, considering how long this game had been going on. But part of him felt a twinge of guilt: what about Scott? But Scott was back in England, and Nathan needed someone tonight. Scott was safe — Nathan had made sure about that — and Kirk . . . well, Kirk was something that Nathan had waited for for a very long time. Putting his conscience behind him, Nathan stepped through the curtain into the chilly Munich night, closely followed by Kirk.

He was so preoccupied with thoughts of what he hoped would happen later that he didn't notice the man on the street corner, giving a running commentary of Nathan's movements into his mobile phone. Nor was he aware of the man following them towards the Ochsengarten.

For once, Nathan had been out-thought. And it was liable to be a lesson that he wouldn't forget.

Four

___

Scott sauntered up Oxford Street, his hands in the pocket of his puffa jacket. It was freezing in London, and part of him was still a bit annoyed that he had been forced to stay at home while Nathan gallivanted around Morocco. Morocco! It wasn't that Scott really wanted to go to Morocco . . . he just wanted to be with Nathan. But Nathan was now some big-shot in the Elective, and Scott was still a student. A student with a degree to finish.

Bloody degree course! His boyfriend was now part of the most powerful organisation on the planet, and Scott still had to get his degree in computer science! He sighed, glancing at his reflection in the window of Next as he passed it. He was a good-looking bloke, he knew that: stocky, with short, almost cropped wavy hair. Okay, so his ears were a bit big, and he looked a bit dopey, but his solid, hairy body made up for that. Well, he'd not had any complaints so far.

So why was he feeling so pissed off? Fuck it – he wasn't that bothered about visiting Morocco, but anywhere had to be better than London in winter – it was bloody cold! And what about Marco and Leigh? They were sunning themselves in Las

Vegas, of all places. Although Scott had been to the States, the circumstances of that visit had been less than pleasant, thanks to Adrian Delancey. It would be nice to visit the country again and really get the chance to have a look around. Oh well, he thought: I'll have to persuade Nathan to go on a business trip to the States when I've got my next break from university. If Nathan can be bothered to take me, he thought bitterly: sometimes he couldn't help thinking that he was an inconvenience to him.

Stop that! He told himself. One of the things that he most liked about Nathan was his tenacity: Nathan never gave up, and this Elective business was simply another example of it. Once everything was sorted out, Scott and Nathan would finally have time for each other – it was simply that: a matter of time.

Suddenly, a movement out of the corner of his eye made him look round. Oxford Street was virtually empty – not unusual for a Tuesday night – but Scott could have sworn that there had been someone there. But not now: the whole stretch between C&A and the Midland Bank was deserted. Scott continued walking, but some instinct in him was making him nervous. Scott had been jumped once, a couple of years ago; although he hadn't been badly hurt – a black eye and a lot of bruises – it wasn't something that he cared to undergo again, and half-glimpsed figures appearing and disappearing wasn't reassuring him.

He started to feel even more nervous as he approached the top of the small alleyway that connected Oxford Street with Great Marlborough Street. What if someone were lurking there? Stop it! he told himself. He was just being silly, over-reacting. Despite that, he took his hands out of his pockets, just to be on the safe side.

As he reached the alleyway, he had almost succeeded in calming himself down. Don't be daft, he told himself. You're jumping at shadows now. Another two minutes and you'll be in the Brave Trader with a well-earned bottle of Hooch.'

'Hello, Scott.'

Scott stopped dead, his heart going ten to the dozen, his way blocked by a darkened figure he had never expected to see again.

The Ochsengarten was remarkably busy for a Tuesday, with standing room only. Nathan wasn't bothered: he just wanted a wall to lean against, somewhere where he and Kirk could let their barriers drop and see what developed between them.

Holding his bottle of Becks and feeling relaxed for the first time since Morocco, Nathan decided to open up the conversation. 'So, why the change of mood?'

Kirk laughed. 'I'm not actually that pissed off about Wolfgang, but I don't want him to know that. I wanted Daddy to see that I was upset, so that he'd tell Wolfgang.'

'You devious bastard!' Before Nathan could say any more, Kirk leant forward and kissed him on the lips, his tongue probing Nathan's mouth with an urgent hunger. As he did so, he put both arms around Nathan and squeezed him, one hand stroking Nathan's back, the other rubbing the back of his neck. Almost immediately, Nathan could feel his cock stirring, fired by the almost certain knowledge that it was going to get something it had wanted for far too long: Kirk.

Kirk finally broke off, and Nathan could see from the tell-tale bulge in his jeans that he had responded in the same way.

'Phew!' Nathan gasped. 'You don't know how long I've wanted that.'

Kirk pursed his lips. 'Oooh – probably as long as I have. Bloody big stroke of luck that you ended up here at this time – another couple of days, and I might have been snapped up,' he said jokingly.

'Too right,' said Nathan, but the little nagging doubt that had begun when Daddy had mentioned Nathan's friend was growing: was he being paranoid? Was it just coincidence that he had turned up just when Kirk was available? The trouble was, Nathan didn't believe in coincidence.

'Do you want to come back to my hotel?' Nathan asked, deciding that now was not the time for subtlety.

'Staying at the usual?'

'Where else?'

Kirk frowned, and it was obvious that something was wrong. Nathan felt his stomach tighten: to get this far, only to see Kirk whisked away yet again . . . It wasn't fair, he thought impotently. Not when something was finally going his way. He decided on the defeatist option – perhaps he could get the sympathy vote?

'Let me guess: the answer's no.'

'Oh, Nathan.' Kirk grabbed Nathan's arms. 'Don't be stupid. Of course the answer's yes. After all this time, did you really expect me to turn you down? But I need to pop to the Grün Bar for about half an hour: I was supposed to be meeting someone, and I can't really let them down.' And, with an almost coy smile: 'I will be back. Honestly.'

A perfectly reasonable answer: Kirk had had no way of knowing that Nathan was going to be there that night, so why shouldn't he have already made arrangements? Nathan knew that he should be grateful that Kirk was actually going to come back, but his inner voice was still nagging at him: *why is he going? where is he really going? isn't it all a bit convenient?*

Before he could say anything that might have ruined the evening totally, Kirk gave him a full kiss on the lips, squeezed his arm again and walked out of the bar.

Suddenly alone, Nathan looked around the Ochsengarten, trying to see if there was anyone he recognised. Unlike the Teddy Bar, however, the clientele of the Ochsengarten was a more transitory crowd: from his own experience, he knew that the chances of seeing the same people on successive nights was fairly rare. And, true to form, there was no one in the bar who Nathan knew.

Suddenly he was aware that he himself was under scrutiny: he could feel eyes boring a hole in the back of his neck – an extra sense that he had developed over years of undercover work as an investigative journalist. Rather than spin round and ruin the moment, Nathan decided to take advantage of the strategically placed mirrors which were dotted around the walls of the Ochsengarten. Within moments, he had located a mirror which showed what – or rather who – was behind him.

To say he was impressed would have been an understatement.

The man was about six feet three, with blond hair, and an unbelievable square jaw – he reminded Nathan of Dolph Lundgren, a perfect example of the Aryan race. The tight grey T-shirt accentuated the solid, muscular chest and biceps, and also revealed the thick covering of hair over the arms. The small tuft of blond hair which poked over the neck of the T-shirt was a clear indication that not only his arms were hairy.

Casually, trying to make his interest obvious – but not too obvious – Nathan turned to face the man, who was standing in front of the door to the ladies' toilet. Although it wasn't the ladies' toilet, of course: it was the darkroom. Nathan attempted a friendly smile, but got nothing in return: the man simply stared at him. But there was something in the stare, something in the eyes, that suggested that the man was actually interested.

That was reinforced, proved, even, when the man pointed at Nathan, then pointed behind him – towards the darkroom. Then the man opened the door and vanished into the gloom beyond.

For a second, Nathan was frozen to the spot: what should he do? Brave and fearless Nathan Dexter, as nervous as a teenager. But he wasn't the only person who had noticed. A small, excitable man in a body harness leant over to him;

obviously he had been watching the events with jealous interest, and Nathan was sex by proxy.

'Go on, follow him!' hissed the little man. 'He's not going to wait for ever.'

Taken aback that he seemed to have become the centre of attention in the Ochsengarten, Nathan acted on instinct, opening the darkroom door and going in.

The darkroom was dark, obviously. But there was enough light from the single meagre bulb to show positions, outlines. But before Nathan could accustom himself to the twilight, he walked straight into a wall of fur.

It was the man's chest, solidly muscled and covered in thick, blond hair. In the moments since the man had entered the dark-room, he had removed his T-shirt and thrown it on to the wash-basin stand, and dropped his trousers round his ankles. Before Nathan could do anything, the man tugged roughly at Nathan's leather jacket, pulling it off and tossing it on top of the discarded T-shirt. Then Nathan's own T-shirt was removed, joining the pile of clothing. Standing there, topless, Nathan gasped as the man's fingers fought their way through Nathan's chest hair, seeking out and finding both his nipples before squeezing them tightly, almost painfully. But it was a pain that Nathan relished, a pain that was closer to pleasure.

As the man continued to play with Nathan's tits, Nathan reached out and grabbed the man's cock, pleased to feel seven inches of thick, veined flesh in his hand. Nathan started to wank it, leisurely strokes which pulled the foreskin back and forth over the already wet helmet.

One of the man's hands dropped from Nathan's chest and sought out Nathan's belt, undoing the leather and pulling at the buttons of his jeans with a frantic urgency. Within moments, Nathan's jeans were around his ankles; his cock, unrestrained by any pants, sprang free. As that happened, Nathan realised that the two of them weren't alone: anything but. Shadows loomed from the darkened corners, shadows which became visible for just seconds at a time: about five men were getting off on the entertainment that Nathan and the German were providing.

As soon as Nathan's cock was free, the German sank to his knees on the cold stone floor. One hand was still squeezing Nathan's tits, first one, then the other, while the other hand reached behind Nathan and started to finger his sensitive ring. Nathan groaned with pleasure, but his groans increased as the German's mouth engulfed his cock and his wet lips slid up Nathan's shaft.

Nathan laid both his hands on the German's broad shoulders and squeezed them, before running his hands through the thick blond hair that covered the German's chest until he found his tits, both pierced with thick silver rings. Nathan tugged on them, harder and harder, urging the German to suck him faster, deeper. The German responded, his tongue sliding across Nathan's helmet, probing his dick-slit and playing with it with his flicking, darting tongue, while his finger forced its way further and further inside Nathan's arse.

Then Nathan detected one of the shadows, detaching itself from the gloom and coming up behind him. He glanced at the man, and was turned on to see that he was a short and stocky man with a fairly hairy chest, heavily tattooed arms, and a long thick cock pierced with a Prince Albert. The man gave a telling look at the tall German, who stopped sucking Nathan and pulled him to his feet.

Nathan didn't object: there was something about the environment, the complete anonymity, which was turning him on far more than the darkrooms of the Harness or the Court- yard ever had. All he wanted to do was submit himself to the two Germans, to let them do whatever they wanted to him.

Almost meekly, Nathan allowed himself to be led over to the washbasin. The blond hefted himself on to the concrete rim of the basin, his legs apart, his cock stiff and proud. The smaller man bent Nathan over so that his mouth was only inches away from the tall German's cock, close enough to see the beads of pre-come leaking from the slit in the red, cut helmet. Nathan knew that he wanted to taste that cock, wanted to run his tongue over the moist helmet and slide his lips along the thick shaft.

Roughly, the smaller man thrust Nathan further forward and bent him down at the same time; Nathan put out his hands to steady himself, grabbing the muscular, blond-haired thighs in front of him. As he did so, he opened his mouth as wide as he could and took as much of the blond man's cock down his throat. Just as he began to worry that he was going to choke, another sensation took over. A sharp burning, as his ring was brutally forced open by the tattooed man's cock. There was no gradual easing in, no gentle penetration: the man slammed his hands on Nathan's shoulders to keep him in place and thrust his cock into him, his balls slamming against Nathan's arse. Nathan gasped; only the blond man's dick in his mouth stopped him from shouting out. It hurt like hell, but the pleasure of being dominated made it more than bearable.

Focusing all of his concentration on the thick cock in his mouth, Nathan tried to relax his arse, forcing the pain to give way to exquisite pleasure as the tattooed man's cock once again buried itself completely inside him. He felt the man's crotch grinding against his arse, the hairy sac of his large balls rubbing against his cheeks. Then the man withdrew, withdrew all the way until Nathan guessed that only the helmet was still inside, then the whole length was slammed back inside, and then out again. As the man built up his rhythm, Nathan matched it: his mouth slid up and down the blond man, and he glanced up to see a look of dreamy rapture on his face. Nathan moved one of his hands up, through the blond hairs of the man's stomach and chest until he reached one of the tit rings.

As the tattooed man's dick slid in and out of Nathan's arse, Nathan began to tighten himself in time to the thrusts, a move which elicited grunts of satisfaction. Simultaneously, he built up his speed on the blond's cock, taking care to run his tongue over the sensitive dick-slit and the ridge just below the helmet. The blond's breathing became faster, and Nathan could see his big balls begin to tighten. Sucking and fucking, both of them seemed about to come. Nathan decided that he had paid them enough attention: it was now time for him to indulge himself. Sucking the blond's cock and squeezing his arse around the tattooed man's almost became automatic, as he concentrated on the feelings that were growing inside him. He tasted the salty pre-come of the blond, his lips felt the hard flesh of the veined cock; his arse allowed itself to fill up with the tattooed man's long thick cock, the helmet stroking away at his prostate, driving him closer and closer to the edge.

As the blond's groans and the tattooed man's grunts became louder and more urgent, Nathan, himself very close to release, glanced to each side and saw the other men in the darkroom, all of them wanking their cocks as they enjoyed the spectacle. Four men, their eyes fixed on Nathan. Four men, their fists beating away at their stiff wet cocks. Four men, their faces fixed in grins of wild excitement.

That did it for Nathan. He dropped his hand from the blond's tit ring and grasped his cock, delivering the last strokes that would bring him off. His load shot against the concrete base of the washbasin, thick drops of white that slowly flowed to the floor. Seconds later, his mouth filled with the warm salty juice of the blond man's orgasm, and Nathan only just managed to swallow each spurt before the next one threatened to choke him. His concentration on the blond was suddenly diverted as a wild, raw yell erupted from behind him. The tattooed man was coming, and Nathan had to steady himself against the blond's thighs as he thrust his cock into Nathan's arse with even more violence that before, pumping that long stiff dick into Nathan's hole, delivering one load after another into his sore abused arse. Finally he finished, and slumped onto

Nathan's back, his wiry chest hair rubbing against the skin of Nathan's back.

Then the others came. The four men moved closer, closer . . . and shot their loads almost as one. Nathan felt their come hit him, spraying over his hair, his legs, his face. The tattooed man seemed to get off on it even more, and wrapped his arms around Nathan, his fingers pulling and tugging at Nathan's chest hair, his tits . . . But even the stocky little powerhouse didn't have that much staying power: he stood up and started to retrieve his clothing.

Nathan allowed the now limp but still impressive cock to slip from his mouth, and then he too stood up. He smiled at the blond man.

'*Dankeshön*,' he muttered lamely. Thank you, even in the blond's native German, seemed inadequate. Nathan grabbed his T-shirt and leather jacket from the floor where they had been knocked.

'No – thank *you*, mate.' The reply was purest East London.

Nathan grinned. 'A Londoner – all the way to Munich and I find another Londoner.'

The blond laughed. 'Bit of a coincidence, eh, mate? Never mind – I'll buy you a drink.'

A few minutes later, when they were fully dressed, Nathan and the blond – Gary – left the darkroom. But Nathan's earlier exhilaration was rapidly fading.

Nathan Dexter still didn't believe in coincidence.

'You bastard!' Scott shouted, punching the man on the arm. 'You almost gave me a heart attack!'

The newcomer was having difficulty speaking through his laughter. 'Sorry – I couldn't resist. You looked so lonely trudging down Oxford Street that I thought I'd give you a surprise.'

'Surprise?' gasped Scott, leaning against the window of Next.

'Surprise?' He shook his head, but couldn't help laughing. 'Still, it's good to see you again. When did you get back?'

Anthony Lynch was one of Scott's oldest gay friends; indeed, he was the person to whom Scott had lost his virginity – quite a while back, come to think about it. Anthony had gone abroad about two years ago, having decided to see the world. Obviously he had returned, in all his glory: six feet tall, muscled, with a blond crewcut – and a very nice tan as well. As Scott's heart settled down, he realised how pleased he was to see him again: the way he felt at the moment, a friendly face was the best medicine.

'Yesterday,' said Anthony. 'I tried to ring you, but the Halls of Residence said that you'd moved. And they wouldn't give me your new address,' he added. 'So I thought I'd check out a few of your usual watering holes – I had a feeling that I'd eventually bump into you.'

Scott grinned. 'Although I'd have preferred it if you hadn't made me jump out of my skin. Anyway – yes, I have moved.' Scott suddenly realised how much he needed to talk to someone, someone outside of Nathan's circle of friends. 'There's so much to tell you, Anthony. Fancy a drink?'

His friend grinned at the suggestion. 'I thought you'd never ask. I presume you're going the same way I am? The Crossed Swords?'

The Crossed Swords on Charing Cross Road was an attractive proposition – it was Scott and Anthony's old hunting ground, and would have been the perfect place to catch up on the last couple of years. But Scott had promised Nathan that he would spend the evening at the Brave Trader, and he didn't really want to piss him off. Besides, Steve was expecting him.

'Actually, no: I'm off to the Brave Trader.'

'The Brave Trader?' asked Anthony in disbelief. 'You used to hate that place. "Full of old men with beards," you used to say.'

Scott smiled. 'I told you there was a lot to tell you.'

'Okay, okay – for once I'm more interested in talking to you than picking up trade.'

Together, they set off for the Brave Trader, unaware of the man watching them intently, talking urgently into his mobile phone as they headed towards the Brave Trader.

From the little that he let slip as they walked down Oxford Street, Scott could tell that Anthony had had a whale of a time during his travels. He was really looking forward to hearing about it, and telling Anthony about all of his adventures as well. It was hard to believe how much had happened in the last year, and something told Scott that his own story was going to be hopelessly outclassed by Anthony's tales.

Opening the door, Scott was surprised to see how busy it was: Tuesday was usually the pub's quiet night, but there was hardly a free space at the bar. For a moment, he considered going somewhere quieter, like the Europa Arms down Old Compton Street, but realised that he had been spotted by the Royal Enclosure. No choice but to stay in the Brave Trader, then.

Stepping into the throng, Scott turned to Anthony. 'Still drinking the usual?'

Anthony nodded. 'Oh yes: a pint of their finest cooking lager.' As Anthony found himself a place to stand, Scott forced his way to the bar, pushing past such old faces as Postman George, Shoeshop Eric, Metal-plate Martin and Big Keith. He couldn't help smiling at the names: giving people their 'pub names' was one of the best-loved games in the Brave Trader, and one of the proudest moments, showing that you had been accepted as a regular: the giving and receiving of names, the welcoming into the community. Then again, not all names were complimentary: Scott's smile faded a bit when he remembered one of his own sobriquets: the Handbagger.

'What can I get you?' asked the barman as Scott reached into his pocket to grab his wallet. His wallet, his money –

despite what the gossips of the Royal Enclosure might imply. With every passing minute, his stress levels seemed to be soaring higher and higher – he definitely needed this drink.

Scott looked up, ready to order, when the words stuck in his throat. The barman was someone that Scott had never expected to see again, simply because he was dead, murdered by the Elective. But there was no doubting it. The barman was about six foot five, with a gingery-brown flat-top, a short beard – virtually stubble – and a slightly dopey expression. A slightly dopey expression that Scott knew only too well.

There, as large as life, serving behind the bar of the Brave Trader, was John Bury.

The *late* John Bury.

Five

———

Scott felt the breath catch in his throat. Almost by reflex, he asked for a pint of Fosters and a bottle of Hooch, and watched in shocked silence as John Bury grabbed a glass and started pouring a pint. This just wasn't possible: John Bury was dead.

It was impossible for Scott to forget the circumstances of John's death: he had followed Scott and Nathan from the Brave Trader to one of their favourite clubs, the Harness, and had successfully attracted their attention. One thing had understandably led to another, and Scott, Nathan and John had ended up having an extremely enjoyable threesome. However, subsequent events had shown that their meeting with John was anything but a chance encounter: John was in the employ of the Elective, who wanted to know how much Nathan knew about the organisation. While Scott and Nathan were asleep, John had ransacked Nathan's files and attempted to hack into his computer.

Nathan had disturbed him, and John had fled into the night. However, that was far from the end of the matter – although it had definitely been the end for John. Under the leadership of Adrian Delancey, the Elective brooked no failures. John Bury's lifeless body had been discovered later that same morning, murdered and carelessly hidden in Hyde Park.

John's death had been the single event that had spurred Nathan on in his quest to uncover the secrets of the Elective: somehow, Nathan had felt responsible for the murder, and that had driven him to defeat Delancey.

But now, standing a few feet away from Scott, was proof that there had never been a murder. John Bury was alive and well and working behind the bar of the Brave Trader. It just couldn't be happening!

'Can I get you anything else?' Scott looked down to see a pint of Fosters and a bottle of Hooch in front of him on the bar.

'Er . . . no, no, that's fine,' he stuttered. It had to be John Bury, it had to be. But the man was staring at Scott without the faintest trace of recognition.

Scott paid for the drinks and made his way through the crowd to Anthony. His shock must have been written all over his face, because Anthony's first words were: 'Are you okay?'

'I'm fine . . . I've just had a bit of a surprise.' Briefly, he explained what had happened, although he was careful to omit all references to the Elective. It sounded fishy enough, without bringing up a shadowy organisation into the bargain.

'So there you have it,' he concluded. 'Someone who died a couple of months ago is now a barman in the Brave Trader. And unless the brewery is in the habit of resurrecting corpses, I can't explain why.'

'Why don't you ask him?' said Anthony sensibly. Far too sensibly for Scott's liking. Didn't Anthony realise how disturbing this was?

'And say what?' he snapped. '"Aren't you dead?" Anyway, he didn't recognise me.'

'He could be acting,' Anthony suggested.

'But why?' What a question. There had to be a logical explanation — there had to be.

'Didn't you say that his name was John?' said Anthony thoughtfully, his eyes looking over Scott's shoulder.

'That's right. John. John Bury.'

'Well, that's not the name he's using now.' Anthony pointed towards the till display, an LED panel fastened to the shelves above the bar. Each barman had an individual till key, and the cost of the order was always displayed there, with the barman's name. John had just served someone, and, through a gap in the crowd, his name appeared.

It wasn't John, though.

It was Mike.

Scott stared deeply into his Hooch, trying to make some rhyme or reason out of what was happening. Of course, it could have just been a case of mistaken identity . . . But no, that just wasn't possible. Scott was proud of his ability to remember faces — and put names to those faces — and it was only a couple of months since he had had sex with John Bury. There was no way that he could be mistaken.

'I wish Nathan was here,' he muttered. 'He'd know what to do.'

'How pathetic,' Anthony retorted. 'Just because your boy-friend isn't here, you go completely to pieces. I always thought that you were the resourceful one — the survivor.'

The attack, although justified, really got to Scott. He needed to prove that he was an independent person, not just an adjunct to Nathan — not just a handbagger. 'All right, I'll do something.' He peered through the crowd, waiting for a gap so that he could see who was holding court in the Royal Enclosure. Satisfied, he turned to Anthony. 'Wait here: I'll be back.'

Pushing through the crowd, Scott made his way to the Royal Enclosure. It wasn't the easiest of journeys, however: since Nathan was one of the more popular and well-known regulars in the Brave Trader, that made Scott equally as well known, and he had to stop and say his hellos at least six times before he could reach the hallowed ground of the Enclosure. But how many of them were saying hello to Scott, and how many were simply trying to curry favour with Nathan? Did Scott have an existence in the Brave Trader without Nathan? Realising that such questions wouldn't help him solve the mystery of John Bury, he said his last hellos and reached the rarefied heights of the Enclosure.

'Evening, young Scott,' said Morgy, raising his pint. Morgy was a pathologist – hence the rather sick nickname. 'Nathan not back yet?'

'Stuck in Germany, I hear.' Steve the landlord appeared at Scott's side, a pint of Beamish in his hand. 'Nate phoned me a little while ago and explained the situation,' he said to Scott quietly. 'If you fancy sitting in the flat and watching TV, Colin's up there.' Colin was Steve's boyfriend, and normally Scott would have liked nothing better than to have sat up there with a drink, flicking through the cable channels or playing a computer game. But not tonight. Not with a face from the grave behind the bar.

'Morocco, Germany ... I wish he booked his tickets through me,' said Suspenders Alex. 'Just think of the commission I could make.' Suspenders Alex, known as such because of his penchant for wearing oh-so-expensive women's clothing beneath his oh-so-expensive Jermyn Street business suit, was high up in some travel firm, Scott gathered. At first, it had been difficult for Nathan to explain why he wasn't booking all of this new-found travel through Alex without mentioning the Elective; only when Alex had taken Nathan to one side and admitted that he was actually a member of the Elective himself, and that his firm actually did book all of the travel for the UK branch anyway, did the situation become easier. Like everyone connected with the Elective, Suspenders Alex was part of their web of lies and deceit.

'I'm with a mate,' Scott explained. 'I'll pop up a bit later.'

He lowered his voice, trying to escape the attention of the Royal Enclosure. Difficult, since they were the pub's equivalent to Jodrell Bank, but it was worth a try. 'Actually, I was wondering about your new barman.'

Steve raised an eyebrow. 'Oh yes? Boyfriend's away for an extra night, and little Scotty's getting lonely,' he said loudly, making sure that the whole of the Enclosure heard. Then he grinned. 'Don't worry, Scott: your secret's safe with me.'

Scott laughed, although he was a bit peeved that Steve was jumping to conclusions – especially conclusions that were being broadcast to the Enclosure. Then again, he should have expected something like that: the regulars and staff of the Brave Trader weren't exactly known for either their underactive imaginations or their discretion. 'No, no, no – it's just that I think I know him.' Couldn't you have made that sound just a little bit lamer, he thought ruefully.

Steve's smile made it quite clear that Scott wasn't cutting any ice. Hardly surprising with sophisticated excuses like that, Scott decided.

'His name's Mike. Mike Johns. He started here last week after Andy left. He works three nights a week, and it seems he's hung like a donkey – according to Ivy. Does that answer all of your questions? Or do you want me to introduce you to him?' he said mischievously.

Actually it didn't: questions such as why does he look like a dead ex-shag still hung in the air. But what was Scott supposed to say? He knew that there were members of the Royal Enclosure who didn't entirely like him: they saw him as a hanger-on, someone who was using Nathan for his own ends. If he continued to make enquiries, word would get around. And, even though Scott and Nathan were fairly forgiving about one another's indiscretions, the last thing that Scott wanted to do was upset Nathan. He wanted Nathan to pay him more attention – he didn't want him firing back accusations. 'No, you're all right,' he answered. 'It's not the bloke I thought it was. Tell Colin I'll see him later.'

Grabbing his pint from the bar and excusing himself, Nathan made his way back towards Anthony. There was nothing else for it: although it was an admission of defeat, it was the only answer. Scott would have to wait for Nathan to get back. As he reached Anthony, he wondered how Nathan was doing. Probably in his hotel room with a good book, no doubt.

Nathan looked at his watch for the umpteenth time. Gary, the East Ender, had left, leaving Nathan to wait in the emptying bar. Where the hell was Kirk? Fair enough, he'd had some brilliant sex in the back room, but that was all it had been: sex. With Kirk . . . well, he knew that it was going to be something different. Nathan took a swig of his beer and was forced to question what he was doing. Fine, so Kirk had been one of his ultimate goals for years but Nathan was going out with Scott. Yes, they had agreed to have an open relationship, but there was something pre-meditated about all of this . . . almost as if it was more than just a coincidence. Like meeting a bloke in the darkroom who lived round the corner from him.

Nathan immediately chastised himself. Ever since learning about Delancey's disappearance, he had been seeing conspiracies and plots in every shadow. This time tomorrow, he would be back in London with Scott. But until then, he was in a foreign city, hopefully about to fulfil a dream that he had been looking forward to for years.

If he turns up, that is, he thought. Fair enough, he'd already got his end away that evening. But Kirk . . . well, Kirk was special.

Draining his beer, Nathan decided to call it a night. Kirk's half-hour had been up a half-hour ago, and Nathan was exhausted. The sooner he got out of Munich, got back to London and saw Scott the better. Things were getting too complicated as it was.

Giving a nod to the barman, he made his way towards the door, pushing through the thinning crowds. It was already two in the morning, and even the pleasure-hungry Germans knew their limits. He said a few goodnights to the 'audience' from the darkroom, who raised their drinks with unabashed pleasure.

'Going so soon?' came a voice in German. Nathan looked up to see Kirk standing in the doorway. 'I thought you were going to wait for me.'

Nathan sighed. Why did Kirk make him feel like he was in the wrong? 'You're a bit late,' he reasoned.

'I know,' said Kirk, a trace of apology in his voice. 'I just couldn't get away. You know what the Grün Bar's like.'

Actually, Nathan did: it made the Ochsengarten look like a tea party, with its four darkrooms, harnesses and wealth of 'equipment'. In many ways, just as the Ochsengarten was like the Collective, the Grün Bar was like the Harness. Nathan wondered whether Kirk had had as much fun as he'd had.

'Do you fancy another drink?' asked Kirk, nodding towards the bar.

Nathan raised an eyebrow. 'I wouldn't mind a drink, but the bar at the hotel's still open. What do you say?'

Kirk grabbed Nathan's arm and ushered him towards the door. 'I thought you'd never ask.'

'You are kidding.' Leigh was nursing a Coke, looking around the interior of the bar in amazement. 'I've never seen anything like it.'

Marco couldn't help laughing. If the truth be told, even he was a little taken aback by the place, even though he'd been warned by his contacts that it was a little . . . unusual. Unusual was an understatement: the Bear's Retreat was like no other bar that Marco had ever seen, anywhere else in the world. And that was saying something.

Firstly, the Bear's Retreat was a members-only bar, and wasn't overly welcoming towards a large Australian and his

English boyfriend, even though they had been back to their hotel and changed into the more acceptable dress code of jeans, T-shirts and leather jackets.

The hostile reception had initially proved a problem: the two bouncers on the door had simply refused to let them in. Only when Marco was able to prove his credentials did they become more amenable: not only was one of the members expecting him, but that member was actually the owner of the bar itself. Finally allowed in, he and Leigh had found themselves in a very different type of bar from anything they were used to.

Inside, it was huge: the small frontage made it look as if it was going to be one of those tiny, intimate bars; instead, the frontage led through to a room the size of a barn — obviously the warehouse that stood behind the frontage.

The walls were corrugated metal, painted black; framed blow-ups of Tom of Finland artwork were everywhere, making it quite clear who the bar catered for. And, just to back that up, it was full: bears, clones, men in cowboy hats and chaps, all of them jostling one another to get the best view of the entertainment. And what entertainment!

At first, Marco couldn't work out what they were looking at: the stage was empty, but everyone was craning their necks for a better view. Then he realised that they weren't looking at the stage, but above them.

Towards the cages.

That was when Marco remembered where he had heard of the Bear's Retreat before. It was infamous for its particular form of live entertainment. The entertainment that was taking place above them, suspended from the ceiling.

Three cages were hanging from the distant metal ceiling of the club: they were about ten feet above their heads. And, in each of the cages, two men were enjoying themselves . . . and each other.

Marco and Leigh ordered their drinks and found a place at the bar where they could get a clear view.

'I didn't want to stand underneath,' said Leigh, settling himself at the rough wooden bar. 'Just in case I get dripped on.'

Marco laughed. 'I see what you mean. But how could I have forgotten about this place? I remember hearing about it in an Elective meeting. Actually, we were considering doing something similar in the Harness, but never quite got around to it.' He estimated the crowd. 'Perhaps we should reconsider: we'd make a fortune.' He looked up at the nearest cage. The two occupants were wrestling with one another: and, fittingly, all they were wearing were skin-tight rubber wrestling suits. One black, one red, the suits were like combined singlets and shorts, showing off their bodies for all to see.

And what bodies! The first man, the one in the black suit, was about six feet tall, with cropped blond hair and a gingery-blond goatee beard. In his mid-twenties, he was broad and quite tubby, the rubber of his suit showing off his large chest and stomach, with the exposed portions revealing a hairy chest, back and shoulders. Despite his extra weight, he radiated strength and power. The other, slightly older man, was dark-haired and clean-shaven, smaller but solid: not an inch of fat on his smooth, sculpted body, every muscle accentuated by the shiny red second skin.

Currently, they were on the floor of the cage, each one trying to gain superiority over the other. The larger one had managed to get on top of the other and was forcing his arms apart, trying to spread-eagle him against the metal bars. Even though there was nothing overtly sexual about it, the sight of two men, each one trying to overpower the other, was giving Marco a hard-on. As he watched, the smaller man slipped from the other's grasp, bounced himself off the bars of the cage and knocked the bigger man to the floor. Despite his size, he was clearly stronger than the man in the black rubber, and immediately had him pinned to the floor.

'Where's this contact, then?' asked Leigh. 'I thought he was supposed to be meeting us here.'

Marco tore his attention from the cage and looked around the bar. Greg, his contact in Las Vegas, was supposed to have met them about half-an-hour ago, but Marco and Leigh's leisurely stroll down the Strip had taken in rather too many hotels and rather too many beers, followed by a madcap dash back to the hotel to get changed, and they were a bit on the late side. Marco wasn't drunk, but he could have done with a clearer head for this meeting. According to the report he had received from Greg, something very odd was happening in the Las Vegas branch of the Elective. Nothing precise, nothing certain, but enough to worry Greg, the Comptroller of the Las Vegas Elective. Enough for him to summon Marco over from England.

Marco shrugged as he replied to Leigh. 'We are a bit late –'

'Whose fault's that?' said Leigh. 'You were the one who wanted to visit the Stratosphere Tower.'

'Point taken.' Marco saw a familiar figure forcing himself through the crowd, one of the few people whose attention wasn't focused on the caged bears. Very tall, very powerful, Greg looked like he had walked out of a Hollywood Western. He was in his early forties, and Marco was amused to see that his trademark ten-gallon hat was, as usual, perched on his shaved head. Greg's mouth was framed by a brown goatee beard, the moustache waxed into two upswept points, making him look like a plantation owner from the nineteenth century rather than a club owner and a Comptroller of the Elective. The rolled-up shirtsleeves of his plain white shirt revealed big, hairy arms, covered in tattoos, while the tight jeans made no secret of the huge packet hiding within. The stories of Greg's sexual prowess were legendary, and part of Marco really wanted proof at first hand.

'How ya doing, old man!' Greg drawled as he approached, grabbing Marco's large hand in an even larger one and almost squeezing the life out of it. 'Thought I'd missed you.'

'My fault,' Marco explained. 'Got a bit carried away on the Strip.'

Greg laughed, a rich, throaty laugh. 'Easily done. Your first time here, isn't it?'

Marco nodded. 'This is Leigh, by the way – my boyfriend. His first time too.'

'Pleased to meet you, son,' said Greg. 'So you haven't seen our resident entertainment, have you?' Greg nodded towards the cages. 'I'll get us some more drinks. Just stand back and enjoy.'

Marco wanted to get the business out of the way, but it would be rude to rush things. Greg was the Las Vegas Comptroller, and the Bear's Retreat was the Elective's base, in the same way that Marco and Nathan's base was behind a locked door at the Harness in Vauxhall. Gratefully accepting the beer from Greg, Marco looked up at the cage.

In the last few minutes, the larger of the two wrestlers had gained the upper hand once more. The smaller one looked exhausted, and was finding it difficult to wriggle away from the other. Finally, he sank back against the metal bars, giving up the fight. Which was when the fun really started.

The cage lowered until it was only a few feet above their heads, giving everyone an excellent view of the two combatants. Marco looked around, and saw that the other cages were lowering: obviously the victories in each of the cages were timed to happen at the same moment.

The black-clad bear grinned at his fallen opponent and reached down: roughly, with a single pull, he ripped the red rubber wrestling suit off him and threw it through the bars of the cage, where an appreciative onlooker grabbed it as a souvenir. The body that was revealed was just as the skin-tight suit had indicated: smooth, with well-defined chest and stomach muscles. But what drove the crowd wild was the cock that sprang upright: free from the restraint of the rubber, nine inches of circumcised dick lay solid and flat against the muscles of the man's stomach.

The larger one urgently pulled off his own rubber suit, showing off his chunky, hairy frame and pierced nipples. Disposing of his own suit to the excited crowd below, he knelt down, his hands still pinning the other's arms to the barred floor of the cage. His head nuzzled at the man's groin, and the crowd beneath had a perfect view of his own cock, short, but thick and erect, poking through the floor bars of the cage.

Marco had a good position: he could clearly see as the blond bear's mouth fastened itself around the dark-haired man's cock. Then, in a rapid manoeuvre, he flipped over so that his mouth was still sucking on the cock, while his own dick was hanging inches above the muscle-man's face. Although the bear's hands were no longer holding the other one down, that was now unnecessary: if the bear's weight above him hadn't been enough, it was obvious that he was now enjoying his captivity. Straining his head upwards, his lips and tongue sought out the bear's helmet, and, moments later, the two were locked together, sucking on one another's cocks like their lives depended on it. As they did so, their hands began to explore one another, fingers stroking chests and stomachs, reaching round and probing into arses.

'You chose a good night to arrive, Marco,' said Greg, knocking back his Bud. 'These two, Simon and Craig, are famous for putting on a good show.'

'Definitely a crowd-pleaser,' agreed Leigh.

Simon, the blond one, was grinding his cock into Craig's face, and Craig was doing his best to take all of it into his mouth. But Marco could see him tensing his body, ready to come, as Simon's tongue flicked over his swollen red helmet. Simon must have sensed it: the crowd fell silent as Simon's lips consumed all of Craig's shaft, sliding up and down the glistening pink flesh, wet with spit and pre-come. Craig's back arched, and Simon took his mouth away as shot after shot of Craig's spunk hit his face, his hair, his beard. Even as Simon gratefully licked a gobbet of come from his beard, he let out a groan and started to pump his cock deeper and deeper into Craig's mouth before sliding it out again, building up an urgent rhythm. Then he yelled out and shoved his cock even deeper, his whole body slumping onto Craig as his did so. A tell-tale dribble of white from the side of Craig's mouth was evidence of Simon's own release.

Finally, both drained, Simon hauled himself off Craig and lay down next to him. The cage began to ascend towards the ceiling, its departure propelled by rapturous applause from the audience. Marco couldn't help but join in. It had been an unbelievable sight, and the pressure that he felt in his shorts was evidence of that: Marco briefly entertained thoughts of asking Greg to arrange a meeting with Craig and Simon, but decided that he didn't really want to pull rank in the Elective, and also Leigh would probably belt him one. Looking around, Marco could see the other cages being lifted up at the same time: quite a feat of timing for the participants.

'I see you enjoyed it,' said Greg with a smile, his eyes dropping to Marco's shorts. Marco gave an embarrassed smile, but could see similar bulges in both Leigh's shorts and Greg's jeans. 'Glad to be of service.' Suddenly Greg's smile evaporated. 'Anyway, time to get down to business: we've got trouble.' He knocked back his beer. 'Big trouble, old man – big trouble.'

Marco sighed. He had expected as much. Unlike Nathan's last two trips abroad, and Marco and Leigh's trip to Paris, the Las Vegas trip had been instigated at Greg's request, after the shadowy Director of the Elective had informed all of his Comptrollers that Marco and Nathan were heading up a full-scale audit of the Elective's operations. And, whatever it was that Greg knew, it was obviously too sensitive to be consigned to the vagaries of e-mail or the phone – which in itself was odd, since the Elective's internal communications network was as secure as they came.

When Greg beckoned Marco and Leigh into his office, Marco knew that it was too sensitive to trust anyone.

Nathan held open the door to his room and allowed Kirk to enter. He still couldn't believe it: after all these years, he was going to get Kirk into bed. He just hoped it wasn't a disappointment: he remembered a similar situation a couple of years ago, when he had finally succeeded in persuading someone who he had been pursuing for ages to come home with him. Years of fantasising, years of dreaming of him while having a wank, had evaporated in one of the most lacklustre sexual performances that Nathan had ever endured. He just hoped that Kirk lived up to Nathan's expectations.

'So, this is your Munich base,' said Kirk, sitting heavily on the bed. 'This is the hotel room that you have always been trying to get me to come back to.' He looked around. 'Nice.'

Nathan poured both of them a vodka from the minibar before sitting down next to Kirk. 'I'm glad you approve.' Then he smiled mischievously. 'I just hope the rest of the evening gets your approval.'

Kirk grinned back. 'After all this time . . .' He reached out and stroked Nathan's knee. 'How could it fail?' He took the vodka from Nathan's hand and put both glasses on the floor.

Nathan put his arm around Kirk's shoulder, and pulled him closer to him; he started kissing him, feeling the German's rough stubble against his own goatee beard. His tongue invaded his mouth, but Kirk fought back, his own tongue colliding with Nathan's, intertwining with it.

Nathan's hand slid down from Kirk's shoulder, stroking his broad, solid back. Kirk wasn't quite as thick-set as Scott, but he was still muscular, and Nathan couldn't wait to see more. Stroking and kissing Kirk, Nathan could smell him, smell that scent that he always associated with Kirk. It was a mixture of

Kirk's aftershave, Fahrenheit, and his natural, musky odour. Overcome by a desire to smell more, Nathan broke off the kiss, and started to removed Kirk's T-shirt, pulling it out of the waistband of his jeans and rolling it up over his body.

For the first time, Nathan saw Kirk's unclothed body, and knew that all of his dreams, all of his fantasies, hadn't come close to matching the reality. Kirk was extremely hairy, thick black hair that covered his chest, his shoulders and most of his back, as well as his thick arms. Unable to resist, Nathan leant forward and started to bite Kirk's nipples – at first playfully, but, when it was clear from Kirk's gasps of pleasure, more roughly, more brutally.

Kirk responded by ripping off Nathan's denim shirt. It was lucky that the shirt was fastened with press-studs, or the buttons would have been pulled off with the urgency. Now they were both only partially clothed, their hairy bodies next to one another as they fell sideways on to the bed, their mouths locked in a deep, passionate kiss.

Nathan couldn't get enough of Kirk: his tongue forced its way into the German's mouth, while his other hand strayed from Kirk's back, down through the thick body hair until it was squeezing his arse. Then Nathan moved his hand round, so it was lying on top of the thick bulge of Kirk's erection which was straining to get free. And that was something that Nathan could accomplish very easily.

His fingers fumbled for a second until he found the top of the zip: then he pulled it down. The bulge forced its way through the fly, a hot bulge, a tell-tale stain of wetness on the blue cotton of his briefs.

Nathan's mouth moved down, from Kirk's own mouth to his chest, straying for a second to chew those tits once more, before carrying on, down, further and further, until his tongue was tracing a line through the hair of Kirk's stomach, but still he didn't stop. Finally, his mouth was resting on the warmth of Krik's erection, the smell of Kirk now so intense that Nathan couldn't resist any longer. His hand pulled down the cotton and allowed Kirk's dick its freedom.

And what a dick: nine inches long, thick and uncut. Nathan greedily took the helmet in his mouth and sucked, licking the moist red flesh, while his hand moved to Kirk's tits and squeezed them, harder than before, hard enough to make Kirk groan with both pleasure and pain.

Before Nathan could do any more, Kirk pushed him off and pinned him to the bed. Then he straddled him and inched his body up Nathan's, across his stomach, across his chest, until his cock was only tantalising inches away from Nathan's eager mouth.

'Go on, suck it again!' Kirk ordered, but Nathan needed no such encouragement. He strained his head forward, his tongue reaching out to flick and tease at Kirk's helmet. Kirk responded by pushing his groin forward, forcing his thick cock into Nathan's mouth.

Nathan took as much of the shaft as he could, sucking the warm, sweaty meat, tasting the sweet pre-come which leaked from the dick-slit.

Another sensation suddenly assaulted Nathan, and his eyes widened with the pleasure. Kirk was undoing Nathan's flies, and the feeling of those fingers, stroking his hard-on, was magnificent. Then he felt his cock released from his jeans and gasped at the freedom. His dick, stiffer than Nathan could remember it ever being, was ramrod straight against his naked stomach.

'That's better,' said Kirk. With his hands behind him, he started to pull Nathan's jeans down; Nathan did the same, roughly pulling at the belt. A few moments later, both were completely naked: for a second, they admired one another, and it was obvious from Kirk's expression that, just like Nathan, this was something that he had been waiting for for a very long time.

Before Nathan could do anything else, Kirk pulled his belt from his jeans.

'No, it's time for a bit of fun,' he said with an evil grin on his face. 'I've been waiting for this for a long while, and now you're in this position I want to make sure that you don't go anywhere.'

He climbed off Nathan and roughly turned him over so he was face-down on the bed. Then he pulled Nathan's hands together and tied them with the leather belt, tied them so tightly that there was no way that Nathan could get out.

'Now I've got you where I want you,' he breathed. Nathan felt Kirk get back on top of him, felt the German's breath on the sensitive spot at the back of his neck. Kirk began to nibble on Nathan's neck, and Nathan gasped at the feeling: that spot was the most sensual part of his body – above his waist – and he had been known to come, simply by having it chewed. But Nathan was determined that that wouldn't happen this time. This was something that he wanted to enjoy.

Kirk's mouth moved down, chewing on Nathan's shoulders, then down to the small of his back, and Nathan found himself twitching as the German's teeth bit into the sensitive skin. All of Nathan's body was on fire now, his skin like another sexual organ, and every bite threatened to bring Nathan to orgasm.

How Nathan held out when Kirk's mouth reached his arse, Nathan just didn't know. The feeling of Kirk's tongue, tracing a line between his cheeks, was exquisite, and Nathan groaned with pleasure, the groan increasing to a frantic cry as Kirk's tongue began to probe his ring. Kirk's hands were on his cheeks, pulling them apart so that his tongue could reach further and further into Nathan, fucking his tight, hot little hole. Nathan's back arched as he tried to push his arse into Kirk's face, wanting more and more of him inside him.

'I think you're ready now,' said Kirk, and Nathan heard the sound of a condom being taken from its wrapper. Then he gasped as he felt the cold wetness of lubricant as it was smeared around and inside his ring.

'I have wanted this for a long time, Nathan,' Kirk breathed. 'I have wanted to feel my cock, sliding in and out of your arse, grinding away at you until I come inside you.'

'Go on – do it,' Nathan urged. 'Please, Kirk, fuck me.'

Kirk didn't hesitate: Nathan relaxed his arse as he felt Kirk's helmet touch his ring, but even he struggled as Kirk's thick German cock forced its way inside him. Nathan yelled out in genuine pain as Kirk rammed more and more of himself into Nathan's arse – it had been a long time since Nathan had allowed anyone that big to enter him. But the thought of Kirk, wonderful Kirk, screwing him was enough for him to bite back the pain, to accommodate as much of Kirk inside him as he could.

It didn't take Kirk long to fill Nathan up, and the pain of feeling as if he were being split in two was overwhelmed by the burning joy of Kirk's helmet, then his shaft, sliding over his prostate. Now fully inside him, Kirk waited a second, waited for Nathan to become used to the entire of his arse being filled by Kirk's dick. Then he withdrew half of his length, and Nathan groaned as Kirk's dick once again stroked his prostate.

'You like that?' Kirk asked, his hands on Nathan's shoulders. 'You like the feeling of my cock being inside you?'

Nathan didn't hesitate: 'I've been waiting for this for so long. Keep screwing me, Kirk. Keep fucking me, keep filling me up.'

Kirk responded by slamming his length into Nathan before brutally pulling it out once more; then he forced it back in, all the way, his balls swinging against Nathan's arse.

Nathan's cock was now swollen and red, and Nathan knew that the slightest touch, the slightest stimulation, would bring him off. But he didn't want that, he wanted to hold off until he felt Kirk's load shoot inside him, until he felt those big balls dumping their hot spunk in his arse. Even if he had wanted to wank himself off, to bring his won release, he couldn't: the tight leather strap of Kirk's belt was cutting into his wrists, preventing him from doing anything that Kirk didn't want. Just the way that Nathan liked it.

Kirk's rhythm was building up now, deep strokes driving his cock into Nathan, followed by withdrawal, followed by yet another brutal thrust. In and out, in and out, as Kirk fucked Nathan, as Kirk did what Nathan had dreamt about for years.

Nathan knew that he couldn't hold out much longer, but, from Kirk's heavy panting, neither could the German. With one final, desperate fuck, Kirk pushed all of his cock into Nathan and then let out a deep, guttural cry of triumph as his come flooded out of him. With a series of grunts, Kirk pushed his cock even further into Nathan, his helmet battering Nathan's prostate again and again until Nathan could wait no longer.

Arched over the bed, his cock twitched and throbbed as he shot his hot white load, drops of come shooting from the raw, red helmet and falling onto the crumpled bedding. Nathan couldn't remember an orgasm ever feeling that intense, that fulfilling. Totally, absolutely drained, he slumped onto the duvet, turning over as he did so.

Kirk was looking at him, his face red with exertion, his forehead damp with sweat. Nathan noticed that Kirk's thick body hair was matted, but then, so was Nathan's. 'Well?' he asked as he undid the leather of his belt, allowing Nathan's hands to go free.

Nathan laughed. 'Are you asking me whether it was worth the wait?'

Kirk nodded.

Nathan reached out and grabbed Kirk, then hugged him and kissed him deeply. Finally, he pulled his mouth away and looked Kirk in the eyes. 'Does that answer your question?'

Nathan's cock was already getting hard again, and Nathan

knew that it was going to be a long night. Just how he wanted it.

'Drink?' Greg indicated a bottle of Jack Daniel's on his desk.

Marco shook his head: something told him that what Greg was about to tell him would require a clear head, and the last thing that Marco wanted was to feel any more drunk than he already did.

'Well, old man, we've got a problem.' Greg knocked back his Jack Daniel's in one go. 'Potentially, the biggest threat the Elective's ever faced.'

Marco frowned. The Elective had survived two world wars, countless recessions, the fall of Communism: all global events that could have undermined the Elective's financial and social success. But the Elective had endured. What could be so serious to make Greg concerned like this? 'Go on,' he muttered.

'As I'm sure you know, Las Vegas is a little different from the other Elective branches in the States —'

'It's the primary communications and computer centre,' Marco interrupted. 'All of the Elective branches across the world link into it.' In an organisation that prided itself on its secrets, the complex was a secret in a class of its own. Only Deputy Comptrollers and above were aware of its existence: an underground base in the Nevada Desert that had taken the fortunes of some of the Elective's finest to build. But without it, the Elective's web of secrecy could never have survived the information age.

Greg nodded. 'Exactly. Cost the Elective close on a billion bucks to build that place. The most secure computer centre outside the US Government – possibly even more secure. And yet —'

'It's been breached.' Marco knew this had to be the reason: the logic all tied up. Why else would Greg have brought them over to Las Vegas? If the Elective's network had been breached, no lines of communication were secure. Whoever had broken into the network would be able to monitor the entire Elective. The network contained everything: addresses, phone numbers, the complete membership list . . . With that compromised, the entire Elective was wide open.

'But why do you suspect that it's been hacked into?'

Greg stood up. 'Not here – we'd better go somewhere a bit more secure. Come on – the helicopter's ready.'

Nathan stared out of the window into the Munich night, his feelings confused. Sex with Kirk had been better than he could ever have imagined – even the best of his wank fantasies could never have matched the sheer pleasure that the two of them had just experienced. But that begged an important question: why?

The trouble was, Nathan was pretty sure that he knew why. When he had first met Kirk five years ago, he knew that there had been an immediate mutual attraction – it had been obvious. But the years of running around, the games and pursuits . . . that's what Nathan had thought it was: a game. The last hour had shown Nathan that it was much more than that. He thought about Kirk, currently in the shower, and the image of him soaping his hairy chest and washing his thick cock started to give Nathan a hard-on. He glanced at his watch: it was nearly five in the morning. He could always sleep on the plane, he supposed. Then he shook his head and sighed. Who was he kidding? More sex with Kirk would only complicate matters, matters which were refusing to sort themselves out in his mind.

Kirk was single now, and there was no denying that he felt the same way as Nathan did. The fact that Kirk lived in Munich was now irrelevant: the resources of the Elective were at Nathan's disposal, and a trip to Munich from London was nothing. Hell, Kirk could even move over to live with Nathan: it would be easy for Nathan to get Kirk a job over there . . .

Nathan sighed. It was all pointless speculation. Nathan

already had a boyfriend, and there was no denying that he loved Scott. He was allowing his flight of fancy to overcome him: the triumph of finally having sex with Kirk was letting him get carried away.

At least, that was what he was telling himself. The sooner he was away from Munich and back with Scott, the better.

Turning from the window, he saw Kirk's jeans lying in a heap on the floor. He absent-mindedly picked them up and started to smooth them out, but stopped when Kirk's wallet fell to the carpet and burst open. Nathan cursed under his breath and knelt down to pick up the scattered contents – and then froze.

Kirk's wallet contained all of the usual detritus that men tended to carry around with them: business cards, credit cards, a smattering of cash . . . but the business card that Nathan was staring at was one that he'd never thought he'd see again.

The name on the card made Nathan's stomach churn, made him want to be sick. Against all of his normal journalistic instincts, he had dismissed his suspicions as being nothing more than coincidence.

But how could it all be coincidence? How could his unexpected stopover in Munich be an act of chance? How could his meeting with a newly single Kirk be nothing more than fate? How could it be – when Kirk was carrying Adrian Delancey's business card in his wallet?

Six

Leigh gulped as the helicopter lurched away from the dusty ground of the helipad and took to the air. He had no problems flying – indeed, he was beginning to realise that he actually quite enjoyed it – but that was when he was strapped into a first-class seat, sipping champagne. Helicopters were something else, especially helicopters which were virtually transparent, with all of Las Vegas spread out below them.

'Are you okay?' asked Marco, squeezing his knee. Was his discomfort that obvious, Leigh wondered. He hazarded a glance through the floor, and watched as the helicopter flew down the strip, passing the huge jutting needle of the Stratosphere Tower, then over the brightly lit hotels with their evening dress of neon. The glittering black pyramid of the Luxor loomed towards them, closer, closer . . . and then the brilliant white beacon on top – apparently the brightest man-made light on Earth – momentarily blinded him as they flew straight through the beam and its glare flooded the interior of the helicopter. It was obvious that the pilot was showing off: Leigh just hoped that his stomach wasn't a casualty.

'Never been in a helicopter before,' Leigh whispered as they left the beam and headed outwards into the darkness of the Nevada desert. 'It's a bit . . .' He trailed off as his stomach threatened to give his hastily snatched hot-dog a repeat performance, and sat back and tried to enjoy the view. He was just grateful that he and Marco had been in too much of a rush to get changed and reach the Bear's Retreat to have had time for anything more than a bit of junk food. And even that was threatening to make a return trip.

'I'm sorry if this all looks a bit mysterious,' said Greg, still wearing his trademark cowboy hat, 'but with the entire communications network of the Elective potentially compromised, I thought it best if we looked at what's happened first hand.'

Leigh felt sick, but it wasn't purely due to the flight: indeed, as the helicopter flew over the floodlit splendour of the Hoover Dam and Lake Mead, he realised that he was actually beginning to enjoy it. What was unsettling him was the unseen presence of Adrian Delancey, the bastard responsible for having Leigh kidnapped and sold into slavery. When the Director of the Elective had consigned Delancey to slavery himself as punishment, Leigh had hoped that that was the end of the matter. But it wasn't: everywhere they went, everything they did, the Elective was all around them, and, by association, the shadow of Delancey. It was almost as if he was constantly watching them all . . . watching and waiting for his moment to strike.

Okay, so he was probably overreacting. Delancey was now a virtual prisoner, and soon, very soon, any trace of his presence in the Elective would have been erased. He just hoped that Marco would honour his promise, and take them as far away from the Elective as he could once all of this was over. He glanced at Marco, staring out of the window as they approached the Grand Canyon, and dreamt of that day when they would be out of the Elective, just Leigh and Marco together. Would that ever happen? Or was there too much of the Elective in Marco, and too much of Marco in the Elective, for them ever to escape?

Greg leant over, straining to make himself heard over the noise of the rotor blades. 'We're nearly there,' he shouted. 'When we get there, you'll realise why I couldn't tell you any of this over the phone.'

The few minutes in between Nathan finding the business card and Kirk coming out of the shower seemed to stretch into eternity, but there was nothing that Nathan could do about it. Silently, not giving a clue, he had to stand there while Kirk got dressed: his long-running desire for the German had evaporated, and he watched impassively as Kirk pulled his T-shirt over his fit body and fastened his jeans. Only when Kirk was ready to leave did Nathan reveal what was on his mind.

'Who's Adrian Delancey?' he asked innocently, his back to Kirk and staring out of the window.

'I don't know what you mean,' said Kirk. Even though he was speaking in German, Nathan could tell that he was lying.

'It's quite simple, Kirk. I found a business card for a Mr Adrian Delancey in your wallet. How do you know him?' Nathan's words were calm and controlled, although within he was almost boiling with anger, with shock . . . and with fear.

'You went through my wallet? I trusted you, Nathan. I thought you were my friend –'

Nathan span round to confront him. 'Spare me your platitudes, Kirk!' he spat. 'I've been in your wallet, I've seen his business card.' Almost without thinking, he marched over to Kirk and grabbed him by the arms. 'Tell me, you bastard!'

Kirk pulled himself away, and the expression on his face stiffened. His voice lost the warmth of friendship, hardening like steel. 'Think you're so clever, Dexter? Then you tell me.'

'It's a trap, isn't it? The whole thing – the plane breaking down, me meeting you . . . All of it's been a trap.'

'Clever boy,' said Kirk sarcastically. 'Your reputation as one of the finest investigative journalists in the world is secure.'

Nathan shook his head. 'But why? What the hell can

Delancey gain by having me stuck in Munich . . .' He fell silent as it became obvious. Blindingly obvious. 'He wanted me out of England.' But why? Then the horrible truth – truth compounded by his earlier intimacy with Kirk – hit him like a fist in the stomach. 'Scott!'

Kirk grinned, but it was an evil, sadistic grin. 'That's only part of it, Dexter, but it'll do for a start.'

'But his cover's been blown,' said Nathan. 'All it'll take is a single phone call to the Elective –'

'But phone calls can be traced.' Kirk's expression was unreadable. 'Phone calls can be blocked.'

Nathan was about to reply; he was about to mention the Elective's own communications network, a network so highly encrypted and secure that even the US Government couldn't hack into it. The communications network that had cost billions to build and would have been the envy of most world powers – if anyone had known about it.

The communications network that was based in the middle of the Nevada desert. Near Las Vegas. Where Marco and Leigh were. Where they had been summoned by the local Comptroller . . .

There was only one conclusion to be drawn: Delancey had done the impossible . . . and hacked into the Elective's network. Under other circumstances, Nathan wouldn't have believed it possible: everything he had been told about the Elective's network made it clear that it was impenetrable. But time and again, Delancey had proved that the impossible was his province. And now, nothing – no bit of information, no phone call, no e-mail – was safe from him. The entire Elective was an open book.

Nathan decided not to pursue that particular avenue: he didn't want Kirk – and therefore Delancey – to think he was worried. Not yet. 'So that's his little game, is it? Divide and conquer?'

Sitting down on the rumpled bed, his demeanour calm,

unworried, Kirk sneered. 'You have no idea of the power we have, Dexter – none at all.'

'More power than I can possibly imagine, no doubt,' countered Nathan. 'Give us a break. I've heard this all before, Kirk: empty threats from Adrian Delancey.' But inside, the seeds of doubt had been sown and were taking root. The last time Nathan had ignored one of Delancey's threats, he had almost lost everything. He tried to appeal to Kirk's better nature, praying that he actually had one. Surely he couldn't have misjudged the German that badly? 'We? We? When you dine with the devil you need a long spoon, Kirk.' He took a step towards the bed. 'Why are you doing this, Kirk? What is he offering you? You do realise that he's using you?'

'Using me? That's good, coming from someone who's been trying to sleep with me for the last five years. All you wanted was sex: the fact that I had split up with Wolfgang, and might possibly be a little upset over it, didn't come into it, did it? No, Nathan Dexter has to get what he wants. At least Adrian is offering me something concrete, something I can take home.'

'Like what?'

'A purpose, Nathan, a reason for everything.'

'A reason to betray your friends, you mean.' But Nathan knew that all he was doing was trading insults, biding for time in a situation that was rapidly spiralling out of control. Once before he had underestimated Adrian Delancey, and the cost of that had almost been more than he could bear. And that time he had had some idea of the resources that Delancey could draw upon; this time, God alone knew what his power base was – although the evidence suggested that it was on a par with those of the Elective. The ability to sabotage one of the Elective's private jets, to know exactly what all of them were doing at any given time . . . the knowledge to hack into the supposed secure communications network, for God's sake! Whatever Delancey was up to, he could have been building up this second power base all the time that he was Comptroller of

PAUL C. ALEXANDER

the Elective, channelling funds and materials into it without anyone being any the wiser. When he had been exposed by Nathan and Marco, financial irregularities had been found; what if those millions had only been the visible tip of a veritable fortune? Before he had risen up the ranks of the Elective, Delancey had been one of the bright boys in the city, one of the most well-respected accountants in London. With his skill, and the billions that passed through the Elective's coffers, who could guess how much he could have hidden away?

But it was time for Nathan to stand his ground. 'So, Kirk, what now? Are you going to kill me? Or is this just a distraction so your paymaster can hunt my friends down?' It was all that Nathan could do not to glance towards the door, to check whether there was some way to escape. But what then? Alone on the streets of Munich, with Delancey's agents hiding in every shadow? Nor could he warn Scott or Marco or Leigh: if the communications network had been compromised, everything, every plan, every counter-measure, every chance of outwitting Delancey would be known before they had a chance to act. Once again, Nathan cursed himself for not paying attention to his instincts.

'Oh Nathan, don't be so melodramatic,' said Kirk, his manner changing, returning to the friendly Kirk that Nathan had fallen for, all those years ago. It didn't fool Nathan for a second. 'Actually, it's quite the opposite. Adrian was very impressed with you when you last locked horns.'

'Impressed? How magnanimous of him,' said Nathan sarcastically. 'I cannot help but be touched.'

'Nathan: Adrian's willing to cut a deal with you. He'll leave you all alone – you, your boyfriend, Marco, Leigh – if you just agree to listen to his proposals.' Kirk held his hands out: 'That's all you have to do, Nathan – listen. And if you don't like what you hear, you can simply walk away. End of story.'

Nathan shook his head, almost unable to believe what he was hearing. He knew of Delancey's love of the melodramatic, but this was going from the sublime to the ridiculous: from industrial espionage to a job interview in one easy motion. 'Are you saying he wants to offer me a job? If it hadn't escaped your notice, Kirk, I already have one.'

'You call the Elective a job? The Elective is old, Nathan, full of old people with old ideas. It needs a man of strength to guide it, to prepare it for the new millennium. A man like Adrian Delancey. But they were frightened of him, frightened of his power. So they deserted him, preferring to walk towards extinction instead of marching towards glory.'

Nathan started clapping, a slow handclap that he hoped would rile Kirk. 'Spoken like the good little Nietzschean that you are.'

'Mock away, Nathan. But you will see that we are right.'

Nathan sighed, saddened by this reappraisal that Kirk was forcing him to do. Over the course of his career as a journalist he had seen it countless times before: people, desperate for a path to follow in life, falling under the spell of a stronger, more charismatic person. And there was no doubting that Adrian Delancey, despite being a complete bastard, was charismatic. Once again, Nathan knew that he had been outmanoeuvred by Delancey – and the only option open to him was to play along until Delancey displayed a weakness.

'Very well – I'll listen to what he has to say. When can I meet him?' Meeting Delancey was the last thing he wanted, but it was inevitable. Delancey wanted a showdown, Delancey wanted to confront Nathan so that he could humiliate him – that much was obvious. Nathan just wanted to be prepared.

'Soon, Nathan: very soon. But it will be at a time and a place of his choosing.' He smiled sadly. 'I like you, Nathan – I really do. I just hope that you come to your senses.'

Nathan ignored the backhanded compliment. 'Am I excused now?' Nathan was tired; yes, he was worried, but there was absolutely nothing that he could do: not from here. Best to check that the others were okay, have a rest, then return to

London tomorrow. Then the four of them — Nathan, Marco, Leigh and Scott — could have a summit meeting, and work out what to do next. He just hoped that Marco, who had worked with Delancey and who knew him far better than Nathan did, would know of some weakness, some way of outwitting him.

Kirk walked up to Nathan and stood only inches away, staring into his eyes. Nathan could have sworn that there was something in there, some last vestige of affection towards him . . . or it could have been Kirk's misguided conviction that Delancey was right. Then Kirk kissed him, a hard, passionate kiss that Nathan pulled away from, even though Kirk's closeness, the freshly showered smell of his body, the feel of his stubble, was making his cock stiffen.

'A pity,' said Kirk. 'We could have been quite a team.' And then he was gone, out of the hotel room and out of Nathan's life.

Nathan watched the door click and then slumped on to the bed, his mind a mass of conflicting emotions. His hurt over Kirk's betrayal was mixed with his worries about the others, and all of that was churned up with the suspicion — no, the proof — that Adrian Delancey was back in business, and clearly more powerful than ever before. Once before, Delancey had used someone that Nathan cared about to get at him: that time it had been Scott. There was no doubting that, as a way of making Nathan follow orders, it worked. And Delancey obviously knew that it worked.

What the hell was he going to do?

He picked up the phone, but then replaced the receiver. Delancey knew where he was; with his access to the Elective's communications, anything that Nathan said would be immediately picked up.

With a sigh, Nathan slumped on to the rumpled bed, the sheets still full of the smell and signs of his and Kirk's frantic lovemaking. All he could do now was wait. Wait and hope.

★

The casino was packed as Marco and Leigh walked through the reception of the MGM Grand towards the lifts, but the enforced amusements of Las Vegas held no attraction for either of them. All Marco wanted to do was get back to their suite, have a shower . . . and then hold Leigh tight for the rest of the night. The sooner that the two of them got back to London with the information they had garnered from their visit, the better.

Only now did Marco realise why Greg's news had been too sensitive to trust to the Elective's secure communications network.

It was because there *was* no secure communications network.

The communications and computing centre that sat at the logical heart of the Elective was in a huge bunker, buried beneath the Nevada Desert – about a mile from the Grand Canyon, to be precise. Greg had been quite the tour guide as the helicopter descended, explaining that it had been built about five years ago, and had cost as much as the US Government's and the Pentagon's own systems put together. Not that that was surprising: the Elective, with its operations in every country in the world, needed that level of computing power. Operatives needed to transfer information securely, at the speed of light; only the billions of dollars' worth of equipment, hidden beneath the desert, could supply that.

Until now.

As Greg had shown them, someone, some agency, had managed to blow the entire system wide open. The Elective was an open book to whoever had had the skills, the expertise, to break into an encrypted computer network such as that of the Elective.

The trouble was, no one had noticed until now. According to Greg, the break-in had happened roughly a month ago – if the Elective's experts had got it right. But the cybernetic burglars had been clever – very clever. They had left no trace, no clue as to their incursion. According to Greg, it was only by chance that the experts had realised what was going on. Marco cast his mind back to their arrival at the computing centre.

The helicopter had landed in the desert, near an unremarkable wooden shack, its surface sand-blasted clean by the desert winds. But that had simply been the entrance. A hundred feet below, the Elective's computer and communications network monitored the whole world. Soon after landing, Marco, Leigh and Greg were sitting in an office just off the antiseptic white of the Elective's computer centre, being told the news that Greg had been unable to tell them until he was sure that they couldn't be bugged or overheard – except by the dictaphone that Marco produced, explaining that he wanted to capture everything to play back to Nathan later.

Marco was fairly computer literate, but even he had had to ask Greg to explain it in words of one syllable. Greg had called in one of the centre's experts, a big bear called Richie, dressed incongruously in Levis, white shirt and leather waistcoat.

'The system's called ENET,' Richie explained in his thick New Jersey accent. 'Not very original, but it serves its purpose. ENET is surrounded by what they call a firewall, which is another computer system designed to prevent the outside looking in and seeing what we do.'

'But this is a communications centre,' said Leigh. 'Surely, phone calls and e-mails are coming in and out of here all the time?'

Richie nodded. 'Exactly. The firewall is just to stop people from seeing how our network – this place, with all of the servers, mainframes and workstations – is put together. For traffic in and out of the firewall, we have to use a different method to ensure security, since that traffic is running over standard channels – commercial phone lines, that sort of thing.'

'Encryption,' said Leigh, clearly desperate to make some sort of contribution to the conversation. 'You encode everything so no one can read it.'

'Exactly. Every phone call, every e-mail, every fax, is encrypted. When it arrives at its destination, you need the encryption key to decode it.'

Marco thought about this, but Leigh was there before him. 'But what if someone else got this key? It isn't difficult to hack into a phone line, is it?'

Richie scratched his beard. 'Nope. Piece of pie if you know how. But they wouldn't have the key. The key is a special combination of things, including the destination of the call or e-mail. And, more importantly, they *never* have the key. It comes from here. When Marco here phones you up, he dials a special code before your phone number.'

Marco nodded, remembering dialling 070564 in front of every call and fax, of typing it into the subject line of every e-mail.

'That code alerts this centre that an Elective call is being made. This centre then follows the call, and then actively decodes it at the other end. This centre monitors every single telephone and computer network in the world. That's why it cost billions of dollars.' He gave them a wave. 'Anyway, better carry on trying to keep them out. Whoever *they* are. Later.'

As Riche left the office, Marco shook his head. 'So this place has a firewall around it that stops outsiders from looking in, and every call that's made under Elective business is encoded, and that code can only be deciphered from here. So why do you think that the network's been compromised?'

Greg held up a hand. 'Because of the evidence.' He pointed to a stack of papers on a nearby desk. 'Each of those sheets refers to an incident over the last two months in which some form of transaction − a financial one, a meeting, the passing of information − has been learnt about, and action taken by person or persons unknown to screw it up.'

Marco couldn't help laughing. 'Things go wrong and you think we've been hacked into? Aren't you being a bit melodramatic?'

Greg suddenly leapt from his chair, his entire body taut with anger. To his credit, however, his voice was unwavering, the obvious anger held in check.

'Last week, my brother Gary, the Comptroller of the Washington branch of the Elective, was due to meet with me here, in Vegas. He was bringing plans for some business expansion that we're about to start in the Far East. He never made it.'

'With all due respect, Greg – why should that indicate that there's anything wrong?' Leigh's tone was tactful, but Marco still wished that he hadn't said anything.

Greg's voice was still calm, but too calm. 'Because I was the only person who knew Gary's itinerary; I was the only person who knew which flight he was catching; I was the only person who knew the value of the papers in his briefcase. He was shot and injured in a drive-by shooting, and his briefcase was stolen.' Greg sighed, and the look in his eyes was dark, hooded. Marco knew that he didn't want to be around when Greg found the people responsible.

'Three days later, another deal was struck in the Far East. A deal that was virtually identical to the Elective's. We were still trying to gather together copies of the paperwork which we needed to close the deal when we learnt that we'd been beaten to it. It was exactly the same deal that we had been planning to do.'

Marco was one step ahead. 'I take it that this is only one of a number of similar cases?'

Greg nodded towards the paperwork on the desk. 'Each of those cases represents some sort of business deal that the Elective has lost out on. And we never lose out on business deals.'

Marco knew that to be true. The Elective could rely on the business, financial and administrative acumen of thousands of the greatest movers and shakers on Earth. There was no way that anyone else could stand in the way of the Elective, unless ... Despite the warmth, Marco shivered. The answer was obvious, but so impossible to believe that he hadn't even considered it.

Until now.

But it was Leigh who spoke, Leigh who voiced the terrible suspicion in Marco's mind.

'It's that bastard Delancey, isn't it?' Leigh's voice was quiet, restrained. But Marco knew what was going through his mind.

Greg stood up. 'Only Elective members of Deputy Comptroller rank are even aware of this complex. I've had every single one of them checked out, and there's absolutely no evidence to link them with this . . . this conspiracy, for want of a better word.'

Marco glanced at Leigh, and was shocked to see how still, how drained, he looked. As close as they were to each other, Marco would never be able to fully understand the true horror of Leigh's enslavement, or the depths of his hatred for Delancey. The idea that the man wasn't safely locked away, but had resumed his machinations, was bad enough for Marco; but what about Leigh? Instinctively, he moved over to his boyfriend and put a comforting arm around his shoulder.

'You feel sure it's Delancey?' asked Leigh quietly.

Greg shrugged. 'Who else could it be? He's the only person who could possibly be in any position to do anything like this. But there isn't any proof; there's absolutely nothing to link Delancey to the Syndicate.'

'The Syndicate?' That was a new one, thought Marco.

'The Syndicate appears to be the organisation behind most of the aborted deals,' Greg answered. 'We haven't got any names or faces; it appears to be a holding company, but one with extensive gay interests.'

'How better to destroy the Elective than by setting up a rival,' Marco muttered. Just the sort of twisted scheme that would appeal to someone like Delancey. The more he heard, the more likely it seemed that Delancey was behind it. 'Who else knows about this?'

'The staff here. And the Director knows about the string of deals going wrong – he couldn't help but notice it – but I haven't told him about this complex being broken in to.'

'Hang on,' said Leigh. 'You still haven't explained why this business-deal stuff means that you've got hackers.'

'Because a lot of the inside information that we were going to use – that the Syndicate *did* use – only existed in the computers here, so the only possible answer, however unlikely, is that we've been broken into. Richie and his team think that they've found evidence in the system logs, but nothing specific. And if that's so, I can't trust any of our systems. When we leave here, I'm taking the first flight over to Europe to see the Director in person, tell him what we suspect is going on. Thankfully, the Director's Codes aren't linked to this system.'

'Is there anything we can do?'

'I'm glad you asked, old man,' said Greg, a touch of his old personality shining through. 'I presume that you're going straight back to England?'

Marco nodded. 'We're due to meet up with Nathan. Actually, I'll be glad of his advice.'

'That's excellent.' Greg raised a finger. 'Are you far from Manchester?'

What an odd question. 'A couple of hours. Why?'

'Because my men here claim that there's only one person who can categorically prove that our network's been compromised. The man who designed it.'

Marco put two and two together. 'And he lives in Manchester?' It seemed rather odd to think that a computer specialist who could build what amounted to the ultimate secured computer network would live in the North of England – you'd have expected him to be in Silicon Valley. But why not?

'I presume you've tried to contact him?'

'Actually, no, I couldn't take the risk. If Delancey – assuming it's Delancey – realised that we were after him, the chances are

102

that he'd spirit him away. Much better to approach him in person. I've got all his details here.' He threw Marco a padded envelope.

'Hang on a minute,' said Leigh. 'If he designed it, who's to say that he's not already in on it? Who's to say that he's not the one who hacked into here?'

Greg smiled. 'That's the main reason why I want you to find him. Because the chances are . . . he *is* the one who did it.'

Now, after another stomach–churning helicopter flight, Marco and Leigh were back in their hotel. Marco had offered to buy Leigh a drink in one of the many bars in the casino, such as the Flying Monkey Bar, or the Brown Derby theme bar, but Leigh wanted none of it. All he wanted was to get back to their room and shut Las Vegas out. And Marco could fully understand why.

'Fancy anything from room service?' asked Marco quietly, standing by the phone. The room was luxurious: the lounge area was dominated by an enormous bed, at least twice the size of a normal double bed, which faced a huge, wide-screen television. A door led off into the marble bathroom, which was as big as Marco's own flat in St John's Wood. One wall of curtains cut off the view of the desert that both Leigh and Marco had admired, as they had watched the sun redden and sink the previous night. The night before they had learnt what was really going on.

It didn't matter how luxurious the hotel was; it didn't matter how exciting or entrancing Las Vegas was. The knowledge that Adrian Delancey was back in their lives was tearing Leigh apart. And that hurt Marco.

Leigh shook his head. 'Food's the last thing on my mind,' he said.

Marco replaced the receiver and sat down next to him on the bed. He pulled Leigh towards him. 'Delancey?'

Leigh frowned. 'I knew it was too good to be true. I knew

that when you agreed to give up all of this Elective stuff, that something would get in the way.'

Marco sighed and squeezed Leigh tightly. He was suddenly aware of the threat that Delancey posed: not just to the Elective, but to Marco and Leigh's relationship.

Leigh stood up and started to take his clothes off.

'It's a bit early to go to bed, isn't it?' said Marco, before suddenly realising what Leigh was up to. 'Sorry – stupid question.'

Marco knew what Leigh wanted. Leigh wanted to be dominated, to be a slave to Marco's instructions. And that suited Marco fine.

Slowly, Leigh removed his shirt, revealing a compact, muscular body with a light dusting of hair over his tits. A vivid green dragon, its wings outstretched, was tattooed on his left shoulder. Then he undid his jeans, letting them drop to the floor.

At the sight of his boyfriend undressing, Marco had taken his cock out, and was grasping it in his hand, slowly wanking it as Leigh put on a show for him. 'Come on, boy!' he ordered. 'Get those boxer shorts off. Show me your thick cock.' Marco knew that Leigh enjoyed their role play, and tonight it might be just the thing to take his mind off Delancey.

'Yes, sir,' said Leigh meekly, and pulled off his boxers and jeans in one go. Standing there naked, his cock was stiff and ready, but Leigh knew better than to touch it without being told to do so. Marco stared at Leigh's cock, desperate to suck it, but knowing that that would come later

'Now, boy – undress me.' Marco stood up and beckoned Leigh to come over. Obediently, Leigh walked towards Marco, his stiff cock bobbing as he did so. But Leigh still couldn't touch it – those were the rules that they observed in their little game.

Leigh started with Marco's shirt, then his boots, then his jeans, until both of them were standing in the middle of the hotel room, completely naked. Marco glanced in the mirror and liked what he saw: solid, muscular Leigh, standing next to Marco's bear-like body with its thick covering of dark hair.

'Now – suck my cock.'

Leigh knelt on the carpet and put his mouth around Marco's stiff cock, his hands clutching Marco's arse-cheeks. Marco felt a shudder of pleasure as his boyfriend's lips slid up and down his thick, fat dick, but that was nothing compared to what Leigh did next. Without being told to, his fingers began to probe Marco's arse, slipping inside his ring and making Marco groan with the sensation.

But Leigh hadn't been told to do that. So he needed to be punished. Marco slapped him round the face. 'I didn't tell you to do that, did I?' When there was no response, Marco slapped him again. 'Well?'

Leigh pulled his mouth off Marco's cock and looked up at him, an expression of fear on his face. 'No, sir. I'm sorry, sir.'

Marco raised an eyebrow. 'For that, you're going to have to lick out my arse, boy.' He walked over to the bed and lay on it face down. 'And I want to feel that tongue of yours right inside me, do you hear?'

'Yes, sir.' Leigh knelt down between Marco's legs, and pulled his arse-cheeks apart with his hands. Marco could feel his ring being stretched open, and couldn't wait for the touch of Leigh's tongue. It didn't take long. The cold wetness of Leigh as his tongue probed Marco's arse was exquisite, as he licked the hairy ring, darting in and out of Marco's arse, probing the warm darkness.

'Now your fingers, boy!' Marco commanded, and groaned with pleasure as he felt Leigh's finger penetrating him, reaching inside him. 'More!' he barked.

Leigh's finger was fully inside him, reaching up so that it was tickling away at Marco's prostate, sending shivers of glorious, wonderful pleasure through him. Leigh knew what he was doing: he stroked it, he teased it, he did what Marco wanted him to do and nothing else.

'Now you're going to fuck me.'

He heard Leigh open the condom packet; he felt Leigh lubricating his arse. Then he felt his ring being pushed open, driven open, as Leigh's cock began to slide inside him. Inch by inch, Leigh drove his dick into Marco's hungry arse, doing it just the way that Marco liked it: slowly. Marco liked to feel his arse filling up, liked to feel every inch of his boyfriend's cock as it entered him. As soon as he knew that all of it was inside him, he tensed his arse muscles, squeezing Leigh's cock with a deliberate rhythm. Marco knew that Leigh liked that, and he had been a good boy for his master, hadn't he?

Marco could tell that Leigh was enjoying it from the gasps of pleasure he could hear from above him. 'Now, boy – fuck me!'

Leigh withdrew his cock a few inches before slamming it back into Marco's arse, then again, and again. Marco gave a satisfied sigh as Leigh continued to slide his hard-on into Marco's ring, the thick cock forcing its way into him. Marco continued to tense his muscles, teasing and exciting Leigh every time all of his cock was inside him. As this was happening, Marco's hand was firmly grasped around his own dick, wanking himself off in time to Leigh's thrusts. He could feel himself getting closer, and, knowing Leigh as well as he did, he guessed that his boyfriend was very close as well, but wouldn't give himself to his climax until Marco gave the instruction.

'You've been a good boy: you can come now.'

Marco felt Leigh building up speed, fucking him faster and faster, his breathing growing more and more desperate. Marco started to wank himself more furiously, feeling his climax building up in his balls and his cock, building up and building up as his boyfriend's cock slammed into him, filling his arse, filling all of him with his fat cock . . .

Marco came, shooting his hot white load on to the bed. As

he pumped his spunk from his cock, he felt Leigh reach his own climax, his dick driving deep within Marco, his come filling Marco until there was nothing left.

With a satisfied grunt, Marco withdrew and rolled over on the bed. 'Thank you, sir,' he said playfully. 'I needed that.'

'Feeling better now?' Marco whispered. He certainly was. He knew what they would be facing when they got back to Britain, the dangers that they could encounter. But tonight it was just Marco and Leigh.

And that was all that mattered.

Seven

Scott looked at his Storm watch for the umpteenth time, glancing from it to the arrivals monitor and back again. He had been waiting in Terminal Three for over two hours, waiting for Nathan's flight from Munich to arrive. Apparently, they hadn't been able to get the Elective's jet repaired, and it *should* have proved quicker to get a scheduled flight. 'Should' being the operative word, as bad weather had unexpectedly gripped Britain.

Scott had woken up on the sofa bed in the flat above the Brave Trader, looked out of the window and seen Poland Street covered in snow. What a homecoming for Nathan.

Thankfully, the display indicated that the plane had just landed; hopefully, it wouldn't take long for Nathan to clear customs. Scott had so much to tell him: Anthony's return to London was one, but the most important was the reappearance of John Bury. Even if Scott had got nowhere, he felt certain that Nathan would find out the truth, find out why someone had apparently returned from the dead.

'Scott!'

Scott whirled round to see a tanned version of his boyfriend running through the arrivals gate. Despite the crowds, he rushed towards him and hugged him as they met.

'Hi ya, hubs – miss me?' Nathan breathed into Scott's ear.

'More than you could know,' said Scott. 'Where to? Home?' He hoped it was home: Scott was feeling as randy as hell. The Brave Trader had had more than its fair share of good-looking blokes last night, but the shock of seeing John Bury had put sex firmly to the back of his mind. But seeing Nathan again, after five days . . . all Scott wanted to do was tear all of his clothes off and see how all-over his tan really was.

'Sorry,' said Nathan, his face falling. Scott knew what he was going to say.

'Let me guess. The Harness?'

Nathan nodded. ''Fraid so. Business to attend to.' The Harness, one of Vauxhall's most popular leather, rubber and S&M bars, actually housed the UK headquarters of the Elective. It had been where Adrian Delancey had orchestrated his slave ring; it was now Nathan and Marco's offices as they rooted out the last vestiges of Delancey's corruption.

'Why?' asked Scott, the disappointment clear in his voice. 'Can't it wait?'

Nathan shook his head. 'Sorry. Won't be for long, I promise. Then I'll show you what I bought for us in Munich.' Then Nathan gave one of his wicked, melting smiles, and Scott knew that he couldn't refuse him anything. 'Anyway, off to Terminal Four.'

'Terminal Four?'

'The next flight from Los Angeles is due in in about twenty minutes. If they haven't missed their connections, Marco and Leigh should be on it.'

The Harness was deserted when the four of them reached it around lunchtime. Not surprising really: the club didn't open until ten o'clock in the evening, and the business of the Elective didn't exactly take place in the open. That was why Nathan had had so much trouble uncovering their secrets: while he had been investigating the Elective, while he had been desperate to find out whatever he could about the shadowy organisation, he had been drinking – and having sex – only feet away from their headquarters.

The taxi drew up along the busy Vauxhall street, and Marco, Leigh, Nathan and Scott clambered out on to the snow-covered pavement, trying not to slip as they did so.

'Bloody cold,' said Marco, pulling his leather jacket round him. 'If I'd known it was going to be like this, I would have sent Leigh on ahead and stayed in Vegas.'

'I know what you mean,' Nathan agreed. Even Munich hadn't been this cold. 'After Morocco –'

'Listen to you two,' said Scott. 'While you've all been off sunning yourselves, some us have been freezing our balls off.'

Nathan laughed, while Marco reached the solid metal door of the Harness, set into the inconspicuous brickwork of an old warehouse. He gave two knocks; moments later, a small grille slid open.

'Oz – it's Marco.'

With that, the door opened. Oz stood in the doorway, the Harness's man-mountain of a bouncer, six feet six of solid muscle, with a shaved head and no neck. He reached out and squeezed his fellow Australian warmly; Nathan gathered that the two of them had been an item a few years ago, and Nathan could fully understand why – from both sides.

Thankfully, the Harness was warmer than the cold streets of London; Oz slammed the door shut behind them and resumed guard duty as the others made their way into the main bar.

Nathan always found it odd being in the Harness – being in any pub or club, come to that – outside of opening hours. It was almost as if the life had been sucked out of the walls and furnishings; or as if time froze when there were no people to be served. Part of it was the lighting: when the Harness was open, the lighting was dim, subdued, conducive to certain relationships. Now, the main lights were on: the dark corners, in which Nathan had had so much fun over the years, were no more; the worn brickwork of the walls was no longer something dirty, something exciting – it was only worn brickwork. Even so, Nathan knew that once the lights were off and the place was full, the Harness would still be able to weave its particular spell over him.

They reached the far wall of the main bar. There were three doors set into the wall: one was the toilet – the proper toilet. The second door led to the playroom, with its slings, manacles and other toys. But the third door . . . the third door was something special.

Marco turned the key in the lock of the third door, pushed it open, and ushered them in.

Even now, it still took Nathan's breath away. Behind the door was another club, another Harness. But different.

While the layout was an identical mirror image of the 'public' Harness, there were fundamental differences, quite apart from the décor – which was of a higher standard than the other bar. Primarily, no money ever changed hands over the bar – all drinks were on the house. That was because this second, secret Harness wasn't open to the public: its facilities were only available to members of the Elective.

Nathan had first been in this bar late last year, when events had conspired to temporarily split up Nathan and Scott. Nathan had gone to the Harness to drown his sorrows, to reassure himself that he was still attractive. Instead, he had walked straight into Adrian Delancey's trap. However, there had been a favourable outcome: he had met Marco, and together they had finally defeated Delancey.

That time. But that was when Delancey had been part of the Elective, when the forces of the Elective could be used against him. Now he was a free agent, with a power base that they could only guess at. Now he was an even bigger threat.

That was the reason why Nathan and Scott were in the

Elective's offices in the Harness, instead of enjoying their reunion as they both wanted to do.

Over much-needed cups of coffee, they discussed their findings. Nathan went first, assuming that his information about Delancey would come as a surprise to the others. However, listening to Marco's recording of the conversation with Greg, he soon learnt that that was definitely not to be the case. He had told them about his confrontation with Kirk, and about the communications network; Marco had revealed the extent of the infiltration. If this mysterious Syndicate knew exactly what the Elective was doing . . .

'Someone has to go up to Manchester,' Nathan concluded. 'We have to locate this . . . What was his name again?' he asked Marco.

Marco checked the information that Greg had given him. 'Andy Burroughs.'

'This Burroughs bloke. Who fancies a trip up North?'

'I wouldn't mind.' It was Scott. 'Having been stuck in London while the rest of you have been gallivanting around the world . . . well, I could do with getting out a bit. Manchester may not be Morocco or Las Vegas, but it's better than nothing.'

Nathan smiled, unable to disagree with his boyfriend. He knew that it had been unfair to leave him behind, but he did have to finish his degree. 'Okay, okay – but you'd better get started quite quickly.' He looked at his watch. 'Trains leave for Manchester every hour or so –'

Scott raised a warning eyebrow, but said nothing. It was Marco who reminded Nathan that not everything in the world revolved around the Elective. 'Surely tomorrow would be good enough?'

Nathan suddenly realised how insensitive he must have sounded. He hadn't seen Scott for nearly a week, and there he was, shoving him off to Manchester without a second thought.

Was the Elective becoming that important to him? 'Of course. Marco – if you could let me know all of this bloke's details?'

'There is something else,' said Scott quietly. 'I think you'd better listen to this.'

Nathan and the others sat there in silence as Scott told them about his encounter in the Brave Trader, and about how he hadn't been able to learn anything more than the man's supposed name.

Nathan broke the silence that followed. 'You are sure that it's John Bury, aren't you?'

'Nathan, I'm not in the habit of hallucinating. It was John Bury – in the flesh.'

'Except that he was murdered three months ago,' stated Marco. 'There has to be some mistake.'

'Then we'll check this out. But later – I'm sure that you two could do with a rest,' said Nathan. 'And we certainly do.' He smiled at Scott, desperately trying to repair his earlier faux pas.

'Okay – let's say we meet in the Brave Trader about nine o'clock?' said Marco.

'Sounds fine by me,' Nathan agreed, rising from the table. 'It's about time I showed Scott what I bought in duty free.'

It was two o'clock when the taxi pulled up outside Nathan's house in Docklands. Nathan opened the door and ushered Scott in, remembering the first time he had invited Scott home, remembering how nervous he had been.

It didn't seem like four months since they had first met in the Crossed Swords on Charing Cross Road; sometimes it seemed like only yesterday, while sometimes it felt like they had known one another for ever. Either way, Nathan knew that he was happier with Scott than he had ever been in a relationship – he just prayed that Delancey didn't have another stab at destroying something so precious. During the flight back to London, Nathan had analysed what had happened between himself and Kirk, and realised that it was the fact that he had got something that he had always thought was unattainable that had been so attractive, so exciting: it didn't compare with the feelings between himself and Scott, and he had been an idiot to doubt it.

Dropping his suitcase on the floor of the living room, he did what he had been waiting hours – no, days – to do. He grabbed Scott and hugged him, gripping him tightly. Scott seemed a little surprised, but Nathan was holding on to the one thing that really meant anything to him, and he didn't intend to lose it. His mouth nuzzled at the stubble on Scott's chin, before moving round to his cheek, to his ear, and then finally to his mouth, his tongue reaching out, probing into Scott's mouth, seeking out his own tongue. Nathan could feel the desperation, the longing: he wanted Scott, wanted to be with him, inside him, have Scott inside him . . .

He stepped back and released him, but said nothing, just looking at him.

'Wow!' said Scott. 'You're keen.'

'I've missed you,' he said. 'I don't like to be apart from you. I'll be glad when all this Delancey stuff is out of the way and the Elective can get back to its day-to-day business.'

Scott frowned. 'But surely, that's when we'll be free of the Elective? Once you've cleaned it up, and got rid of this Syndicate, you can go back to being a journalist. Remember: brave and fearless Nathan Dexter?'

'Go back . . .' Nathan suddenly realised that it was something that he'd never even thought about. He was a good journalist, he knew that. Indeed, many thought he was an excellent journalist. But there was something about being part of the hierarchy of the Elective, something about being part of an organisation with so much influence, that Nathan liked. Yes, he could go back to being a journalist, but why? Why go back when the Elective was a way forward? But the look on Scott's face made it clear that this wasn't the answer he wanted to hear, and this really wasn't the time to open that can of worms.

'Let's get all this shit with Delancey out of the way first,' he said. 'Anyway, I've brought us a present.'

'Us?' said Scott. 'What is it?'

Nathan opened his suitcase, and rooted around in the crumpled clothes until he found what he was looking for. He pulled it from the case almost triumphantly, holding it aloft.

'What do you think?' he said, a mischievous twinkle in his eye. 'Fancy helping me road-test it?'

Scot grinned. 'I'd love to.'

Nathan went to go upstairs, but Scott grabbed his arm. 'Where are you going?'

'I thought –'

Scott raised an eyebrow. 'I think down here is as good a place as any, don't you?' He pulled off Nathan's jacket, and threw it over the sofa, before throwing his own over the top. Then he reached out and started to undo the buttons of Nathan's shirt. Nathan started to do the same, but Scott stopped him.

'Ah-ah,' he said. 'I want to do all of the work this time. I want to show you that there isn't anything that this Kirk's got that I haven't.'

Don't worry about that, Nathan thought. He hasn't got anything to compare with you. He gasped as Scott ran his hands through Nathan's chest hair, his fingers teasing at his nipples. His hands went lower, reaching down the waistband of Nathan's jeans and playing with the hair around his cock, before undoing the belt and fly buttons and allowing Nathan's jeans to fall round his ankles.

Kneeling down, Scott forced his face into Nathan's groin, his tongue snaking through the cotton of Nathan's boxers. Nathan felt a wave of pleasure pass through him as his boyfriend's lips caressed his cock, which was now rock solid, both in response to Scott's actions and in anticipation of what they were about to do.

After long, exquisite moments of teasing, Scott yanked

Nathan's boxers to the floor, allowing his cock to spring free. But it wasn't free for long: Scott ran his tongue along it, from base to now moist tip, before engulfing as much of it as he could in his mouth. Nathan shuddered as Scott's tongue flicked over his helmet, and he found himself forcing his groin into Scott's face, forcing him to take more and more of his cock. But Scott had a different idea: he pulled back, leaving Nathan's cock to spring up almost vertically.

'Feeling ready to try out the present yet?' Scott asked, standing up.

Nathan glanced at it on the floor, but there was something he wanted to do first. His hand stroked the bulge in Scott's jeans, making it even larger. Urgently, Nathan undid Scott's zip, and pulled out Scott's firm, large hard-on. He gripped it in his fist and began to wank it, slowly at first, squeezing out drops of pre-come. Then he knelt before him and returned the favour, sliding his lips up and down the thick shaft, drinking the salty clear liquid which was lubricating the big helmet. Scott gave a little groan of pleasure as Nathan continued to suck him off, his tongue exploring the sensitive ridge and dick-slit, while his hand slid up Scott's shirt and stroked his flat, hairy stomach, something which Nathan knew was guaranteed to get Scott going.

'Now I'm ready,' he said finally, getting to his feet. Scott needed no encouragement: he was already taking off his boots and removing his trousers. Nathan watched as Scott pulled off his shirt, and once again wondered what he had been thinking about with Kirk. What had the German had that Scott couldn't provide?

Naked, Scott sat down on the floor, his legs slightly raised, and indicated for Nathan to do the same. Nathan quickly took off the rest of his clothes and sat down opposite Scott, his legs assuming exactly the same position, before reaching out and grabbing another object from his suitcase – a bottle of lubricant. He squirted a large pool of it into his palm, and then handed the bottle to Scott, who did the same. Then he began to rub the lubricant into Scott's arse, his fingers sliding easily into Scott's hot, waiting hole.

Nathan gasped with pleasure as Scott's fingers penetrated his arse, lubricating it, relaxing it. As they explored one another's rings, Nathan leant forward and kissed Scott on the lips.

'I love you,' he muttered.

'You too, mate,' breathed Scott. 'You too.' Then Scott grabbed the object that had been patiently waiting on the floor, the item that Nathan had seen and just known that he wanted to buy. A double-ended dildo.

Each of the two dildoes was about ten inches long, and about two inches thick, solid, flesh-coloured latex. A solid metal bar marked the point where the two were joined.

Slowly, Nathan began to insert his end of the dildo, pulling it inside him with the metal bar, relaxing himself so that he could accommodate it. He fought back the hot pain, willing the burning to turn into that special pleasure that he lived for. With a gasp, he felt the dildo's helmet stroke his prostate, and stopped.

'Your turn,' he said breathlessly.

Scott raised his arse and manoeuvred his ring into position; then he guided the latex cock inside him, his face initially grimacing with the pain. Nathan watched intently as the latex buried itself inside Scott, until finally the whole of the thick length was gone. Scott gave a satisfied sigh and grinned.

'Feels great,' he said.

'Too right,' Nathan agreed. 'Now the fun begins.' Nathan grabbed the handles of the dildo, and indicated for Scott to do the same; then, suitably braced, he slowly slid the dildo halfway out of his arse. Scott did the same, revealing the glistening, lubricated latex. Then, simultaneously, they pushed their arses against the dildo's two ends, moving closer to one another as the latex cocks vanished inside them. Nathan groaned as he felt the helmet brush his prostate, and began to build up to the rhythm that he knew would bring him off.

Scott was doing the same, grinding his arse against the latex filling himself up with the thick, artificial cock, and Nathan found the sight, coupled with the feeling of the dildo inside him, rubbing the hot nut of his prostate, almost more exciting than he could bear. Although he preferred the feeling of Scott's hot thick cock filling him up, this way he could see his boyfriend pleasuring himself as well, fucking himself, driving himself to climax.

Scott was already breathing heavily, and Nathan knew that his boyfriend wouldn't be able to hold out much longer. But then again, nor could Nathan: even though he was deliberately not touching his own cock, almost painfully stiff, wet with pre-come, the sensation of the dildo inside him, the sight of Scott fucking himself, was too much, far too much.

With a huge yell, Nathan came, his cock twitching and throbbing as he shot one, then another load, thick white come shooting over his chest. As he grunted with the release and grabbed his cock with his hand, he watched as Scott gave way to the same temptation and squeezed his own orgasm out of him. Load after load of hot come flew from Scott's dick, spraying over Scott's muscular torso, over Nathan's stomach, over the carpet.

Finally drained, his hands slick with lubricant and come, Nathan sighed.

'What do you think?' he whispered. 'Was it worth buying?'

Scott, his forehead damp with sweat, his voice exhausted, smiled. 'Better than two hundred duty-free cigarettes, that's for sure.'

Nathan laughed and leant forward, hugging and squeezing his boyfriend. He had been silly to have any doubts: Scott was what counted, and he would never forget that again.

So why were his thoughts already straying back to the Elective?

Eight

It was only as Scott and Nathan were getting ready to leave
that Nathan remembered that Wednesday was Bear Night in
the Brave Trader. On the plus side, it meant that the pub
would be packed to the rafters with very attractive men;
unfortunately, it also meant that asking discreet questions would
be difficult. Oh well, that would be a hurdle that Nathan
would cross when he had to.

'You do believe me, don't you?' said Scott as the taxi
entered Soho.

'About John?' Part of Nathan was convinced that Scott was
mistaken, but how could that be possible? The two of them
had spent hours in the man's company, had had sex with him.
Even if that hadn't been sufficient to make his face stick in
their memories, his subsequent murder had been enough of a
shock to ensure that they remembered him. Besides, he was six
feet five, for God's sake! It was another mystery. And, given
the current machinations of Adrian Delancey, it was one
mystery too many.

'Scott,' he said calmly. 'If you say you saw him, then I
believe you. There could be a simple explanation: he might

not have died. For all we know, Delancey might have staged John's death to frighten me off.' He trailed off as the taxi slowed. 'Anyway, we're here. We'll soon get to the bottom of this,' he said, with a lot more confidence than he felt.

As Nathan pushed open the door of the Brave Trader, he was confronted with a wall of furry bodies, bearded faces analysing the new arrivals. Bear Night in the Brave Trader.

'Any sign of Leigh or Marco?' Scott shouted over the background roar of the conversation and the jukebox, which was currently blaring out the greatest hits of the Eurovision Song Contest. Nice.

Nathan peered through the crowd, but to no avail. For some reason, the Brave Trader's Bear Night tended to attract the tallest bears in the neighbourhood; Nathan wasn't short, but he felt positively dwarfed.

'No sign of them.' He pulled Scott closer to him. 'I'm going to the bar.' With that, he pushed his way through the solid wall, aware of the thick heady smell that filled the bar. Stronger than the smell of beer or the smoke, it was the musky smell of too many men in a confined space. For a brief moment, Nathan wished that he had been there on his own: there were at least five men in the crowd that he would have loved to have taken home with him. But he was in the Brave Trader for a purpose.

'Sorry, Ian,' he yelled, as he pushed past Ian the actor, sitting at his usual place at the bar sipping his pint of Strongbow.

'Don't worry, dear heart!' he called out, but Nathan was too concerned about the person he was looking for to answer.

And there he was. Standing behind the bar, pouring a pint of lager shandy for Dartford Dave, was John Bury.

'The usual, Nathan?' asked Ivy, but Nathan said nothing. He just stared at someone that he knew was dead . . . But then the rational side of his mind kicked in. *Come on, Nate*, said his inner voice. *You're brave and fearless Nathan Dexter, journalist.*

Either it's John Bury or it isn't John Bury. Do what you're best at – investigate!

It looked like John except that there was something not quite right about him. Something that didn't tally with the John Bury that Scott and Nathan had had a threesome with. Nathan tried to drag up a more vivid picture of the man who had shared his bed, before trying to break into his computer for the Elective.

'Earth to Nathan?' Nathan dragged his attention away from 'John' and grinned at Ivy. 'Sorry, Ivy: I was admiring your new barman.'

Ivy raised an eyebrow and smirked. 'If you're that interested, there'll be time for that later, when he's off duty. He reckons he's going to the Junction when we finish here.'

Ah, the Junction, thought Nathan. The Junction, over in King's Cross, was the venue for the Wednesday night club for big blokes and bears – Brute. Nathan hadn't been there for a while, but it was always fun. Perhaps tonight called for a trip to King's Cross . . .

As Ivy poured a pint for Nathan, Nathan was planning his next move. 'John' had looked at him directly twice, but there hadn't been the slightest flicker of recognition in his face. Either 'John' was a consummate actor or, as Nathan suspected, there was something else. He checked the pub clock: 9.10 p.m. Hopefully, the friend he needed to talk to would still be at work. And if he could come up with the answer that Nathan expected, that would make this Wednesday's Brute more than entertaining. Paying for his round, he made his way back to Scott.

'Well?' asked Scott, taking his Hooch. 'What do you think?' It was clear that Scott wanted some sort of explanation, some sort of proof that he wasn't going completely mad.

'It looks like him. I must admit, it looks like him. But don't ask me why, but I don't think it actually *is* him.'

Scott narrowed his eyes. 'But –'

121

Nathan held up his hand. 'I'll explain later. Don't get too drunk, by the way: we're going to the Junction in a while.'

Scott grimaced. 'The Junction? Why?' Nathan remembered that Scott didn't like the Junction. He found it too dark and intimidating. Nathan, on the other hand, loved it. And tonight, just for once, Nathan wanted to indulge himself.

'Because,' said Nathan, 'I fancy a bit of sleaze. Anyway, hold this for a second.' He held out his pint. 'I need to make a couple of phone calls.'

Unsurprisingly, Marco and Leigh had decided to have a night in – jet lag, and whatever else they had been up to, had taken its toll. But Nathan wasn't too worried, though: if his suspicions were correct, he would be able to see them tomorrow morning with the answer to at least one of their questions. This was one part of the investigation that he felt happier handling on his own – and besides, he would have just the audience he needed when he got to the club.

The Junction was out near King's Cross station, but you wouldn't have known it was there unless you had been there before – which was just the way that the management and the clientele liked it. It was down a small side street about five minutes' walk from the station, an unremarkable door in an unremarkable row of houses. Unremarkable all round . . . until you went in.

'Are you going to explain what's going on or not?' asked Scott, a trace of annoyance in his voice. Nathan knew that he was being mischievous: it was obvious that Scott was really worried about 'John', and it was only fair to let him in on his suspicions. But Nathan felt like a bit of drama. The chances were, this would be the last time he would be able to indulge himself before they would have to deal with Adrian . . . and Nathan somehow doubted that fun would play much of a part in that.

Nathan pulled open the door, and the two of them stepped

into the club. Neither of them had to pay: that was one of the perks of being members of the Elective. Joe, who ran Brute, waved them through without question.

'Upstairs or downstairs?' asked Scott.

'Downstairs,' said Nathan. 'That's where we're supposed to meet him.'

'Him? Who, John?'

'Not yet,' Nathan replied, as they descended into the Underground Bar of the Junction. ''Just an old friend.'

Upstairs at the Junction was nothing out of the ordinary: a friendly pub atmosphere, a couple of fruit machines, and that was about it. No, the big draw for the people who flocked to the Junction was the Underground Bar.

As Nathan pushed open the door into the bar, the first thing that struck him, as it always did, was the smoke, a thick bank of it that filled the Underground Bar. Not cigarette smoke – that was swamped by the cloyingly sweet smell of the smoke that billowed out of the smoke generators, the smoke that was carefully and subtly lit to make the Underground Bar look more like the underworld. Dark corners were only vaguely visible, and then only through the shadowy red haze. The archway that led to the darkrooms was lit in blue, while the way to the bar itself was a sickly amber. Nathan peered into the gloom, but was unable to make out anything save a few dark figures that slowly moved through the night. Dark, smoky and anonymous.

Nathan loved it.

'I'll have a pint,' he said to Scott. 'And while you're there, I'll have a look for my friend.'

'I'll do you for this, Dexter,' snapped Scott; although the tone was playful, Nathan knew that his boyfriend wouldn't take much more of this secrecy. For a second, Nathan felt a twinge of guilt: he had just spent a week away, and even the excellent sex that they had just had wasn't enough to make up for it. But Scott would have to learn that the evil that Delancey represented just had to be stopped: if Nathan didn't stop him, who else could? Then he saw a familiar figure through a break in the fog.

Graham. Nathan's friend. But in this case he was here in a different capacity: as Nathan's solicitor.

Not that Graham was any old solicitor. Nathan and Graham had a history, a history forged in hot and heavy weekends over the last few years. They were more than friends, but less than lovers, a fact that had been one of the factors that had almost split Scott and Nathan up a few months ago. But Graham, as well as being one of Nathan's best friends, was also extremely useful: as a solicitor, he could access information that Nathan could never get near, or that would take far too long to access. And hopefully, that was exactly what he had done tonight.

'Graham!' Nathan gave him a warm, tight hug, then stepped back to admire his friend. As well as being a solicitor, Graham was also a skinhead: tonight, he was wearing a red Fred Perry, and white, skin-tight jeans, held up with thick white braces. With his black DMs and his complete crop, he looked a threatening figure to anyone who didn't know him.

Graham grinned, and Nathan once again felt a trace of the affection that he held for Graham. He looked into Graham's wide, innocent eyes, shocked as always that someone whose face was so open, so harmless, could be capable of some of the best and some of the dirtiest sex Nathan had ever had.

'How are you doing, Nate?' he asked, before looking over Nathan's shoulder. 'Is this who I think it is?'

Scott appeared at Nathan's side, and then handed him a pint.

'Scott, this is —'

'Graham?' Scott's voice was icy, unemotional; but who could blame him? One of the things that had driven Scott out of Nathan's life and into Delancey's web had been the knowledge that Nathan and Graham had had sex the day after John Bury had died. Nathan's excuses had fallen on deaf ears: as far as Scott was concerned, Nathan had turned to someone else for emotional support instead of his boyfriend. That had been a difficult crime for Scott to forgive. Nathan suddenly wondered whether his desire to make this evening so melodramatic was actually one of the biggest mistakes he could have made. He wasn't prepared for Graham to take the initiative and start talking.

'So, you're Scott,' he said. 'I suppose you must hate me?'

'What?'

'Unless Nathan's been lying to me, one of the reasons that the two of you split up last year was because of me.'

Scott opened his mouth, but was unable to speak. Nathan was secretly pleased: by bringing it all out in the open before Scott could escalate matters was a stroke of genius.

'Well, although I can't turn the clock back, and I do love Nathan dearly – as a friend – I want you to know that I'm sorry. Nathan is one of my best friends, and I realise that I hurt him through hurting you. So yes, I'm sorry.'

Scott sighed. It was a sigh that he must have been holding in for months ... ever since it happened. 'I don't hate you, Graham. If anything, I've always been a bit afraid of you. You know Nathan better than almost anyone, and you two were also lovers. I think I was, well, afraid of losing him to you.'

Nathan put his arm round Scott and hugged him. 'No danger of that – no offence, Graham,' he laughed.

'Here – just in case you ever need any help.' Graham handed Scott a business card, which Scott then put in his wallet. 'None taken. And no, Scott – there is no danger of that. I know exactly how much you mean to Nathan. Anyway, when does the fun start?'

'Did you find out what I'd hoped you'd find out?' asked Nathan, still being mysterious. He just hoped that Graham wouldn't blow it before the main attraction turned up.

Graham nodded. 'You were on the nail, Nate. I must admit, I am intrigued – intrigued enough to miss my Wednesday night meeting with the guys for this. I just hope it's worth it.'

Nathan had once been to one of Graham's 'meetings with the guys': a room full of randy gay skinheads. It had been heaven.

'Nathan!' hissed Scott, and urgently gestured towards the doors.

Nathan glanced round and saw a familiar figure coming down the stairs, six feet five, short ginger beard, dopey expression . . . John Bury.

Except that Nathan now knew that he wasn't.

The three of them stood in silence, observing the man as he plunged into the smoke and made his way to the bar. The sudden change in atmosphere in the Underground Bar made Nathan give an involuntary shudder: the presence of the mysterious 'John', the luminous fog, the shadows that lurked within shadows . . . To Nathan, it all seemed strangely unreal.

And then 'John' came back through the smoke.

'Excuse me,' said Nathan politely. 'Don't you work in the Brave Trader?'

'John' frowned, then smiled in recognition. 'Fosters and a Hooch, isn't it?' Even though Nathan was sure that Graham had uncovered the truth, it was uncanny. The resemblance was perfect. But then again, of course it was.

Nathan grinned. 'That's right. Your name's Mike, isn't it? Mike what?'

The tall man looked slightly spooked, but answered anyway. 'Mike Johns.'

Nathan glanced at Scott, mainly to make sure that he had his full attention. 'Johns? Are you sure it's not Bury?'

'John' took a step back. 'What do you mean?'

'John Bury was your brother, wasn't he? Your twin brother?' When you have eliminated the impossible, whatever remains, however improbable, must be the truth. Wasn't that what Sherlock Holmes had said? Well, the impossible – that John Bury had been resurrected from the dead – was easy to eliminate. That left the improbable. Guessing that there was some chance that John had had a brother, Nathan had asked Graham to use his contacts to check the birth records. And Graham's curt agreement was all the proof that Nathan had needed.

Mike squeezed his eyes shut, the admission obviously painful. After long seconds, he opened them again, but there were tears in them. 'Did you know John?' he asked quietly.

Nathan sighed. 'I'm afraid so. Do you know how he died? *Why* he died?'

'That's the reason I've come down here from the Midlands,' he said. 'To find out the truth about my brother.'

Nathan put a reassuring hand on Mike's arm. 'I think we all need to have a chat.'

Sitting in the upstairs bar at the Junction, Mike sipped from his lager, but didn't taste it at all. After weeks of dead-ends, of trying to find out the truth, it had suddenly confronted him. He had hoped that the knowledge would bring him some sort of comfort, some sort of release . . . but it didn't.

All he could think about was revenge. Revenge against the person who was responsible for all this.

'I knew that he'd been a rent boy,' he said softly. 'I tried to stop him, but it was no use. Once John made up his mind, that was the end of it: we're both as stubborn as hell, and telling either of us not to do something usually means that we'll do just that. Then I got a call from him, telling me that he'd met this bloke who was going to look after him. I told him to be careful – it all sounded too good to be true, but he wouldn't have any of it. Told me to mind my own business, and that . . . Well, that was the last time I spoke to him.' Mike looked at Nathan with sad, hollow eyes. 'I'm sorry for what he did to you.'

Nathan shook his head. 'It wasn't him, it was that bastard Delancey, Mike.'

Nathan had explained a little about this mysterious Elective to Mike, although he was still confused as to how Nathan had gone from investigative journalist trying to uncover the truth about the organisation to second in command of it in one go. But all that mattered was getting Delancey. Mike was determined to get the bastard to pay for his twin brother's death, if it was the last thing he did.

Nathan looked at his watch. 'Anyway, we'd better be going. Scott's off to Manchester tomorrow.'

'Business or pleasure?' asked Mike, more to make conversation than anything else.

'Business of a sort,' asked Scott.

'Anything to do with Delancey?' He had come down to London, hoping that his resemblance to John would bring the truth crawling out of the woodwork. Now it had, he wasn't going to stop until it was all over . . . and Nathan, Scott and the Elective offered the best chance of exactly that.

Scott glanced at Nathan, and Mike got the impression that he was asking for Nathan's approval. This was reinforced when Nathan gave a slight nod.

'Yes,' Scott agreed. 'We're trying to find out if he's got his claws into someone else, and I need to go to Manchester to check.'

Mike slammed his glass down on the bar, eliciting curious stares from the men standing close by. But he didn't care – Mike didn't care about anything now. He had come to London to find out the truth. Now he had the truth, and he knew exactly what the next step was.

'Then I'm coming with you. Okay?' He hoped that his tone would brook no argument.

It didn't. Nathan smiled. 'I suppose it would be pointless to try to get you to change your mind?'

'I told you I was stubborn.' Then he frowned. 'What about the Brave Trader? I don't really like leaving Steve in the lurch.'

'Don't worry about that,' said Nathan. 'I'll deal with Steve. You just make sure that you look out for one another up there.

If Delancey is involved . . . well, we've all suffered thanks to him.'

'Too much.' Mike had wanted the truth to comfort him, to reassure him. It hadn't. Instead, he felt an inner strength, a new confidence. His life had been on hold since John had died. Now he could start it again.

Nathan echoed his thoughts. 'Early start, then.' He looked round at Graham. 'Coming?'

The skinhead – Mike found it hard to believe that he was a solicitor – shook his head. 'Now I'm here, I might as well have a bit of fun.' He nodded towards the door that led to the Underground Bar. 'I think I'll check out what's on offer,' he said, unable to restrain a broad grin. 'Saw a few potential new clients while I was waiting for you – I'll see if they want the benefit of my potential advice.'

Leaving Graham to descend into the Underground Bar, Nathan, Scott and Mike made their way out of the club. As Mike reached the door, he gave the club a last glance. When he had decided to visit the Junction, all he had expected was a bit of sex. The last thing he had imagined was that he would finally stumble on to the truth.

Graham entered the Underground Bar with a smile. It was good to see Nathan again, even if Scott had been with him. Graham hadn't been entirely truthful when he had told Scott that there was no danger: Graham knew that, one day, he and Nathan would enjoy one another again. But he also knew that that was something between Nathan and himself.

Even so, the images of Nathan, tied to the bed, with Graham's large cock sliding up his arse, sliding in and out of that warm, wet hole . . . Graham could feel his erection growing within his tight white jeans, and knew that he would have to do something about it soon.

The smoke was still everywhere, but Graham knew the Underground Bar well enough to locate his destination, even in the red-light gloom of the far wall. The archway looked like it belonged to some ancient castle, but Graham knew only too well exactly what lay inside. Knew, and wanted it.

The darkroom was dimly lit by the luminous fog outside, and Graham could easily see what was going on. One of the Junction's regulars – another gay skin called Toby – had stripped off, revealing his muscular little body, completely smooth, with tattoos up both arms. His cock was short but fat, and Graham had many pleasant memories of having that dick shoot its load into his mouth – Toby was another regular at Graham's 'nights with the boys'. At the moment, that cock was the centre of attention for two others: a tall clone with a blond flat top and a bodybuilder. They were taking it in turns: at the moment, the clone was sucking Toby's cock, while the body-builder had Toby's balls in his mouth.

Oh well, thought Graham – the more the merrier. Walking over to Toby, he kissed him roughly on the lips. At the same time, he got his own cock out: a few strokes and the sight of Toby being sucked was all it took to bring it to its full seven inches.

This immediately got him noticed. The bodybuilder stopped sucking on Toby's balls and started on Graham, taking his hard-on in his mouth and sucking it.

Standing there in the darkroom, kissing Toby, having his cock sucked while Toby's cock was in the clone's mouth, Graham was grateful for the diversion. Still kissing Toby, he started playing with Toby's tits: both of them were pierced, and Graham knew that Toby liked having them squeezed and bitten – the harder the better. He twisted both of the tit rings, and felt Toby's muscular body stiffen with the pleasure that Graham knew he was causing him. But Toby also knew that Graham liked just the same thing, and his hands sought out Graham's tits.

As Toby squeezed them, Graham felt the pain turn into exquisite pleasure, waves of it passing through his body. At the same time, the bodybuilder's mouth was driving him wild as he teased at Graham's helmet with his tongue. Graham couldn't wait any longer: he pulled his cock from the bodybuilder's mouth and gave it the final few strokes that would give him release. Pulling away from Toby, he let out a groan as he came, his come shooting out in thick gouts over the bodybuilder's white singlet, over his face, in his hair. Graham sighed. He had needed that – especially after tonight.

He buttoned up his jeans and wiped the last drops of spunk on to the white denim, hoping that it wouldn't show too much. Okay, so that little session hadn't been as good as many of his nights with his fellow skins – that was sex of a totally different calibre – but it had been necessary. He had needed something to take his mind off what else was going on in his life.

'Feeling better?' The voice came out of the fog, and Graham felt his stomach tighten. He had been pretty certain that he would try to contact him – he just hadn't expected him to be so brazen as to appear in person.

Adrian Delancey came out of the red-tinged smoke, almost like a pantomime demon. But there was nothing comical about the erstwhile Comptroller of the Elective, especially not with his bodyguard, James, behind him.

'What do you want, Delancey?'

The blond-bearded man, dressed only in jeans and a leather upper body harness, laughed. 'What I always want, Mr Wilson: information. Well?'

Graham was tempted not to answer, but in the presence of James – a big, stocky, tattooed thug – Graham told Delancey about Nathan's discovery; about Mike joining forces with them to seek revenge. And their trip to Manchester.

'Manchester?' repeated Delancey, a puzzled expression on his face. 'Why Manchester, I wonder?' Then his eyes widened. 'Names, Wilson. Did they give any names?'

Graham thought back, but couldn't remember anything. 'No.'

'Damn. It looks like the Elective has started the ball rolling. Oh well – time for the Syndicate to make its move.' He turned to leave, before hesitating.

'Well done, Wilson. I hope we can do business in the future.' And, with that, he was gone.

Graham shuddered. He had set up Nathan, his best friend. Sold him to the Syndicate, all so that he could keep his job.

Delancey had found him, had told him that the senior partner in Graham's practice was a friend – a friend who could ensure that Graham would not only lose his job, but never work in the legal profession again.

As Graham left the Junction, one thought echoed through his mind: the price of betrayal.

Nine

The train slowly pulled out of Euston, already an hour late thanks to the remnants of the snow. Scott leant back in his seat and couldn't help staring at Mike. Even though he now knew that he was John's twin, he still couldn't escape the feeling that John had come back from the dead.

'How long will the journey take?' Mike asked, staring out of the window as the train cleared the platform and set off for Manchester.

'Three hours, I think. Not that I mind. It's good to get out of London, and it's not often I get to travel first class.'

'But I would have thought that you travel everywhere first class,' said Mike. 'What with you being part of the Elective. From what Nathan was saying last night, the Elective seems to have unlimited wealth, and all its members enjoy unimaginable luxury. Cushy number.'

Scott couldn't help but notice the bitterness in Mike's voice. It was understandable – the Elective had effectively murdered his brother – but Scott worried that that might now prove to be a liability. Scott himself wasn't entirely comfortable with his and Nathan's new roles in the Elective, but they needed that level of support, and the luxury that came with it, to carry out their task, to ensure that no one else suffered like John and Leigh had done.

'Actually, it's Nathan that does most of the travelling,' and Scott was surprised at how bitter he sounded too. 'I have to stay here and finish my degree, so all this flying around the world is out of the question.' And all the sex that Nathan has while he's away, he thought. Okay, so they had an open relationship, but the odd incident of cottaging, or an afternoon in the sauna, hardly made up for Nathan's Moroccans, or sex in a Munich darkroom. The agreement was that they wouldn't go off with other people in each other's presence: the problem with that was, it was Nathan who got to travel, leaving Scott stuck in London, with the gossips from the Royal Enclosure watching his every move. Nathan had told him this morning that Steve had mentioned Scott's interest in Mike the other night – Scott couldn't even fart without it all being logged and noted.

'You don't sound happy about that,' said Mike. 'Are things okay between you two?'

Scott was about to answer almost out of instinct, before hesitating: up till now, he had taken his relationship with Nathan for granted: they were together, and that was that. But all this travelling did appear to be taking its toll on them both; Nathan didn't seem to be as warm, as responsive, now as he had been once. Scott was tempted to put it down to their relationship settling down, the initial fires dying down to be replaced by something deeper, more secure, but a voice in his mind told him that this wasn't the case.

Nathan was growing distant because he was devoting more and more of his energies to the Elective. The Elective, the pursuit of Delancey, the threat of the Syndicate: all of them were becoming more important to Nathan than Scott was.

Scott just hoped that they could clear this business up and get on with the rest of their lives.

'Tickets! Tickets, please!' The deep voice startled Scott from his reverie. He looked up to see the ticket collector standing over him, and was pleasantly surprised. In his experience, ticket collectors tended to be on the old and ugly side, but this one was anything but: Scott estimated that he must have been about twenty-five, with spiky blond hair and a square-jawed face. His uniform couldn't disguise his physique: although he wasn't big, there was an impression of a well-honed body under the blue jacket and white shirt.

According to his name badge, he was called Dave. Scott smiled as he handed over his ticket, but Dave seemed preoccupied. Then Scott realised what it was: he was staring at Mike.

As Mike showed Dave his ticket, Dave briefly touched his hand and smiled; Mike broke into a grin. Then Dave was off, heading towards the front of the train.

'You're in there,' said Scott, craning his neck to see where Dave was heading. Sure enough, he was waiting at the top of the compartment. 'Go on!' Scott urged.

Mike frowned for a second, then shrugged. 'Who am I to let down one of my fans?' he said, before getting up.

Scott slumped back into his seat and smiled to himself. It was going to be a very interesting journey.

As Mike stood up from his seat, part of him wondered what he was doing. Of course he liked to have sex and yes, he was as horny as hell at the moment, but there was something unreal about the whole thing. In a first-class compartment of the London to Manchester, of all places! But the ticket collector certainly seemed keen, and Mike hadn't had sex since Jason the other night. He hadn't even had a wank, come to that.

The ticket collector – Dave, Mike remembered – was standing by the automatic door, just far enough away so as not to open it. As Mike approached, his trace of a smile turned into a grin.

'I was hoping you'd get the message,' he said quietly.

Mike shrugged. 'It's a long journey. Got to do something to pass the time,' he said laughing.

Dave took a step towards the glass door, which immediately opened. 'It's not exactly luxurious,' he said apologetically, as he opened the toilet door.

Mike didn't mind. He didn't care. There was something about this Dave that was giving him one hell of a hard-on inside his jeans. Whether it was the cheeky grin on that square-jawed face, or the muscular body beneath the uniform, or even the uniform itself, but Mike knew that he had to have him. He followed Dave into the toilet, unable to take his eyes off the compact, solid arse, and locked the door behind him.

Dave didn't waste any time. He grabbed Mike and pulled him towards him, and Mike leaned down slightly so he could kiss him full on the lips. Suddenly, nothing else mattered: all he wanted to do was rip off the ticket collector's uniform, and slide his hard cock between the tight cheeks of that perfect arse.

His tongue fought with Dave's, forcing its way into Dave's mouth. Mike could feel the stubble against his own short beard, could smell the aftershave, could feel Dave's strong hands massaging his back. Mike's hands moved from Dave's shoulders to his back, and then down so that they were grabbing, squeezing that arse.

Dave pulled back and stared into Mike's eyes. 'You're as eager as I am,' he breathed.

'Too right I am,' Mike replied. With that, he pulled on Dave's tie, which came away in his hand. Throwing it next to the sink, Mike took off Dave's jacket and began to undo the buttons of the man's shirt, his hands almost fumbling in his haste. As the shirt came undone, Mike was pleased to see that his guess about Dave's body had been an understatement: the ticket collector definitely knew how to look after it. From the broad shoulders to the perfectly defined, smooth chest, down to the flat, muscular stomach, his body was perfect.

'Like what you see?' said Dave.

Mike said nothing. Instead, he reached out and took Dave's nipples in his fingers and squeezed, first gently, then harder and harder. Dave gasped, but the enraptured smile on his face made it plain that he was enjoying it. Mike let one hand drop from Dave's chest and moved it down to the fly of his trousers. In one go, he unbuttoned them and unzipped them, allowing them to fall to the floor.

The impressive bulge in Dave's briefs was almost too much for Mike: he wanted to drop to his knees and suck on that erection through the cotton, the damp of his spit mixing with the pre-come. But Mike's height, coupled with the lack of space in the toilet, made that difficult. Mike settled for stroking the bulge, and he was turned on to feel it grow even larger under his hand. He cupped the balls, big heavy balls trapped inside the cotton. He could soon rectify that.

He yanked the briefs down, and watched as the cock sprang free. It was about six inches long, but thick and veined. Dave was uncut, but the foreskin had rolled back over the red helmet, and a clear bead of pre-come glistened on its tip. Mike grabbed the cock in his hand and squeezed, his thumb resting over the dick-slit. Then he started to rub the helmet, smearing the pre-come over the hot flesh.

Dave groaned, and responded by undoing Mike's fly and pulling out his dick. It was as hard as Dave's, hard and sensitive, and desperate to bury itself in Dave's hot tight arse. Mike was just working out how to ask Dave if he could fuck him when Dave solved the problem.

'I want that inside me,' he said. 'All of it.'

Mike said nothing – his smile must have said it all. He reached into his back pocket and took out a condom. Urgently, he tore open the foil and pulled out the rubber, before rolling it over his stiff cock.

Dave was keen: he already had his back to Mike, and was bending over the sink so that his arse was in the right position.

Mike opened the packet of lubricant and smeared half of it over his hard-on; the rest he squeezed onto his fingers.

Dave let out a grunt of pleasure as Mike's fingers rubbed the cold lube around his ring, and another as Mike entered him to deposit the rest.

'Are you ready for this?' Mike breathed into Dave's ear. Dave nodded.

Mike placed his hands on Dave's shoulders, gripping the muscles as he manoeuvred himself so his cock was in the right place. Then he moved himself slowly forward, until his helmet was just brushing Dave's ring.

'You want me to fuck you?' said Mike. 'You want to feel my cock inside you?'

'Yeah. Oh yeah,' Dave gasped. 'Go on, screw me.'

Mike needed no further encouragement. He pushed himself forward, and felt his cock parting Dave's ring as he forced himself inside. Dave's arse was quite tight, and Mike had to push himself past quite a lot of resistance as he slid further and further inside, inch by inch, until finally all of his length was pushing into Dave's arse.

'That's it,' whispered Dave. 'All of you inside me.' Mike felt him squeeze his arse muscles around his cock, and sighed with the feeling. Now it was time to really get going. He gradually pulled himself out, withdrawing almost half of his cock, before slamming it all back in. Dave grunted as Mike once again buried himself inside him.

Mike could feel his cock rubbing against the hard nut of Dave's prostate, and the groans of pleasure as he rubbed it were further proof that Mike could play Dave like a musical instrument. He slid half of his cock out once more, before grinding it back inside, pumping away at Dave's tight arse, being turned on by his gasps and groans and the feeling of that hot arse around his cock. He moved one hand from Dave's shoulder and slid it down his muscled chest until he found his nipples, then squeezed them, tightening his fingers around them each time all of his cock was inside. He increased his rhythm, forcing his cock into Dave with faster and faster strokes; his hand moved further down until he was grabbing Dave's cock. Each time he was fully inside Dave he gave his cock a hard, slow wank, until he was fucking and wanking at the same time.

Dave's breathing was getting faster and faster, but then again, so was Mike's. His cock, forcing its way into Dave's hot dark hole; Dave's cock, stiff and red and ready to shoot . . .

With a series of deep grunts, Mike felt his balls churn and then explode, his come shooting from his dick again and again, inside Dave's tight arse. Dave couldn't hold off any longer either: with a cry of release, his come shot from his hard dick, spraying the wash basin, the floor, the mirror with its thick white gouts.

Finally, Mike was spent. Gently, tenderly, he pulled his cock from Dave's arse, and turned the man round. Dave was red with exhaustion, his forehead damp with sweat, but the smile on his face made it clear that he had thoroughly enjoyed it.

Probably almost as much as Mike had.

Mike grinned back. 'Thanks,' was about all he could think of to say.

Dave grinned. 'All part of the service, sir,' he said politely.

Marco handed Nathan a can of beer before opening one himself. 'So, what do we do now?' he asked. The two of them were sitting in Marco's flat in St John's Wood, a shrine to minimalism, which Marco blamed on spending years travelling and being unable to buy more than he could carry. Leigh was at work in his graphic design studio in the West End, leaving the two of them to focus on Elective business.

Nathan chewed his bottom lip before replying. 'We need to know the scope of this Syndicate. So far, we suspect that they can access the Elective's communications systems –'

'I'd put it a little stronger than suspect, Nate. Greg seemed pretty convinced. And why are we saying "they"? We know it's Delancey.'

Something started to tug at Nathan's mind – something he knew was significant, but he couldn't remember what or why. 'Because that's the only way that we're going to defeat him, Marco. The last time, we used the Elective against him. This time, we have to do the same. If he wants to fight the Elective in the boardroom, or on the world's financial markets, then so be it. That's the way we have to play this game.'

Marco swigged from the can before he replied. 'Except it isn't a game. People died the last time – John Bury, Poor Ledge the leather queen, all the others who never made it out of Delancey's slave ring. Greg's brother's been crippled – who's to say that he isn't just the first of many?'

Nathan could tell that Marco was getting agitated: his Australian accent, dulled by years in London, was coming to the fore. 'I know it's not a game, Marco – but that's exactly how Delancey sees it. If he wanted to destroy the Elective, he could. He has all the information he could ever want, with his direct route into our computers.' *Our computers.* Not for the first time, Nathan realised how easily he had taken to his role as Deputy Comptroller, how easily he had become part of the organisation that he had once sworn to tear apart with his bare hands.

'Why else would he have staged that little act with Kirk in Munich? That wasn't the strategy of a master businessman, attempting a corporate takeover, Marco. That was a flourish, a touch of high drama. That's how we must play it as well – on one hand the trading floor and the boardroom, on the other . . . well, leave that to me.'

'Whatever we do, we're going to have to move quickly. From the look of those case studies that Greg had, the Elective is haemorrhaging money almost hourly. If we don't stop the Syndicate within the next week, there's a serious danger to the Elective's trading abilities.'

Nathan knew exactly what he meant. The Elective had been founded at the turn of the century by a consortium of gay millionaires – back when a million dollars really was a million dollars. By using their business acumen and creating a series of holding companies and investing heavily on the stock market, they had created an organisation which was completely self-funding. There was no market on Earth that the Elective didn't back, distributing its wealth for two reasons. One was philanthropic: the Elective didn't want to unbalance any particular industry. But the other reason was self-preservation: by spreading itself across the world, it was able to avoid local catastrophes. Recessions, depressions, wars . . . none of them affected the Elective.

As well as re-investing its profits, the Elective also grew by recruiting new members. Not just members with money, but members with particular skills which could be harnessed. Together, the members of the Elective invested their money or their knowledge, and enjoyed the fruits of their investments in the form of business and social contacts which they could use, and a support network when they needed it.

Nathan had once thought of the Elective as a sinister, Freemason-like organisation; since joining, he realised that it was more like a cooperative. But if it started to go wrong, if the holding companies started to spiral into debt, if the good trading name of the individual parts of the Elective was tainted, it wouldn't take long for the entire system to simply collapse.

'I wonder, if we . . .' Nathan trailed off as something struck him. 'Of course! The tape!'

'What about it?'

'Can you dig it out?'

A few minutes later, Nathan was fast-forwarding through the conversation between Greg, Marco and Leigh, until . . .

'Thankfully, the Director's Codes aren't linked to this system.'

'What are the Director's Codes, Marco?'

Marco frowned for a second and then replied, 'I can't tell you.'

'What?' This was ridiculous. 'Why the hell not? Do you want to help the Elective, or don't you?' Nathan shocked himself with the amount of feeling in that outburst. Did the Elective mean that much to him?

'Because I'm a Comptroller, and you're only a deputy.' Marco's tone was almost apologetic. 'There are some things –'

'Some things a deputy is not meant to know. Spare me the crap, Marco. We're in this together. If you want me to help you in this, I need to know everything.'

Marco obviously thought very heavily about this before answering. 'The Director's Codes contain the details of the holding companies which make up the Elective. That information only exists on paper, and there is only one copy of it – and that's with the Director. That information alone would be enough to totally –'

'To totally destroy the Elective. Exactly. Don't you see – that's why Delancey's playing it like this. He wants the Director's Codes!'

Marco pondered this for a second. 'But he can't get them. The Nevada complex isn't the only bit of hi-tech in the Elective, you know. The Director's Codes are held in a secured vault at a secret location. Only the Director knows where they are.'

Nathan suppressed a laugh. 'Oh come on, Marco – this isn't James Bond! The Director can't be the only person. What if the Director dies without passing on his deathbed secrets? The Elective might be mysterious, but it isn't stupid. Someone else must know.'

'Well, I suppose the Deputy Director and the Elective Accountant would be probable candidates.'

'So, that's three people who know the location, as well as a couple of dozen Comptrollers who know of the Codes' existence. Interesting – that would explain a few other things as well.'

'Such as?'

Nathan realised that he was racing ahead. 'Now that we know about the Syndicate, we can take steps to stop the sabotage. We can re-encrypt the Nevada complex, or route information via other means. Delancey must have known that we'd uncovered his tap into the complex – that was why Kirk could be so brazen about it. He must be ready to move on to stage two – and that must involve the Director's Codes. I reckon he hacked into the Nevada complex to see if the Director's Codes were there. The rest of it was nothing more than a very damaging distraction.'

Marco took another drink of his beer. 'So we should just sit back and do nothing, and wait for him to show his hand again. Is that what you're saying?'

'No. Delancey may be many things, but he's determined, and he's quite intelligent. If we're not careful, stage two will hit us and we won't be prepared. No, we need to go on the offensive. And . . .' This was it. This was the $64,000 question.

'I need the Director's Codes.'

Marco's mouth dropped open. 'Man, you are kidding. Tell me you're kidding.'

'Not in the slightest. It's the only way to stop Delancey once and for all. Believe me.'

Marco let out a deep sigh. 'Nate, man, you really have lost it this time.'

Manchester had been even colder than London when Mike and Scott got off the train at Piccadilly Station, an icy wind blowing through the concourse.

'What's the plan of action?' Mike had asked.

'Hotel first, then we'll try to find this Burroughs bloke. According to the map, he lives a short taxi ride from the city centre.'

Even though it had been early afternoon, Manchester seemed bathed in gloomy twilight. Scott remembered Nathan telling him that Manchester was a city best appreciated at night, and, from the look of it, he'd been absolutely right.

Unfortunately, the address that they had been given hadn't been. Or rather, it was out of date: the mysterious Andrew Burroughs had moved from that address over a year ago, and the less-than-helpful new occupants didn't have, or were unwilling to give, a forwarding address. Sitting in Scott's hotel room, Mike and Scott tried to decide their next move.

'No joy here,' said Mike, throwing the telephone directory on to the floor. No "A. Burroughs" to be found anywhere in Manchester.'

'Bugger it,' hissed Scott. 'You would have thought that this Greg would have done his research. If this bloke is so important, you'd think that they'd have kept better tabs on him.'

Mike frowned. 'Perhaps they thought they were. If he has fallen in with Delancey and his lot, moving without the Elective knowing would have been exactly the sort of thing that Delancey would have arranged. Remember: he must have been planning this Syndicate stuff for quite some time.'

Scott had to agree. It would have been child's play for Delancey, effectively using the Elective against itself. If Burroughs was part of Delancey's scheme, falling out of sight would be an ideal solution.

'So, it's a dead-end.' Mike shrugged. 'Bit of a wasted trip, then?'

Scott smiled. 'Not completely. Nathan's not expecting us back until tomorrow, and we do have this hotel room for the night.' Scott moved over to the window, and drew back the curtain. Night had fallen over Manchester, and Scott didn't want to waste it.

'You brought a change of clothes, didn't you? Let's have some fun.'

★

Nathan had needed to get some fresh air — and wanted to give Marco a chance to think over his proposal. Jumping into a taxi, he had asked the driver to take him back to Docklands; he fancied some familiar surroundings. However, after ten minutes of bouncing off the walls of his house, he just knew that he had to get out.

It was still early afternoon, but the streets of Docklands were deserted. His hands in the pockets of his leather jacket, Nathan sauntered aimlessly past Rotherhithe tube station, down towards Jamaica Road.

Actually, they weren't quite deserted. In the distance, Nathan could see a man hanging around by the entrance to the Rotherhithe Tunnel. For a second, he was puzzled — then he remembered that there was a public lavatory there.

A rather popular public lavatory.

Normally, Nathan wouldn't even have thought about going cottaging, but this afternoon . . . well, it was better than sitting indoors, banging his head against a brick wall — which was how it had felt while he was trying to convince Marco of the validity of his plan.

A couple of minutes later, he had reached the top of the toilets: a square of black metal railings with an open gate on one side. The steps led down into the darkness.

Nervously looking around — Nathan could never fully escape feeling guilty about going cottaging — he walked down the steps.

It wasn't actually dark in the toilet: a single electric light bulb illuminated the scene. And what a scene! In one corner, he could see a man in a suit, with someone else — who looked like a builder — on his knees in front of him. All of the cubicles were full; the only other option for Nathan was to stand at the stalls.

He stood next to a bloke in his early twenties who was standing there giving his long, thin cock a slow measured wank. Nathan got his cock out and did the same, teasing it until it was fully erect. The boy next to him was obviously impressed: he moved slightly closer to Nathan, and then reached out with his hand to grab Nathan's cock. Nathan said nothing – he knew the etiquette of cottaging – he simply put his hand around the boy's cock and squeezed. The boy grinned: he had short, wavy hair and wide expressive eyes. His chin was covered in a few days' growth of stubble, and Nathan was sorely tempted to invite him back. But that wasn't the point of coming to places like this. Cottages were all about faceless, anonymous sex – and that was exactly what Nathan felt like that afternoon.

Unfortunately, it didn't take long for the boy to come: Nathan must have only given his cock about five or six wanks before he shot his come over the white porcelain of the urinal. He gave Nathan a smile of thanks and then made his way out of the toilet, leaving Nathan with a raging hard-on and a whole load of frustration.

Nathan suddenly realised that there was someone new standing to his right. It was the man who looked like a builder, the one who had been sucking off the businessman.

Now, this was more Nathan Dexter's stock in trade. He was in his thirties and big-built. Although it was a cold February afternoon, he was only wearing a T-shirt, which showed off his thick hairy arms. Hair was also sprouting from the neckline of the T-shirt, and appeared to run all the way down his back. As Nathan watched, he pulled his dick from his jeans, and looked Nathan straight in the eye.

The cock was about six inches long, thick and uncircumcised. The builder already had a partial erection: Nathan held it in his hand for a moment and felt it stiffen in his grasp. The man grinned, and took Nathan's cock; standing there, side by side, they started to tug on one another's dicks. The attentions of the boy earlier had brought Nathan quite close; the feeling of this big rough builder, pulling on his cock, while Nathan wanked on his, was too much for Nathan to hold out for long.

146

But the builder must have been close as well – perhaps the blowjob was responsible – because, as he gave Nathan's cock the final decisive wank that brought Nathan to climax, Nathan brought him off as well. Standing there in the toilet, the two men shot their come against the urinal, both grunting as they came. Nathan carried on wanking the man until he had no more come left, while the builder gave his cock one last tug before letting go.

Nathan sighed as the builder put his dick back into his jeans, gave him the thumbs-up, and left the toilet. That had got the dirty water off his chest, as an old friend of his had once described it.

Now it was time to get back to St John's Wood. And hope that Marco had come to the right decision.

The Dutch Master was packed when Mike and Scott got there, a busy Thursday night in one of Manchester's more popular bars. In their biker's jackets, denim shirts, 501s and DMs, both Mike and Scott fitted in perfectly with the majority of the crowd, and the fact that they were new faces meant that they drew quite a lot of attention as they made their way to the bar.

'Well, well, well: if it isn't Scott,' came a familiar voice. Scott looked up to see Nigel, the erstwhile landlord of the Brave Trader, standing behind the bar. Nigel was in his early thirties, about six feet tall, with cropped ginger hair and a bushy ginger moustache; he had left the Brave Trader about a month ago, having decided to return to his native North. Despite his legendary rudeness to just about anyone, Scott had become very fond of Nigel, and had been quite sad to see him leave. Seeing him now was quite a pleasant surprise – Scott hadn't been sure which pub he had gone to.

'Nigel – how's it going?'

'Very well. Can't say that I miss the Brave Trader. A better class of punter in Manchester. Anyway, who's the friend? Playing around behind Mr Dexter's back, are we?'

Scott laughed, knowing that there was no malice in Nigel's comment, just straightforward bitchiness. 'His name's Mike, he's a friend, and he works at the Brave Trader, believe it or not.'

Nigel smiled. 'You have my sympathy,' he joked. 'Anyway, what can I get you?'

A few minutes later, Mike and Scott had found a space on the far side of the bar and were enjoying their Hooches.

'Not a bad place,' said Scott, looking around. The décor was faintly at odds with the clientele, creating an almost chintzy backdrop to the leather jackets, beards and moustaches, but there was a tangibly friendly atmosphere. And an awful lot to look at. That was the nicest thing about going to a different city, or even just a different pub: not just the same old faces.

'He's quite nice,' said Mike, trying to subtly indicate a chunky bear on the other side of the bar, near the toilets. 'I wouldn't say no to him.'

'Seen someone you fancy?' Nigel was standing behind them, a large vodka and tonic in his hands. 'Thought I'd take my break now, and sort out your love lives.'

'Mike was admiring that bear over there,' Scott explained.

'What, you mean John?' Before either Mike or Scott could react, Nigel was beckoning him over.

'Nigel!' Scott hissed, but it was too late. The man had joined them. He was in his early thirties, with a short full brown beard, and short hair, and slightly on the tubby side. He gave Nigel a toothy smile.

'Yes, Nigel,' he said with an air of resignation in his voice. From his accent, he was clearly a native. Mike got the idea that the regulars of the Dutch Master were used to Nigel's machinations, just as those in the Brave Trader had been.

'John, I'd like you to meet Scott, an old friend of mine, and his friend Mike. Mike wanted to meet you.'

Mike visibly reddened, but still held his hand out. 'Nice to meet you,' he said. With that, the two of them started chatting, the general interchange of information that meant absolutely nothing. Scott smiled: he'd known that Mike was feeling randy – indeed, he'd been half-tempted to offer his own services, but was still a little thrown by his resemblance to his late brother – but he hadn't expected Mike to click quite so soon. Then again, he hadn't counted on Nigel coming to the rescue.

'One down . . . just you to sort out now,' said Nigel. 'So, who d'you fancy, Scott?'

Scott looked around. The Dutch Trader had more than its fair share of good-looking guys: leathermen, clones, bears . . . Scott suddenly stopped. There was a man standing about five feet away, staring at him intently. And Scott didn't mind – the bloke was gorgeous.

At first glance, he wasn't really Scott's type: he wasn't visibly hairy, but was extremely muscular, with classical good looks – what many gay people would call a Muscle Mary. But there was something about him that Scott found attractive.

'I see you're getting the eye from our Andy,' said Nigel. 'Lucky boy.'

'Who is he?'

'Ask him yourself – he's coming over.' Oh well, Scott thought, it beats spending ages eyeing him up.

'Evening, Nigel,' he said warmly. Then he turned to Scott. 'I'm Andy.'

'This is Scott,' Nigel explained. 'A friend of mine who's come to sample our Northern delights.'

Andy grinned, and the look he gave Scott suggested that he was offering Northern delights of his own. This close up, Andy looked even more stunning, with penetrating blue eyes, a blond flat top, with short blond stubble covering his square jaw. He was wearing jeans, boots and a white singlet, which showed off his tanned, muscular body.

'Hi, Scott – well, what do you think of life up North?'

Scott laughed. There was something in Andy's voice and

manner that put him at his ease, and suggested that he wasn't full of himself like some muscle-bound men were.

Smiling in triumph, Nigel made his exit. 'Have a good evening, boys,' he said warmly, before returning to the other side of the bar. Scott looked at Andy, and realised he was staring at him with just as much interest.

Scott glanced over at Mike, only to see him in a tight clinch with John. Oh well, though Scott. It looks like it's going to be an interesting night.

Ten

'Gran Canaria? The Director's Codes are in Gran Canaria?'
Nathan shook his head. He'd imagined that they would
have been somewhere mysterious, not on the Spanish island
famous for its gay scene, its clubs, dunes and beaches.

'Apparently,' Marco said, rereading the letter. While Nathan
had been out, Marco had finally seen the wisdom of Nathan's
plan, and had sent an e-mail to the Director of the Elective,
explaining the situation. Aware of the possibility that Delancey
could pick it up if he sent it from home, he had posted the e-
mail from a public internet café in Greenwich. And here was
the response: the Director wasn't taking any chances either,
and had sent it by courier.

Nathan's argument had been very persuasive, obviously: not
only did the Director agree, but he was making another of the
Elective's private jets available to take Nathan and Marco to
Gran Canaria.

There was only one snag: they had to leave immediately.
Apparently a car was already on its way to pick them up.
Nathan was pleased that the Director was taking this so
seriously. Then again, given that the alternative was the end of

the Elective, he'd have been a fool not to. And if there was one thing that Nathan had learnt about the Director, it was that he wasn't a fool.

'How long do you reckon we'll be there?' asked Marco, heading into his bedroom to pack.

'A couple of days?' Nathan glanced at his watch. 'Damn – I haven't got time to get back and pack anything, the car will be here in ten minutes.'

'Don't worry about that. It's a good job we're roughly the same size. You can borrow some of my stuff,' Marco called out.

Suddenly, Nathan remembered Scott. 'Damn!' He glanced at his watch, knowing full well that Scott and Mike would undoubtedly be clubbing it by now. He thought about leaving a message at the hotel, but his natural paranoia warned him against it. The last thing he wanted was for Delancey to get wind of the trip and follow them there, before Nathan had had the chance to prepare for the inevitable confrontation. Oh well, Scott should be back from Manchester tomorrow. He'd leave a message for Leigh at the flat, asking him to pop round and explain the situation to Scott.

Marco came out of his bedroom with two rucksacks; he threw one of them at Nathan, who expertly caught it. 'There, that should do.' He smiled. 'I've always wanted to go to Gran Canaria, you know.'

'Marco,' Nathan warned, 'remember that we're going there on business, not pleasure.'

'Nathan,' said Marco in a shocked voice. 'How could you think that I'd ever mix the two?' But the evil grin on his face made it quite clear that that was exactly what he planned to do.

Oh well, thought Nathan, this should prove . . . entertaining. At that moment, the sound of a car horn came from outside. It was time to go, however inconvenient.

But if things worked out the way that Nathan planned, this

might prove to be one of the last times that Delancey's actions ever inconvenienced them.

Mike and John had vanished, somewhere between leaving the Dutch Master and Scott and Andy arriving at Bondage, the underground leather bar. Then again, given the way that they'd virtually been eating one another since they'd met, it was hardly surprising.

Andy had proved to be intelligent and witty as well as really good-looking: he did something in computers, and seemed genuinely interested in Scott's computer science degree course. But Scott knew that that part of the conversation was nothing more than window dressing: he wanted to do exactly what Mike and John were doing, but was too nervous to ask.

The club was packed, and Scott recognised most of the faces from the Dutch Master. After Andy paid for them to get in, they descended the staircase into the main club area: a large room with a long bar, a place to stand, and a dance floor.

'So, when are you going back?' Andy asked, after they had got some drinks.

'I'm supposed to be going back tomorrow . . .' He trailed off. He *was* meant to be going back to London tomorrow, but what was the hurry? He could easily extend his stay in the hotel, and it wasn't as if Nathan would even notice that he'd gone. No, Nathan would probably be up to his ears with Elective business, and Scott would simply be in the way . . .

Scott stopped himself following that line of thought. If it was bothering him that much, then he and Nathan should sit down and talk about it. Brooding on it wasn't going to do either of them any good, was it? Besides, there was something about Andy that was too good, too attractive . . . one night stands were one thing, but, as both Nathan and Scott had found to their cost last year, once emotional attachments crept in, that spelt trouble. It was fairly likely that he would end up having sex with Andy, but Scott knew that he should leave it at that. Anything more would be asking for trouble, and trouble was the last thing he wanted at the moment.

'No, I can't really spend too much time out of London. I've still got my degree to finish.'

Andy laughed. 'I remember my own degree. I'm surprised I ever got it, the amount of partying that I did.' Casually, he placed one muscular arm around Scott's shoulders, and Scott felt a shudder of excitement travel through him. The feeling of that thick, solid arm around him, holding him, protecting him . . . It emboldened him enough to make him turn round to Andy.

'Do you fancy coming back to the hotel?'

Andy raised an eyebrow. 'You're a bit keen, aren't you?' Then he grinned. 'Actually, I was thinking exactly the same thing, although, well, would you come back to mine? I've got a few . . . a few things there that you might be interested in.'

Scott got the feeling that Andy wasn't talking about the latest computer magazines. 'Yes, I'd love to.' At the very least, it would take his mind off his problems with Nathan − whatever they were.

The jet was well on its way to Gran Canaria; the pilot estimated that they would be there in about two hours. Nathan and Marco were sitting back in the soft leather chairs, enjoying a glass of whisky. The décor was luxurious, with thick carpets on the floor, an extensive video and CD library, and a permanent chef. And, of course, a drinks cabinet to die for. Another example of the benefits that the Elective offered.

'Are you going to let me in on this little plan of yours, then?' asked Marco finally, having been putting off asking Nathan until now. 'I mean, I'm the one putting my neck out for you, aren't I?' Marco had quite a good reputation in the Elective: while Delancey had been using the Elective for his own devices, Marco had made sure that he was whiter than white, totally untainted. And it seemed to have worked: the

Director had trusted him enough to make him Comptroller, and now he was trusting him with the ultimate secrets of the Elective – the Director's Codes. But while Marco could see why and how Delancey could make use of them, he couldn't see how Nathan could use them to stop Delancey.

Nathan stared into the amber of his whisky for a moment before replying. When he did, his voice was quiet. 'We thought we'd stopped Delancey the last time, didn't we? But we hadn't, and now he's more dangerous than ever. This time round, we have to stop him once and for all. That means not only removing any influence that he still has with the Elective – which thankfully isn't very much, by the look of it – but destroying this Syndicate as well. We've got to make sure that he's got no people, no power base, no power. And, if necessary . . .' Nathan trailed off and looked out of the window, into the empty night sky.

Marco's eyes widened. Surely Nathan didn't mean what it sounded like he meant? 'Kill him?' he gasped. He knew that Nathan had his reasons to hate Delancey, but surely even he wouldn't consider that?

Thankfully, Nathan laughed. 'Good God, no – what sort of a person do you think I am? That would make me as bad as him. No, we need to make sure that he's out of the way – and I'd like to see him locked up for a very long time.'

That was better. Marco couldn't help but notice that Nathan had changed over the last couple of months, becoming more single-minded. It was an indication of those changes that Marco could almost have believed that Nathan was capable of such a final sanction. Almost – but not quite. Relieved, he continued. 'So, you're going to set him up?'

Nathan smiled, but it was a cold, almost icy smile. 'No. He's going to set himself up, and I'm going to use the Director's Codes as bait.'

Marco whistled through his teeth. 'Bait! Good God man, think of the risk! What if it backfires? What if Delancey actually gets his hands on the Codes? Think of the damage he could do!'

'Marco, it's the only way. There is nothing to link Delancey directly with anything he did when he was Comptroller – he was too clever for that. Everything – John's murder, the slave ring – was done under the auspices of the Elective. To try to blame Delancey for any of it would blow the Elective's cover, and we can't do that. So we have to get him for something he does now, and it has to be something absolutely watertight.'

Marco knew that he sounded as if he was picking holes in everything that Nathan said, but he had to be certain that it was going to work. The stakes were too high for anything less. 'What if he sends one of his minions, like your friend Kirk?'

Nathan's eyes narrowed. 'Careful, Marco – you don't want to go there.'

As Marco had suspected, Kirk's betrayal was like an open wound. All the more reason to be careful. If Nathan was acting out of revenge, that was when mistakes got made. And mistakes were something that they couldn't allow, not with the Director's Codes at risk. 'Sorry. But it's a valid point.'

Nathan leant forward in his seat. 'Delancey won't send a minion. Not for this one. I understand him, Marco, I know what makes him tick. Getting the Director's Codes will mean the destruction of the Elective. Delancey won't take the risk that anything will go wrong – he'll be there in person. And that's when we'll get him.'

'It's risky, Nathan – very risky. But . . .' Marco knew he had to decide: to follow Nathan, or to call the whole thing off. Then he thought of Leigh, prisoner of Delancey's slave trade; he remembered the look on Leigh's face when he realised that Delancey was back in action. There really was no alternative.

'Okay, okay – you've convinced me. Just don't fuck this up, Nathan – too much depends on it.'

Nathan raised an eyebrow. 'Don't worry, Marco, nothing is going to go wrong.'

As Marco and Nathan refined their plan, the Lear jet flew on to Gran Canaria. But the pilot was unaware of the other private jet on a parallel flight path. A jet registered to Simonson Industries.

Part of the Syndicate Group.

Andy lived in a house about five miles out of Manchester, but they managed to get a taxi almost immediately. As they were driven out of the city, Scott wondered what Andy had meant by saying that he had a 'few things' at home. Whatever they were, Scott was intrigued.

Scott was impressed by the house as the taxi pulled up outside: it must have cost Andy a fortune. When they got inside, Scott didn't change his opinion: if anything, he was even more impressed. All of the furnishings looked brand new, and of the highest quality. It reminded Scott of Nathan's house in Docklands ... He briefly thought about Nathan, and wondered what he was doing. Whatever it was, he probably wasn't thinking about Scott.

'At the risk of sounding forward ... do you want to go upstairs?'

Scott laughed. Yes, it did sound forward, but it was nearly three o'clock in the morning. And Scott felt as randy as hell.

'Why not?' They made their way to Andy's bedroom, which was just as well-furnished as the rest of the house, with one of the biggest beds Scott had ever seen.

'Do you like being tied up?'

Scott looked at Andy, not sure what to say. Under normal circumstances, he would have been uncertain about allowing a relative stranger to tie him up, but tonight ... tonight, that was exactly what he wanted. 'Oh yes,' he answered.

'Get on the bed,' said Andy, his tone changing. That hadn't been a request, that had been an order, and Scott had no choice but to oblige. He got on the bed, still fully clothed.

'Put your hands above your head.' Once again, Scott did as he was told.

'Good,' said Andy, reaching beneath the bed. He pulled out two sets of handcuffs, and began to fasten them around Scott's wrists. 'I'm going to make you do everything I tell you to,' he hissed in Scott's ear as he locked the handcuffs around his wrists. 'You're mine tonight – totally mine.'

As he fastened the second set around Scott's ankles, Scott could feel his erection growing. Being secured with handcuffs, still being fully clothed, having to do exactly what Andy told him to do . . . It was really turning him on.

'Right – now we can get started.' Andy took all of his clothes off, and Scott was impressed with his physique. Scott trained, but Andy was not only muscular but toned, the muscles rippling under the tanned skin. As he removed his jeans and briefs, his cock was revealed: about eight inches, thick and uncut, already erect. Scott wanted Andy to shove that in his mouth, in his arse, to take him however he wanted. But whatever Andy wanted to do, Scott would have to obey. He had no choice.

Andy got on to the bed and started to undo Scott's jeans. As he pulled them down, he smiled at Scott's dick.

'I like the look of that.' His mouth greedily descended on Scott's hard-on, licking at the moist helmet, while his hand reached underneath and found Scott's ring. A finger slid inside, probing and penetrating him. 'Good,' he said finally, taking his lips from Scott's dick. 'I know what you're ready for.'

Getting off the bed, he went over to the wardrobe and opened the door. After a few seconds, he emerged with something that made Scott smile with anticipation. It was a large dildo, about ten inches long and over two inches thick.

Scott wasn't sure whether he could take something that big, but there was something about tonight that made Scott want to try. He wanted to feel that dildo inside him, and he would do everything he could to accommodate it.

'You're going to take all of this, aren't you?'

Scott nodded. Andy squirted some lubricant on to his fingers and greased up the dildo, before spreading the rest of it around and inside Scott's arse.

'This is going to hurt you, but you're going to take it all,' said Andy, clearly getting excited by the thought of inserting that huge plastic cock into Scott's tight arse. 'Get ready to take it,' he ordered, and Scott lifted his legs slightly so that Andy would be able to drive it into him more easily.

'Right.' Andy touched the dildo to Scott's arse. 'Relax, boy – take all of it. I'll be gentle with you.' With that, Andy began to steadily drive it into Scott's arse.

The pain was excruciating – Scott had never had to take anything that big inside him, and even though he was as relaxed as he could be, that just wasn't enough. The dildo bullied its way into him, forcing his arse apart, forcing his arse muscles wider than they had ever been before. There was no pleasure, simply burning, agonising pain – and then it stopped. Suddenly, Scott realised that the whole of the dildo was inside him, filling him up with its length and girth. He squeezed his arse around it, and felt the pressure on his hot little prostate. No more pain, just a warmth and a pleasure.

'Good boy,' said Andy. 'Let's have a play around.' He began to slide it out, slowly, carefully, and Scott groaned as he felt the latex rub against his prostate again. His cock twitched with the sensation – something that didn't go unnoticed by Andy.

'You like that, do you?' He struck the dildo's base with the palm of his hand, forcing it back inside Scott. Scott bit his lip with the pain, but refused to cry out, waiting for the burning to give way to pleasure. It didn't take long.

Andy was obviously getting off on screwing Scott with the dildo, and he started to wank himself as he pulled the dildo out again before driving it back into Scott's sore yet willing arse. Scott was beginning to get used to the pain-pleasure-pain, and

159

wished that he could wank his own cock. But his hands were securely fastened above his head.

'You've been a good boy, so I'm going to make you come now.' Andy climbed on top of Scott, and positioned himself in such a way that his cock was exactly over Scott's. He grabbed both cocks with one hand, while the other hand continued to slide the dildo in and out of Scott's arse. Then he started to wank them both off, firm strokes in time with the dildo's fucks.

Both Andy and Scott were as excited as one another: Scott felt his release building within him, and, from the look on Andy's face, he wasn't far off himself.

Andy drove the dildo in one last time before his cock throbbed in his hand, showering Scott's own cock, his hairy stomach and chest, his face with hot spunk. The feel of that landing on him, coupled with the dildo violating his arse, was too much for Scott: Andy was continuing to milk his own orgasm, and was still wanking Scott: Scott came, shooting further than he could ever remember, a stream of white hitting the wall above his head. The next shot hit his chest, mixing with Andy's, while the third and fourth dripped on to his stomach. He sighed.

'You liked that?' said Andy, slumped on top of Scott, his face inches from Scott's own.

Scott was too exhausted to do anything apart from nod.

'Good. It's my turn next.'

Nathan stared out of the window as the jet flew on, knowing that a lot more rested on the outcome of the next couple of days than just the defeat of Delancey. He had been hiding the truth from himself, but it was blatantly obvious to anyone who knew Nathan and Scott that there were serious problems developing between them. For a time, Nathan had justified his absences by saying that Scott understood how important all of this Elective business was.

But that was crap. Scott was Nathan's boyfriend, and yet Nathan saw more of Marco than he did of Scott.

Unless he did something soon, he ran the very real risk of losing Scott, and that was something that he didn't think he could bear.

The plane flew on.

Scott sank back on to the bed, utterly exhausted. Sex with Andy had been better than he could ever have expected, and he made a mental note to try a few of those things out with Nathan in the future – perhaps he could persuade Nathan to buy one of those ten-inch dildos.

If there was a future: he thought of the pleasure that Andy and he had had, the hot, sweat-drenched passion they had shared, and part of him – too big a part of him – wondered whether Andy was where the future was going to take him.

No, he decided. Even lying there in the afterglow, he knew that Andy didn't represent an escape from Nathan: despite their inability to communicate, Scott was going to try to work things out, to make sure that the relationship succeeded. Andy was just a bit a fun, a sweet distraction for an hour or two. Nothing else.

Wasn't he?

'Fancy a beer? Haven't got any Hooch I'm afraid.' Andy came into the bedroom bearing two cans of Stella and nothing else, and the sight of that muscular body, that solid chest and stomach, the thick cock, was enough to make Scott's dick begin to stiffen once more. But no, he'd already decided that he wasn't going to stay the night. He wanted to get back to the hotel . . . and ring Nathan.

To his credit, Scott did make an effort to sound genuinely sorry. 'Actually, I really need to get back to the hotel. I've got stuff to do,' he explained. Okay, so it sounded a bit lame, but so what? Scott felt sure that, as far as he was concerned, Andy saw him as nothing more than another one night stand.

However, the expression of genuine disappointment on Andy's face suggested otherwise. Oh dear, thought Scott. I really don't like doing this to him, but I haven't really got any choice.

Especially since I never even told him that I had a boyfriend.

'Can I give you my number?' Andy asked. 'It would be really nice if we could meet up again.'

Really nice, yes. But also dangerous. But there was no harm in getting his number. It wasn't as if he *had* to ring him, was it? 'That would be great,' said Scott, trying to stop himself from feeling guilty as Andy walked over to the dressing table and pulled a card out of his wallet.

'Here you go. Give me a ring if you're ever in Manchester – but try not to give the number out. I'm ex-directory. And if I'm ever in London, I'll pop into the Brave Trader.'

Shit, thought Scott. That would be just perfect – he could imagine what the Royal Enclosure would make of that! He idly glanced at the card . . . and then swallowed. No, that couldn't be. It was too much of a coincidence, surely? But there it was, in black and white on the business card.

Andrew J. Burroughs.

Scott frowned, before looking up at Andy, standing there, unashamedly naked, a puzzled look on his face. 'Is everything okay? You look a bit . . . well, surprised.'

Scott got out of bed, aware that he was also naked. This was hardly the way that he had hoped to confront the person he had come to Manchester to see; indeed, it was all faintly ridiculous. But it had to be done.

'Are you *the* Andrew Burroughs?'

Andy laughed. 'What an odd question. Well, I'm the only one that I know. What exactly do you mean?'

Okay, Scott, be blunt – it's the only way. 'Are you the one who designed the encryption system for the Elective communication complex in Nevada?'

The look on Andy's face was priceless: he went visibly white, his jaw dropping.

'How the hell do you know about that? No one knows about that. No one!'

'I suppose I'd better be honest,' Scott said, hoping that Andy wouldn't take this too badly. 'I have a boyfriend. A boyfriend who happens to be the Deputy Comptroller of the Elective in Britain.'

Andy sat down on the bed, shaking his head. 'I don't believe this. I don't –' He looked up at Scott, and Scott was shocked to see that there was genuine fear on his face. 'Has *he* sent you?'

'He? Who do you mean?'

'Well, if you're going out with Marco, then you must know who I'm talking about. Delancey – Adrian Delancey.'

Suddenly, it all started to make a bit of sense. If Andy had gone undercover, tried to get away from the Elective, then it was unlikely that he would have learnt about the changes in the Elective.

'You're a bit out of date,' Scott said, trying to reassure Andy, who seemed on the point of going to pieces. 'Delancey's not the Comptroller any more – Marco is. My boyfriend's called Nathan – Nathan Dexter.'

There was a flicker of recognition on Andy's face. 'The journalist? Well, well, well. But I'm still puzzled – and worried. Why *are* you here, if Delancey isn't involved?'

Delancey not involved? If only. But Scott would get on to that later. 'I must confess – I did come to Manchester to find you. But this was a total coincidence. So, why are you so worried about Delancey?'

Andy sighed. 'Do you know him?'

Do I? thought Scott. 'I'm afraid I do.'

'Then you know he's a ruthless bastard. When I designed the encryption routines for ENET, I was contacted directly by the Elective in the States, and they paid me handsomely for my efforts – and for my silence. And, at the risk of blowing my own trumpet, it's still one of the most secure methods of

163

encryption in the world. I could have patented it, but the Elective was worried that someone might put two and two together and work out a way to hack into it. So I took the money and ran.' He opened his can of Stella and took a deep swig from it. 'Then, one day, Delancey came to see me. I knew him because he'd been the person who'd been the go-between between me and the Elective in the US once they'd initially contacted me. At first, I wasn't suspicious – well, no more suspicious than anyone would be if they were dealing with an organisation like the Elective.

'But after a while, Delancey started to ask some bloody odd questions. He wanted to know if it was possible to break into the system, claiming that he had been asked by the Elective to ensure that it was secure.

'Of course, I checked. I phoned up the people in the US who had commissioned me. I was careful not to implicate Delancey – I still wasn't entirely sure what sort of a set-up I was dealing with, but they pleaded ignorance.'

Andy took a sip from his beer can before continuing. 'That's when I started to get worried. Not just worried – bloody terrified. I realised that I was being followed – there was always someone there, watching me. You know that feeling.'

Scott knew that feeling only too well. When he had thought that someone was watching him the night that he met Anthony, he had put it down to paranoia. Now he wasn't so sure.

'I got so frightened that I moved house but I didn't want to leave Manchester. I lay low for a while – I've only just started going out on the scene again.' He sighed. 'I knew it was too good to be true. I knew Delancey wouldn't give up.'

'So you think it's Delancey's who's been following you?' It was the obvious answer. Andy's reply showed that he thought that as well.

'Who else? So why did *you* come looking for me?'

'Because someone did hack into ENET. Someone did find a way.'

Andy groaned and buried his head in his hands. 'It was always possible. The plan was for me to upgrade the security every so often, but that never happened. I suppose the Elective sent you here?'

'The people from the complex itself, actually. I think they want you to repair the damage, make them watertight again.'

Andy frowned. 'And you say that Delancey's gone ... So where does he fit into all of this? I mean, if he's not the Comptroller any more? Why is he still following me?'

'It's all a bit complicated, but he appears to have set up a rival organisation. He's trying to use it to bring the Elective down. And we think that it's this rival organisation which has hacked into ENET.'

Andy shook his head. 'He's a bastard. When I told him that I didn't want to help him, he made all sorts of threats. I –' Andy broke off as the doorbell rang.

'Who the hell can that be at this time of night? Hang on a minute.' Andy quickly wrapped himself in his dressing gown and went downstairs.

Scott still found it all a bit of a coincidence, but at least he'd found the person they were looking for, even if Scott had had the arse fucked off him into the bargain. Hopefully, Nathan would be grateful; finding Andy might even cheer him up a bit.

With a bang, the bedroom door was thrown open, and Scott was shocked to see a policeman standing in the doorway. The noise from downstairs sounded suspiciously like someone being unwillingly dragged out of the house.

'Get your clothes on,' the policeman growled. 'Now!'

'Why?'

'Because you're under arrest for possession of drugs, that's why.' He held up a small plastic bag of white powder. 'You're going to have to come with me.'

'But –' But then Scott realised that resistance was futile. Whether he had any drugs, whether any of this was anything to do with him, it didn't matter a toss.

Once again, he had been set up by Adrian Delancey. God alone knew how he was going to get himself out of this one.

The jet arrived at Las Palmas airport at about four o'clock in the morning. As Marco and Nathan got off the plane, Nathan was suddenly taken back to the first time he had visited Gran Canaria, years ago. The warmth, the exotic smells in the air, the sound of crickets coming out of the darkness. Ah, Gran Canaria, he thought wistfully. It's great to be back.

'There's the car,' said Marco, pointing at the Merc. Grabbing his borrowed rucksack, Nathan followed Marco towards it. Despite what he had said about mixing business with pleasure, just being back on the island was enough to convince Nathan that all work and no play would make Nathan a very dull boy indeed. And that just wouldn't do.

Sitting in the tiny cell, Scott was pissed off. More than pissed off. There was no sign of Andy, and the policeman didn't appear to even know who Scott was talking about. Clearly something odd was going on.

Scott needed to talk to Nathan. There were things that could be done. Okay, so it might mean the Elective putting pressure on a few people, a bit of money changing hands, but he was supposed to be an Adjutant of the Elective. Surely that was supposed to count for something. And, even if it didn't, his boyfriend was the Deputy Comptroller. Hopefully, they would come along soon and allow him to make his one phone call. Then Nathan could hotfoot it to Manchester and sort everything out.

He looked up as the cell door opened, hoping that it was a policeman. But it was another poor innocent victim being pushed into the cell.

As he came in and Scott got a better look at him in the harsh fluorescence of the cell lights, Scott realised that he didn't look that innocent after all. He was in his late twenties, stocky, roughly shaven with almost completely cropped hair. Despite the freezing-cold night, he was wearing a T-shirt, showing off muscular, hairy arms – but these weren't muscles built up through nights at the gym. These were the results of physical labour. Scott could see that both his shoulders were tattooed. From the way he was standing, Scott guessed that he'd been picked up for being drunk and disorderly. Great – so I'm spending the night with a pissed-up straight bloke, he thought. Oh well, if I'm lucky, I might make it through till the morning without having my face smashed in.

'Hey,' Scott called out as the policeman started to close the cell door. 'When am I getting my phone call?'

'In the morning – we're a bit too busy to deal with wasters like you at the moment.' Then the cell door slammed shut, and the little flap over the viewing hole was drawn across.

'Great,' he said. 'Just what I wanted to hear.' Could things get any worse? Knowing the way that Scott's luck had been going lately, almost certainly.

'Don't worry, mate,' said the other man in a thick Mancunian accent. 'It'll only be a couple of hours. What have they got you in for?'

'Someone planted some drugs in a house that I was . . . that I was visiting. It's a mistake –'

'Of course it is, mate, of course it is. They reckon I was pissed up but I told them, I'm like this after one pint. The fact that it's the tenth is neither here nor there.' He grinned, and Scott realised that he was actually quite good-looking, in a rough, straight-bloke sort of way. 'Anyway, I fancy a bit of shuteye.' He sat heavily on the bunk opposite Scott, about four feet away. 'Hope you don't mind, but I'm going to have a wank – it's the only way I'm going to get any sleep in this place.'

167

Scott found it difficult to repress a smile. How the hell he was going to repress his excitement when this rough-looking builder was wanking himself off, he didn't know. Unless he was completely brazen about it . . .

'Actually, that seems like a good idea. I think I'll have one as well.'

'Suits me, mate,' the other growled. 'My name's Danny, by the way.'

'Scott.'

Scott allowed Danny to make the first move. He watched as the thick-set man undid his torn, dirty jeans and pulled them to the floor, revealing muscular, tree-trunk-like legs covered in black hair. There was a tattoo of a sword on his left shin. Then Danny took off his T-shirt, showing off his body. His chest was muscular, and covered in thick black hair, although it wasn't thick enough to hide the tattoo of a bird on the left-hand side, which matched the tattoos of a puma and a heart on his left and right shoulders. The hair continued down his stomach, which was just turning to fat, and vanished beneath his briefs.

Scott's erection was already forming in his jeans, the pressure pushing his cock against the denim. Since Danny was now undressed, it seemed to be the right time for him to do the same. He pulled off his denim shirt, and was aware that Danny was looking, although he was trying not to make it too obvious. However, when he pulled down his jeans, Danny made no attempt to hide his interest, especially since Scott wasn't wearing any underwear.

Danny pulled his own briefs down, and a thick, stiff cock sprang upright. It was about seven inches long, and quite fat. The circumcised helmet was red and glistening.

Without saying a word, Danny grasped his cock in his hand and began to wank it, never taking his eyes off Scott. Scott put his dick in his fist and did the same, really turned on watching this straight bloke wanking in front of him.

'You've got a fit body,' said Danny. 'Do you work out?'

Scott nodded. 'Yours isn't so bad. What about you?'

'No, mate – building site.' He stepped closer to Scott, still wanking, never taking his hand off his cock. Then, without saying a word, he reached out with his other hand and ran his fingers through Scott's chest hair, down, past his stomach, stopping just as he got to Scott's dick.

'Can I . . . I mean . . . well, I've never touched another bloke's dick before,' he said nervously. 'I just wondered what it was like.'

Scott tried to prevent himself from smiling – what an excuse! But he removed his hand from his cock, and allowed Danny to touch it. It felt good, having the man's rough hand caressing his dick. Danny started to wank it, gently at first, as if he was afraid to hurt Scott.

'Do you want me to . . .?' Scott left the question floating in the air, but his meaning was obvious. Danny looked into his eyes, and it was clear that he was trying to decide whether allowing it would make him queer or not. His desire to come must have won. He nodded. 'I'm not a poof, you know. I like women. It's just that I'm feeling really horny tonight.'

'That's okay,' said Scott. He took Danny's cock in his hand, that thick warm cock. The pre-come was already beading out of his dick-slit; Scott moved his thumb so that it was over it, then smeared the clear liquid around, rubbing Danny's helmet.

Danny gasped. 'That feels good. Oh, don't stop.'

After a few moments of pleasuring Danny that way, Scott decided to chance his arm. He sank to his knees and took Danny's cock in his mouth. It tasted really good – the sweat smell mingling with Danny's own natural odour, the taste of his pre-come – and Scott greedily sucked on it, his tongue flicking around Danny's slit, the ridge of his helmet, the shaft . . . Danny started to groan, and, from the tightening of his balls, it was obvious that he was about to come.

Scott squeezed Danny's balls, and sucked him harder and faster, his mouth running up and down that thick shaft . . .

Danny let out a guttural yell, and pushed his cock even further into Scott's mouth, coming as he did so. Scott had difficulty swallowing it all, load after load of hot, salty come, hitting the back of his throat, filling his mouth . . . But he managed it. Finally, Danny stopped shooting and made to pull his cock out; Scott gave it one last suck, cleaning the remaining drops of come from the still thick, still stiff cock.

'How was that?' he asked.

Danny gave a shy grin. 'Can I . . . well, can I do the same to you? I mean . . . well, I owe you one, mate.'

Scott shrugged, and Danny took this as a yes. He went down on his knees, and stared at Scott's cock, which was bigger than his own, thick and veined with the intensity of Scott's excitement. Then, tentatively at first, he moved his head forward, and licked the red, moist helmet, his tongue lapping up the droplets of clear precome. He smiled, and took the whole helmet in his mouth, obviously turned on by the taste of Scott's dick.

Although Danny gave the impression of never having done this before, he was a natural at it. Scott gasped as Danny's lips massaged his sensitive helmet, before they slid further up his shaft. Danny's hands were stroking his body, his fingers running through Scott's chest hair, while his mouth continued its action on Scott's excited cock.

Scott placed his hands on Danny's solid, hairy shoulders, and watched as the stubbly face ground itself between his thighs. The thought that this man had never done this before, had never taken another man's cock in his mouth, was almost as great a turn-on as Danny's big hairy tattooed body, or the sensation of his mouth as he sucked and licked on Scott's hard-on.

Scott's hands moved from Danny's shoulders and began to stroke that broad back, feeling the muscles under the skin, muscles forged on building sites as Danny laboured away. Did Danny look around at his mates and wonder what they would be like in bed? Did he go home at night and wank himself off while fantasising about his straight mates, dreaming about fucking them, about taking their hot, sweaty dicks in his mouth and drinking their come?

The vivid image of Danny and his builder mates was too much for Scott. Unable to stop himself, he forced his cock even further into Danny's mouth as the first load of his orgasm shot into the straight bloke's eager, waiting mouth. Another load, and another, all gratefully swallowed by Danny. Scott gasped with the intensity of his orgasm as he continued to come, and Danny continued to drink all of it.

Finally, Scott was spent. He stepped backwards from Danny and sat down heavily on the bed, exhausted. Danny stood up and wiped a droplet of come from his mouth with the back of his big hairy paw. He was grinning.

'I've always wondered what that was like,' he said, sitting down. Scott noticed that he was making no move to get dressed again. 'Er . . . can we do it again?'

Scott smiled. Being locked up did have its advantages after all.

The next day was unbelievably clear and bright, especially after the cold and snow of London. Nathan stood on the balcony of the apartment that had been provided for them by the Director's office and admired the unbroken view.

In the distance he could see the sea, glinting and glittering in the warm sunlight, and he hoped that he would get the chance for a swim before they went back. Slightly closer, he could just make out the Yumbo Centre, the concrete shopping mall that, strangely enough, was also the centre of the gay scene in the resort of Playa del Ingles. At least, by night it was.

'Morning,' mumbled Marco, coming up behind him. Marco looked slightly green around the gills, but he had polished off a lot of whisky after they had reached the apartment, claiming that he couldn't sleep and wanted to watch the sun rise over the island. Nathan had gently pointed out that he wasn't actually on holiday, but this had fallen on deaf ears as the contents of the bottle gradually diminished.

'How are we feeling this morning?' he bellowed into Marco's ear. He was amused to watch Marco recoil in obvious pain. 'Dearie me – hung over, are we?'

Marco grunted but said nothing, heading off into the kitchen, presumably looking for painkillers in the fully stocked cupboards. And he would undoubtedly find some: the Elective seemed to be prepared for every eventuality.

He decided to break the good news to Marco. Perhaps it would make him feel a bit better. 'Anyway, you can have your holiday – well, at least a day of it.'

'A day? Why?' said Marco quietly. Very quietly.

'Because of the message I got while you were still in a coma. Our contact was delayed flying over from Brussels. He's not going to be here until tomorrow.'

Thankfully, the news appeared to have a very positive effect on Marco. He even broke into a grin. 'Okay, okay – the beach this afternoon, then.' Marco started to make his plans, his hangover almost miraculously abating. While Marco planned his entertainments for the day, Nathan walked into the well-appointed lounge of the apartment, with its comfortable sofas, wide-screen satellite TV and video, and picked up the telephone. It was almost eleven o'clock, so it was probably a bit early for Scott and Mike to have returned from Manchester, but Nathan still wanted to leave a message.

He just hoped that Scott was having a good time.

Scott replaced the handset and shook his head. 'There's no one at home, just the answering machine.' Damn it. He was still stuck in the police station at eleven o'clock. Even Danny had been let out, although he had looked decidedly guilty when he had woken up, having slept off the night before.

The bored-looking duty sergeant shrugged. 'Is there anyone else you can call? If there isn't, you're stuck here, mate.'

Scott was about to say no, when he thought of the one person who could help. Indeed, the one person who would be perfect in this situation. Graham Wilson, Scott's solicitor. He asked the sergeant for his wallet; he hoped Graham's card was still where he'd put it. Although he didn't like to bring outsiders into this whole Elective thing, Nathan trusted Graham. And if Nathan trusted him, then that was enough for Scott.

Eleven

The dunes were busy for this time of day, Nathan decided. Usually the gay holidaymakers and locals didn't surface until later, but today they were virtually swarming. Marco and Scott had been lucky to find a place to sit.

Set about five minutes' walk behind the gay section of the beach, the dunes were a labyrinth of tangled trees, secret places and urgent, sweaty trysts. Just what Nathan felt like that morning. After the pace at which they'd set off for Gran Canaria, it was good to have a rest before the real work started – and Nathan knew that it was going to take all of his resources to set this one up.

Marco and Nathan were dressed in their shorts, sitting on towels, watching the scenery. And very nice scenery it was too: in the ten minutes since they had set up camp in the shade of one of the huge trees, three bears had sauntered by, two very muscular blonds who Nathan guessed were Germans, and a very sweet-looking clone.

'What do you think?' he asked, before taking a long drink from the water bottle.

Marco smiled as he started to pull down his shorts. He was

174

still feeling a little delicate, but he did seem to be regaining his enthusiasm. 'I liked the taller of those three bears, but the little blond was quite horny. Hopefully he'll wander by when I've got a little bit more of my strength back.'

A noise made Nathan turn round. There was a figure, watching them both from the shadows of a nearby tree. Nathan couldn't make much out: he seemed to about of average height, and quite well built. But even though he was difficult to see, there was something about him, something in his build and his general poise, that made Nathan want to see more.

'I'm just going for a little wander,' he told Marco. Marco gave him a little wave and then laid his head down on the towel; he had now removed his shorts, and was lying there with his dick semi-erect, obviously hoping that the world would come to him. Well, Nathan preferred to be a little more proactive.

Trying not to burn his feet on the hot sand, Nathan made his way towards the mysterious figure in the shadows. But when he had covered half of the distance, the figure moved away.

Fine – I'm in the mood for a bit of a run-around, Nathan thought. He guessed in which direction the man had gone and decided to be a little devious. He knew the dunes fairly well – this was at least the twelfth time he had been to Gran Canaria – and if the man was heading where Nathan thought he was heading, there was a short cut that Nathan could take to head him off.

Setting off through a gap in the tangled trunks of a copse, Nathan squeezed his way into what was effectively a tunnel of trunks, taking great care not to scratch himself or accidentally tread on one of the little lizards that had a habit of running around the base of the trees.

Successfully managing both, he reached the other side of the copse and was pleased to see that his guess had been correct – he was now ahead of the man, who was backing towards him.

This time, he was able to get a clearer view, even though it was only his back: he was thick-set, with a nice firm arse, and muscular arms and legs. His light brown hair was cropped quite short.

Nathan decided that he didn't want to give the man a heart attack, so he gave a discreet cough. The man spun round, and Nathan was pleased to see that his instincts had been correct.

He wasn't quite as well built as Nathan or Marco, but he obviously looked after himself. His chest was smooth and solid, with a ring through his right nipple. He was clean-shaven, with a friendly, almost astonished expression. Nathan decided that he looked quite sweet.

'Hi,' said Nathan nonchalantly. 'How are you doing?'

The man gave a couple of tries before he could answer. 'How did you get here so quickly?' There was a strong accent to his voice, which Nathan placed as something Scandinavian.

'I knew a short cut. I'm Nathan.'

'I am Gunnar. Hello.' Before Nathan could reply, he came over to Nathan and kissed him roughly on the mouth, while his hands squeezed Nathan's tits so tightly that it was only Gunnar's mouth over his that stopped him from yelling out. In response, Nathan grabbed Gunnar's tit ring and pulled it and twisted it, while his other hand grasped Gunnar's cock, which was already becoming erect. As Nathan squeezed it, it grew larger and harder, until it was a respectable eight inches of fat, pink meat.

Gunnar's other hand ran through Nathan's hairy chest, and the look of satisfaction on the man's face made it clear that he approved of hairy men. He stroked Nathan's stomach before finally reaching Nathan's cock, which was already ramrod-straight. His hand wrapped itself around Nathan's erection and started wanking it, slow strokes that made Nathan shiver with anticipation. That continued for a few moments, until Gunnar stopped and gently eased Nathan to his knees, so that his fat pink cock was only inches away from Nathan's mouth. Nathan needed no further encouragement: grabbing the dick with one hand, he placed his mouth over the moist pink helmet and ran his tongue over the hot skin, teasing the dick-slit and gently biting the sensitive ridge below.

Then he moved his lips further up the shaft, trying to take as much of the thick meat into his mouth as he could. He felt the helmet tickle the back of his throat as he squeezed his lips around the flesh, before sliding his mouth back to the helmet.

Gunnar suddenly pushed Nathan backwards on to the hot sand, so that he was lying there with Gunnar's cock still in his mouth. Gunnar was now crouching over him, his heavy balls almost resting on Nathan's chin. Then Gunnar moved himself around so that his arse was above Nathan's face, before leaning down and taking Nathan's own hard dick in his mouth.

Nathan would have gasped if his mouth hadn't been full of thick Scandinavian cock; Gunnar's tongue was flicking over his helmet, sending a spasm of pleasure through Nathan. Nathan placed both his hands on Gunnar's back, both stroking his smooth body and urging him to continue, to carry on sucking and licking him. As he did so, he kept sucking Gunnar's cock, tasting the sweet pre-come that was issuing from his dick-slit.

The two of them managed to synchronise their movements, their mouths sliding up and down one another's cocks at the same time. Nathan wondered whether Gunnar was as close as he was: he could feel that tight sensation building up in his cock and balls, and knew that it was only a matter of moments before he filled Gunnar's mouth with his come.

That moment, Nathan got his answer: the Scandinavian's cock throbbed in his mouth as the balls tightened, flooding Nathan's mouth with thick salty come. Nathan struggled to swallow the wave after wave of come as Gunnar forced his cock even further into Nathan's mouth.

The taste of Gunnar inside him was the final straw for Nathan: he allowed himself to come, his groin bucking up into Gunnar's face as he shot his load into his mouth. Gunnar sucked greedily on Nathan's dick as Nathan continued to come, until there was no more left in either of them.

They stayed in that position for a few minutes, both of them completely drained, but enjoying the sensations of having each other's dicks in their mouths. Eventually, Gunnar pulled himself off Nathan and got to his feet.

'Thank you,' he said politely. 'Perhaps I see you later? In the Yumbo?'

Nathan smiled. 'Anything's possible,' he said enigmatically. But it might be good to see Gunnar again – he'd always had a thing about Scandinavians. With that, Gunnar vanished back into the shadows, leaving Nathan alone in the little clearing.

Drained but very satisfied, Nathan wandered back to where he and Marco had set up camp, only to find the hairy Australian fast asleep. And he was the one who wanted a holiday, Nathan thought with amusement. Oh well, I suppose I'd better wake him up. He'll never forgive me if he misses out.

Graham had come through for Scott. Although he hadn't been able to get up to Manchester himself, one of his colleagues had turned up within the hour. Half an hour later, Scott had been freed, although there was still a possibility of charges against him.

Now, wandering through the slush-covered streets of Manchester, he thought back over what had happened. He didn't doubt that it had all been a set-up: Delancey's lot must have been watching him, watching what he did, and he had led them straight to Andy – who was now God knows where. Even if they couldn't force Andy to help them, they could make sure that he couldn't help the Elective. The very fact that the Elective wouldn't be able to guarantee the security of their communications network was enough of a difficulty to cause serious problems.

No, this time Scott had seriously fucked up. He just hoped that Nathan would be able to sort something out.

He reached the hotel and went up to his room to have a hot shower before facing Mike. He turned the key, walked in . . . and realised that Andy's house hadn't been the only place to have unexpected visitors. Scott's clothes were all over the floor, his rucksack had been turned inside out . . .

'What the hell's happened?' asked Mike, who was standing behind him in the doorway. 'I heard your door open,' he explained.

'Three guesses. Anyway, before I tell you my little adventure, how was John?'

Mike frowned. 'There was no John. He did a runner. Unfortunately, we were already on our way out of the city by taxi when he got out at some traffic lights and vanished. By the time I was able to get back, you were nowhere to be seen.'

Divide and conquer – wasn't that Delancey's credo? He had set Mike up so that he wouldn't be around in case he was able to help Scott or Andy. Scott sighed. This was getting worse by the second.

'I suppose I'd better call Nathan,' he said, moving over to the phone. 'And I don't give a flying fuck if Delancey's listening in.'

'Er . . . Nathan's not at home,' Mike said hesitantly.

'What?'

'When I got back at about four in the morning, there was a message at reception for us. Marco and Nathan had to go abroad, although it didn't say where.'

Brilliant. Just brilliant. Scott sighed. 'Wherever it is, you can bet that it's hot and sunny.'

At about five o'clock, Nathan and Marco decided to call a close on their dune adventures. Once he had been woken up, Marco had taken full advantage of all there had been on offer, including all three of the bears they had seen earlier – at once.

Although Nathan hadn't directly taken part, he had had a good long wank as he watched the four of them, their hot, hairy bodies taking one another, penetrating one another. Despite his earlier delicate condition, Marco more than made up for lost time: Nathan watched in awe as the big Australian screwed two of the bears, his big cock sliding in and out of their willing arses, while the third of the bears was inside him, his short fat cock pumping away at Marco's ring, until finally all four had come, their spunk shooting everywhere.

Nathan had just about managed to hold out, but the sight of Marco's chest, back and arse covered in white come, while the bears took it in turns to lick it off, was too much for him to take, and his own come flew from the end of his dick and landed on the hot sand.

After that, Nathan had a fairly quiet afternoon – after Gunnar, and Marco's side-show, he was drained. He just lay back on his towel and watched the world go by . . . although he did let a rather sweet Spaniard suck him off a little later, while Marco was being fucked by a tattooed German skinhead.

Back in the apartment, the two of them dined splendidly on seafood paella, courtesy of the contents of the fridge and Nathan's culinary skills. If it hadn't been for the knowledge that they were there for a reason, they could almost have been holidaymakers. But Nathan couldn't forget that they were due to met someone from the Director's office the next day – nor could he forget why.

'So, what's the plan for tonight?' Marco asked. 'Party time?'

Nathan thought about it. The representative from the Director's office wasn't due until lunchtime, so a spot of excitement in the Yumbo Centre wouldn't go amiss. And besides, he wanted to catch up on some of the friends he had made on his frequent visits over here. He remembered something that Scott had said to him a couple of weeks previously, just after Nathan had returned from yet another trip abroad.

'I don't get it,' he had said. 'You go to all these really great places, places that most people would love to visit. You don't have to pay a penny, you stay in the best accommodation . . .

and yet you come back here acting like you've just spent the day in the office.'

Nathan had tried to protest, but Scott had continued. 'Okay, I know that you have difficulty letting your hair down sometimes, but you're not the Nathan Dexter that I started going out with. At least he knew how to have fun.'

At the time, Nathan had been a little upset, but he had put it down to the fact that he kept going abroad without Scott. But perhaps Scott had a point. Perhaps Nathan should learn to let his hair down . . .

He broke into a broad, evil grin. 'Why not. Watch out, Gran Canaria – Marco and Nathan are in town!'

Dressed in jeans and Ben Sherman shirts, courtesy of Marco's wardrobe, they reached the Yumbo Centre around ten thirty, just as the party atmosphere was beginning to pervade the concrete pavements and the wide stone staircases. The Yumbo Centre was about ten minutes' walk from their apartment, and, as they had set off, they had quickly realised that they were joining a mass influx of fellow gay people who were converging on the centre. Nathan even recognised a few of them.

The idea of a gay scene centred around a shopping mall had struck Nathan as being faintly ridiculous when he had made his first visit to the island – it was like going into the Brent Cross Shopping Centre in London and finding Heaven, the Harness and the Brave Trader next to W. H. Smith and Marks & Spencer. But somehow it worked: during the day, the gay scene was based around the beach and the dunes; by night, everyone was in one of the dozens of clubs or bars on the many floors of the Yumbo.

The two of them entered the centre and headed towards the main square on the lowest level, passing the German Bear Bar, with its crowd of leather-clad bears and clones milling around outside, and the open-fronted Hummel-Hummel, where the cabaret was in full swing. Part of him was very drawn to the

Bear Bar – last year, he had spend a number of his evenings in the darkroom there – but there were social niceties to attend to. If they had time, they might pay it a visit, but towards the latter part of the evening – or rather, the early part of the next morning when there would be the traditional exodus from the lower levels to the upper levels.

Nathan would be no different: later, Nathan would take Marco to XL, or the King's Club, both on the second level, where the evening really would get going; but first he wanted to drop in on his old friend Phil, the eponymous proprietor of Diamonds bar.

In many respects, Diamonds was virtually an outpost of the Brave Trader: in fact Miss Gilbert, the head barman, had held his leaving party at the Brave Trader a couple of years ago, Nathan remembered. Diamonds had become almost a home from home for both ex-pats and tourists alike, and Nathan was no exception.

Striding across the open square of the Yumbo, he could see that Diamonds was as busy as he always remembered it to be. People were sitting at the tables outside, enjoying the beer and the lovely warm evening, the colour of their tans a clear indication of how long they had been in Gran Canaria. Nathan could see Miss Gilbert, middle-aged with a thick moustache, ferrying out a tray of drinks, while Gary, the stocky blond Mancunian barman, was collecting glasses. But the person Nathan really wanted to see was standing in the centre of it all, surveying his own private empire. And the smile on his face made it clear that he was loving every minute of it. Phil Diamond, the owner.

As Nathan and Marco got within shouting distance, Phil spotted Nathan and waved warmly.

'Well, well, well,' he called out to them. 'Look what the cat dragged in.'

As soon as they got to the front of the bar, Phil gave Nathan a friendly hug. Phil was in his late forties, with swept-back grey hair and a fruity yet imperious expression. His clothes were always exquisite and usually completely over the top: tonight he was wearing a black silk shirt edged with silver and gold sequins, with his glasses hanging by a chain around his neck.

'Why didn't you tell me you were coming?' he asked, and Nathan was suddenly reminded of Kirk's similar comment. One of the fringe benefits of being Deputy Comptroller of the Elective seemed to be that he kept dropping in on friends unexpectedly. Friends? He felt a slight twist of anger when he thought about Kirk, and tried to banish his memory of his betrayal. He was in Gran Canaria to make sure that such betrayal never happened again – even if it was the last thing that he did.

'Last minute decision, Phil,' he explained. 'Got some business to deal with on the island.' He introduced Marco, taking pains to ensure that Phil didn't get the wrong idea. 'Anyway, how's business?'

Phil gave one of his twinkling smiles. 'Not too bad – a lot more bars this season though, a lot more. Competition's tough.' But obviously not too tough: inside the bar, there wasn't a free space. Nathan recognised more than one familiar face from the Soho scene. 'Anyway, enough of that – this calls for a celebration. Miss Gilbert – the champagne, please!' He pursed his lips. 'Only Moët, I'm afraid. If you'd warned me, I'd have got the Krug in.'

Nathan smiled. It was evenings like this, relaxing with old friends, that made him realise why he had decided that the Elective was worth fighting for.

But in making that decision, had his priorities changed? Where did Scott fit into all of this?

By half past eleven, Nathan, Marco and Phil had finished their second bottle of Moët and Chandon, and Nathan decided that they'd better be off to the upper levels before they were too drunk to negotiate the great stone staircase. He definitely didn't fancy tottering up to the second floor after another bottle, and he knew what Phil's hospitality was like.

'Time to go, Phil – the upper levels await.' Nathan placed his empty champagne flute on the bar. 'If we're still around tomorrow, I'll be in,' he said. Okay, so the Bear Bar might have offered more of an adventure, but Diamonds was the perfect place to mellow out before the evening's entertainments got into full swing.

'I look forward to it,' said Phil. 'I'll see about getting that Krug for tomorrow.' He gave Nathan another hug, and launched a friendly wave towards Marco.

'What a great place,' said Marco, as they sauntered, not too steadily, towards the staircase that would take them to the next level of the Yumbo. 'So, where to now?'

Before Nathan could answer, Miss Gilbert came running up to them. 'Sorry, Nathan, I meant to tell you, but it went right out of my mind. Someone was asking about you earlier.'

Nathan knew. He didn't have to guess, he didn't need to ask. In what was an action replay of Munich, his enemy was already here. Somewhere in Gran Canaria, Adrian Delancey was watching, waiting. For all Nathan knew, he could be in the Yumbo Centre at this very moment.

But this time Nathan would be ready for him.

'What do we do now?' Mike asked. He and Scott were in the living room of Nathan's house in Docklands, having arrived back in London late that afternoon. The hours since then had dragged by, as Mike and Scott relived their manipulations at the hands of Delancey. Afternoon had given way to evening, but both of them still felt aimless.

Scott shrugged. He was still worried about the events of the previous night. Not so much the impending court case – he trusted the Elective to get him out of that one. No, he was more concerned with Andy's fate. Andy had seemed a nice bloke, and, even if he hadn't been, Scott wouldn't wish anyone into the clutches of Adrian Delancey.

So why had Nathan and Marco chosen exactly the wrong moment to swan off to Gran Canaria? It just seemed that everything was conspiring against Scott at the moment. He banished that thought: Nathan was the paranoid one around here, wasn't he? At that moment, the doorbell went.

'That'll be Leigh,' said Scott, going over to the front door.

Leigh came in, looking as miserable as Scott felt.

'Cheer up,' said Scott.

'You can talk – you look like a wet weekend.' Leigh held out his hand to Mike. 'And you must be Mike. I'm Leigh.'

The introductions over, Leigh sat himself down in the leather sofa. 'So, what are the poor boyfriends going to do while their menfolk are sunning themselves in Gran Canaria, then?'

It was Mike who answered. 'Look, it's a Friday night. We're in London. I have no intention of just sitting here, wallowing. Let's party!'

Scott had to agree. Sitting around, dwelling on their various misfortunes and misgivings, was not going to do any of them any good. 'Point taken – so, where shall we go?'

The one venue that all three agreed that they wanted to avoid the Harness: it was too closely associated with the Elective, and that was something that they really wanted to forget about, if only for one night. Other options were suggested and dismissed, until they finally agreed on the Crossed Swords. It fulfilled all the criteria: it was open late, and always packed on a Friday night. And it was only a short taxi ride away.

Their destination agreed, Scott even phoned Graham, to see if he wanted to come along – Scott felt that he owed him one for getting him out of that mess in Manchester. But Graham was busy. Oh, well, perhaps another night.

Feeling slighter better now that they were actually doing

something, Scott went upstairs to get ready. He got the feeling that it was going to be a good night.

Marco was worried about Nathan. Since Miss Gilbert's message, he had lapsed into a cold, single-minded silence, as if he were sending his mind out across the Yumbo Centre in an attempt to find Delancey. They were standing outside the XL Club, on the wide concrete walkway of the second level. As with the majority of the clubs and bars in the Yumbo Centre, the front of the club opened out on to the walkway, and the clientele spilt out as well. High energy from the leather bar a few doors down was partially drowned out by the dance music from the XL and the conflicting house from the level above them. But Nathan obviously wasn't in the mood for dancing.

Naturally, Marco wasn't exactly thrilled to find out that his old boss was somewhere near by: quite apart from what he had done to Leigh, there was the matter of the Director's Codes to contend with.

Somehow, Delancey must have intercepted the message from the Director, although Marco couldn't see how. But he *was* here: how were Nathan and Marco going to get the Director's Codes back to England, without Delancey intervening. Unless Nathan's plans could be brought forward, the entire mission appeared to be in jeopardy.

'Well?' Marco asked. 'Are you going to stay like that all night? If I didn't know better, I'd swear that you were sulking.'

'I'm not ready for him, Marco.'

'So? Improvise, for God's sake! You managed well enough in Amsterdam, didn't you?' Virtually exiled to Amsterdam by Delancey, with the threat of something nasty happening to Scott, Nathan had still managed to turn the situation around and come out triumphant.

Nathan sighed. 'Wherever he is, standing around moping isn't going to help. You're right.' He drained his bottle of Heineken and placed it on the ledge. 'Another beer?'

Marco couldn't help smiling. The fire was back in his friend's voice, the fire that suggested that Delancey didn't hold all of the winning cards.

Perhaps they could triumph after all.

As expected, the Crossed Swords was packed: when Scott, Leigh and Mike got out of the taxi, they saw that there was a queue of people waiting to get in, a line that stretched all the way back to the top of the little parade of shops and bars on Charing Cross Road.

'Bugger,' muttered Mike. 'We're going to be here for ages.'

Leigh smiled. True, the regular punters were going to have to wait for about a quarter of an hour in the light yet unpleasant drizzle, since people could only be let in when other people left. But being an Adjutant of the Elective had its privileges, and this was one of the times when Leigh felt no guilt about using it. 'Watch this,' he said, jumping the queue and going straight up to the black-clad bouncer.

A few moments later, they were making their way through the smoked glass door into the crowded interior. Despite jumping the queue, they still had to push their way to the bar to get served. Mike was at an advantage here: Leigh decided to let him force his way through while he stood out of the way with Scott.

While they were waiting for their drinks, Leigh looked around, trying to see if there was anyone he knew. The clientele was, as ever, a complete mixture: Muscle Maries stood back to back with clones, pretty boys and businessmen in suits, everyone relaxed and enjoying an almost party atmosphere away from the cold Friday night outside the black glass façade.

'Drinks up!' bellowed Mike, easily carrying three bottles in his large hands. 'Where shall we stand?'

'What about the Round Table?' said Scott. 'There might be space there.'

Pushing past a couple of bodybuilders in jeans and grey

jogging tops, they reached the small raised area towards the back of the ground floor of the Crossed Swords, set back from the main bar. At the right side of this back bar was an area known to all as the Round Table – basically because that was exactly what it appeared to be.

But there was a lot more to it than that. The Round Table was effectively the Crossed Swords' version of the Royal Enclosure in the Brave Trader, although perhaps not quite as exclusive. Leigh could see that at least one of the regulars was there: Mother, who said very little, but seemed to know everything about everyone. A useful person to know. Leigh could also see Neil and Paul, two university friends of Nathan.

'No Nathan?' asked Mother as Leigh, Scott and Mike positioned themselves around the table. Mother was aware of Nathan and Marco's activities, since he too was a member of the Elective.

Leigh briefly explained that Nathan and Marco had decided to take a short break; he couldn't say any more, even if he had wanted to, since he was as much in the dark about what was going on as the rest of them. Then the conversation sailed into safer waters, as Mother filled them in on the latest gossip from the Crossed Swords.

Looking around the Crossed Swords, Leigh started to think about Marco. He knew that there were problems between Nathan and Scott: although Scott hadn't said anything specific, it was obvious that this unexpected jaunt abroad was virtually the final straw, especially because of Scott's troubles in Manchester. Scott felt bitter that Nathan hadn't been around to help him, and who could blame him? But Scott was just one of the casualties: he had just overheard Neil and Paul asking Scott how Nathan was: the three of them had once been inseparable. Everything and everyone now seemed to be secondary to Nathan's quest – even his own boyfriend.

Leigh was beginning to tire of it, especially since Nathan was always dragging Marco into his schemes: he just hoped that

Marco kept his promise when this was all over, and allowed their own relationship a chance to grow outside the luxurious prison of the Elective. Perhaps Nathan would take the hint and do the same.

Leigh was suddenly aware that someone new had entered the orbit of the Round Table: a tall man in his mid-twenties, broad-shouldered, wearing a plain grey T-shirt that showed off a wiry physique. He was handsome in a willowy sort of way, with short, dark spiky hair.

And he was staring at Leigh. Oh well, thought Leigh, we're here to enjoy ourselves. Why not? With that, he smiled back at the man and walked over to talk to him.

By one in the morning, Nathan actually felt relaxed. The beer had helped – that went without saying – but it was the knowledge that Delancey was finally moving openly which had clinched it. Matters had to be reaching a climax for Delancey to come out of the shadows, and that would be when he was at his most vulnerable. There would never be a better time to put paid to him once and for all.

And the thought of that made Nathan a very happy man indeed. He looked around the club and wondered where Delancey was. Would he be prowling the Yumbo Centre, or would he be waiting for a time and a place of his choosing?

'You look pleased with yourself,' he said to Marco, as the Australian came out of the toilet. Of course, the doorway didn't just lead to the toilet – a side branch led to the darkroom – and it didn't take a genius to work out what had happened. Especially since Marco had been in there for over twenty minutes. Nathan looked over Marco's shoulder and saw a short leatherman and a clone leaving, both of them obviously worn out.

'You should try it, Nate!' he hissed. 'It's wild in there.' He turned to the bar. 'Anyway, I deserve a drink after that.'

Why not, thought Nathan. Why shouldn't I enjoy myself? 'I might just do that,' he replied.

'Then you'd better hurry – I haven't left that many people for you in there!' he joked, sauntering off to the bar.

Nathan walked over to the doorway with its curtain of beaded metal and pushed it to one side with a satisfying clatter. The interior was dim, with subdued lighting – but more than enough to see where you were going . . . and what you were doing.

Passing the doorway to the toilets, Nathan made his way to the darkroom, remembering the first time he had visited this particular club, and the fun that he had had. Hopefully tonight wouldn't be a disappointment.

The darkroom in the XL was civilised by any standards: the first room you found yourself in had a row of three benches, facing towards a television screen. Nathan smiled when he recognised the video that was being shown. It was actually one of Nathan's favourites, and he had often wanked himself off over it.

But Nathan wasn't the only one watching it. There were four other people in the room, watching the video and watching each other: they were sitting in two of the rows – the front one and the one behind. A short, compact Spanish guy with a bushy moustache; a skinhead; a big bear with a cropped black beard – possibly German; and a clone. Nathan smiled: any one of them looked like fun, although he was particularly taken by the skin. For a moment he was reminded of Graham, and he wondered how he was. Oh well, once all of this Elective business was over, Nathan could rekindle all of those friendships which his single-minded quest had forced into the distance.

Then he caught a movement on the bench: the skinhead had undone his flies and had pulled out his cock. It was clearly visible in the light from the TV screen: about six inches long, circumcised and quite thick. Looking at the Spaniard, the skinhead started to wank himself off, slowly with measured strokes.

The Spaniard reached out and grabbed the skin's cock, squeezing it tightly before continuing the wank. As he did so, he released his own dick, five inches of uncut meat. The skin grinned at him and took it in his hand.

Watching all of this, Nathan felt his own excitement growing in his crotch. He sat down between the bear and the clone, and boldly placed his hand on the bear's knee. The bear grabbed the hand, and for one embarrassing moment Nathan was afraid that he was going to remove it. Instead, and much to Nathan's relief, he moved it to his own crotch and pushed on it, making Nathan feel the erection that was beneath the denim.

The clone, who was in his thirties, with a bushy moustache and cropped dark hair, put his hand on Nathan's thigh for a moment before sliding it up to his crotch; then he started to undo the buttons of Nathan's 501s, groping inside for Nathan's cock.

While the clone was taking out Nathan's cock, Nathan was at work on the bear. As Nathan had suspected, the bear was German: he must have been in his late twenties, with short brown hair, and wide, puppy-dog eyes. His beard was full but short, and there was something almost adorable about him.

Unzipping his flies, Nathan pulled out the bear's cock: it was about seven inches long and uncut, with a big, mushroom-like helmet. It was already wet with pre-come, and Nathan smeared it with his thumb, causing the bear to grunt with pleasure.

Suddenly it was Nathan's turn to grunt: the clone was wanking him, his hand pulling Nathan's foreskin back and forth over his moist red helmet. But although Nathan was enjoying it, and enjoying wanking off the bear, the person he really wanted to get close to was the skin – but he was preoccupied with the Spaniard.

Taking his hand away from the bear's cock, Nathan stood

up and stared at the skin, trying to attract his attention. After a couple of seconds, he obviously realised that he was being watched and looked up. Nathan grinned, and turned on his heels, walking slowly but directly towards the room that lay beyond the video room.

The true darkroom.

Although the lighting wasn't quite as good, it was still possible to make everything out. Nathan looked around, and nostalgically remembered the first time that he had set foot in here.

It was a very long room, but quite narrow. Every few feet, there was a discreet alcove, steeped in darkness; between the alcoves were low benches.

Hearing footsteps, Nathan turned round. He hoped that it was the skinhead, but any of the others would do: he fancied having his cock sucked, and he didn't really care which of the four did the honours.

The figure came up to him, coming out of the darkness that pooled around the entrance to the darkroom and stepping into the faint illumination. Nathan was extremely pleased to see that it was the skinhead: he must have been about nineteen or twenty, with piercing blue eyes, a four-zero crop, and a cheeky grin.

'Hi,' he whispered in a very English accent. Then he pulled off his tight T-shirt, to reveal an impressive, muscular body, with the faintest trace of hair around his nipples and his stomach. There was a tattoo of the Union Jack on his left shoulder.

Nathan did the same, unbuttoning his Ben Sherman and laying it on one of the benches. The skin came up to him and pulled him close, forcing his mouth against Nathan and driving his tongue into Nathan's mouth. His fingers found Nathan's tits and started to play with them, squeezing them and teasing them.

'I want you to fuck me,' the skin hissed in Nathan's ear. 'I want your cock inside me, screwing me. You gonna do that?'

Nathan smiled. Then his smile hardened. 'Get those jeans down. I want to see your cock and I want to see your arse. Go on!'

The skin did as he was told, visibly aroused by the orders. Moments later, he was naked, apart from the jeans that were pulled down around his twelve-hole DMs.

Once again, Nathan had the chance to admire the skin's cock: six inches of fat, uncut meat. Nathan reached out and grabbed it roughly with one hand, while the other hand took the skinhead's balls and squeezed them tightly. The skin grunted with pain.

'I don't care if that hurt, you little cunt,' Nathan growled. 'When my cock is inside you it's going to hurt a whole lot more.' He wanked the skin roughly, still gripping his balls. 'You like this, don't you?'

'Yes,' whispered the skin.

'Yes, what, you little shit?'

'Yes, sir.'

That was better. The sound of a rough little skin calling him 'sir' was a major turn-on. Nathan let go of the skin's cock and balls.

'Go on: take my jeans off and start sucking my cock.'

The skin knelt down in front of Nathan and unbuttoned his jeans, before pulling them down. Since Nathan wasn't wearing any boxers, his erect cock, eight inches of stiff cock, was revealed; the skin moved forward and placed his mouth around the helmet and started sucking.

Nathan looked down and watched as the skin sucked him: the young skin's cropped head moving back and forwards as his mouth slid up and down Nathan's shaft. Nathan placed his hands on the skin's muscular shoulders, feeling the strength and the power in the boy's body. As the skin continued to lick and suck Nathan's dick, Nathan thought about what the boy was doing here, here in Gran Canaria. Was he over here with his straight mates? Had they all gone off to one of the nightclubs, while he had sneaked away to do what he really liked to do, suck off men and feel their cocks in his arse? Or were his mates into that as well? Were they in the Yumbo Centre, looking for men to shag and be shagged by?

What happened at the end of the night? Did they all go back to their apartment, the apartment they shared, and tell one another what they had been doing? Nathan could just imagine that: four or five skinheads, all sitting there, drinking lager and smoking joints, telling one another about the sex they'd had. Then they'd start to get horny again; first one, then another, would get their cocks out and start wanking slowly and deliberately as they listened to one of the others talking about the man that had forced his big cock into their arse, how his dick had slid in and out, fucking away until he had shot his load inside them. How the skin had been forced to take that dick inside him, forced to do what he had been told.

Then one of the other skins would lean over and start sucking them off, his cropped head bobbing up and down on the thick cock, tasting the remnants of the come that had shot from that skinhead dick only hours ago. Another of the skins would get his dick out, and yet another one would suck that. All of them, rough little skinhead boys, sucking one another off, their skinhead mouths tasting skinhead dick, until finally they couldn't take any more.

One after the other, they would come, shooting their hot come into each other's mouths, swallowing their mates' come, getting off on the salty taste that their mates were pumping into their eager mouths . . .

Nathan had to stop imagining that – besides the fact that it reminded him of the evening that he had spent with Graham and his skinhead mates, the images were bringing Nathan too close to coming, and he was saving that for this little skin's hot, hungry arse. Pushing the skinhead away, he forced him to bend over the nearest bench.

'Right – I'm going to fuck that skinhead arse. Is that what you want, you little bastard?'

'Yes . . . yes, sir!' was the obedient reply.

Grabbing a condom and some lube out of the back pocket of his jeans, Nathan rolled the latex of the rubber over his stiff, ready dick. Then he smeared it with some of the lube, before spreading the rest about the skinhead's ring. Brutally, he forced his finger inside him, and was surprised to feel how tight he was.

Slowly, he eased his cock into the skinhead. It was difficult at first: he just about managed to get his helmet inside, but the boy was really tense.

'Open that arse, boy!' Nathan commanded. 'Come on!'

Slowly, the skin's ring relaxed, only slightly, but enough for Nathan to continue driving his cock inside. Inch by inch, he forced himself into the skinhead, forced all of his cock inside that tight little skinhead arse. Finally it was all in, his balls resting against the cheeks of the skin's arse.

'Do you like that? Do you like the feeling of all of my cock inside your arse?'

The skinhead simply nodded, and Nathan could see from the way he was biting his lip that it was still hurting. Good. He wanted the boy to hurt. He wanted the boy to cry out as he took his arse with his dick, as he rammed all eight inches of his cock into him.

Without any trace of gentleness, he pulled his cock partially out, then slid it all the way back in. Then out again. Each time he drove it back in, he drove it in harder, more violently, feeling his cock sink into the boy's hot arse, feeling the tightness of the boy's arse muscles squeezing and tightening round his cock. As he built up his rhythm, he moved one hand so that he was wanking the skin, wanking the skin's thick cock in time with the deep thrusts of his own cock into his tight arse.

By now, the skin was enjoying it, the feeling of Nathan's cock inside him clearly turning him on. His dick felt stiffer, thicker in Nathan's hands as Nathan continued to wank him, faster and faster in time with the deep desperate thrusts of his cock into that arse.

Suddenly, Nathan realised that someone was behind him. It was the bear from the video room, standing there, totally naked. His chest was covered in thick brown hair, and his cock, that gorgeous, seven-inch cock with the big red helmet, was standing proud. Nathan knew what the man wanted, and knew that it was just what he wanted. He felt the coldness of the lubricant as the man rubbed it over his ring and up inside him, and relaxed himself. Moments later, he felt the stranger entering him, that seven-inch dick sliding into his arse. It felt good, having his cock inside a skinhead, having a bear's cock inside of him; as soon as the bear had filled him, Nathan started to fuck the skinhead again, hoping that the other man would match the rhythm of Nathan's strokes, hoping that he would drive his cock into Nathan as Nathan's cock drove into the skin.

Nathan groaned as the man's cock was pulled out, only to be thrust back inside him, and Nathan matched his own rhythm to the one he set.

For long moments, the three of them fucked like a machine: Nathan inside the skin as the bear was inside him, Nathan's hand wanking the skin in time to his own cock, their cocks grinding into one another, harder and harder, faster and faster . . .

Nathan couldn't hold out any more. With a final shove, he came inside the skinhead, shooting his load again and again. The skin came at the same time, hot spunk covering Nathan's hand, then dripping on to the stone bench.

With a blood-curdling yell, the other man shot his load, and Nathan felt the thick dick throb inside him, pouring its spunk into his arse once, twice, three times. Then the man sighed, and gently eased his dick out of Nathan's sore but satisfied ring. Nathan did the same, then pulled off the condom and threw it on the stone floor.

The skin turned round and grinned. 'That was fucking great . . . sir.' Then he retrieved his T-shirt and left the darkroom. Nathan nodded at the bear, who smiled warmly, before putting his clothes back on.

All very civilised, thought Nathan. And very, very dirty. He loved it.

Walking out of the darkroom, Nathan was unable to disguise the grin on his face. That had been something: the three of them, taking pleasure in one another's bodies . . . He looked around for Marco, but there was no sign of him. That was odd, thought Nathan: he hadn't been in the darkroom, and it was unlikely that he would have left the club without saying anything to Nathan.

Buying another beer from the bar, Nathan walked out of the club and on to the walkway. It was nearly two in the morning, but the club was still busy, and it took Nathan a couple of seconds to make out Marco, standing by the ledge which overlooked the central square of the Yumbo.

'Marco?' he asked.

'Nathan, I . . .' The Australian shook his head, a look of absolute horror mixed with disbelief on his face. 'I think you'd better look at this,' he said, pointing to the far corner of the square.

Nathan peered into the gloom, trying to focus.

When he did, the breath caught in his throat. It had been a long time since he had last seen the man standing in the shadows, but not long enough. In a perfect world, Nathan would hope never to see him again, but it wasn't a perfect world – far from it.

And there, in the central square of the Yumbo, was the epitome of all that was imperfect in Nathan's life.

Adrian Delancey.

Then the shock passed, to be replaced with a feeling of excitement. He was here, out in the open.

Vulnerable.

'We've got him!' Nathan hissed.

'I'm afraid it's harder than you think,' said Marco quietly. Nathan suddenly realised that Marco really was in a state of shock.

'What's the matter, Marco?'

'That man that Delancey's talking to. The shorter one with the moustache.'

'What about him?'

'I know him,' said Marco, his voice almost a whisper. 'I know who he is.'

'So?' Nathan didn't understand. What was so special about him?

Marco's reply was a simple statement of fact, but it brought Nathan's entire plans crashing down around him.

'It's the representative from the Director's office. He's the Elective Accountant.'

Nathan grabbed the ledge to steady himself. Their contact from the Director's office, standing there with Delancey like an old friend. Which perhaps they were.

The scene in the square could mean only one thing.

Far from being almost free of corruption, the Elective was anything but. And, worst of all, the corruption reached right to the very top, right to the Director's office.

Twelve

Nathan took a deep breath to calm himself. How could he have been so stupid? There was no way that Delancey could have got away with his perverted, evil slave ring for so long unless he had help in the highest places. The only way that such a scheme could have operated, the only way that Delancey could have used the resources of the Elective, was if he had the sanction of the Director himself.

So why was he trying to destroy the Elective? What was the purpose of the Syndicate? Questions, questions . . . and there was only one person who could supply the answers.

He made to move off, but Marco grabbed him by the arm. 'What d'you think you're doing?' he hissed.

'I have to speak to him, I have to confront him –'

'No!' Marco barked. 'If you do that, you'll blow the whole thing.'

Nathan virtually deflated. Leaning with his back towards what was going on in the square, he gave Marco a pleading look.

'Then what do we do? The contact from the Director's office –'

'The contact from the Director's office is actually the Elective's accountant, Ian Burke. But I would never have guessed that he was in league with Delancey.'

Nathan tried to hang on to something, tried to find a still point that would allow him to collect his thoughts. His mind went out to Scott, but he was horrified to realise that it wasn't enough. Scott had been his anchor, his still point . . . but no longer. His hatred of Delancey was all he had left.

'When are we supposed to meet Ian?' asked Marco.

'Tomorrow lunchtime. In a restaurant just outside the Yumbo,' said Nathan absently. But what was the point of getting the Director's Codes now? If Delancey was in cahoots with the Elective's accountant and the Elective's accountant had access to the Codes, then what was the point of having them as bait?

'Then we do things exactly the same. We meet Ian, and then you ask a few pointed questions. Perhaps we can find out what's going on.'

Nathan sighed. He didn't like it, but Marco was right: a direct confrontation now, without all of the facts and without the Director's Codes, would be useless; they would be showing their hand and giving Delancey the advantage. At the moment, Delancey didn't know that they knew of his continuing influence in the Elective.

Perhaps they could use that to their advantage.

Scott looked around for Leigh, and quickly found him deep in conversation with a fairly good-looking bloke in a grey T-shirt. Oh well, at least Leigh's scored, he thought with just the slightest trace of jealousy.

'How ya doing?' It was Mike, back from yet another trip to the bar.

'To tell you the truth, I'm a bit bored, actually. I could do with a bit of excitement.' To be more truthful, he could do with someone simply showing him a bit of attention. Leigh had his new admirer, and there was no shortage of people interested in talking to six-feet-five-inch Mike, was there?

'Be careful what you wish for,' said Mike. 'It often has a habit of coming true.'

Scott laughed. 'Thank you, Mr Philosophical. But that's just it: Nathan's so wrapped up in the Elective –'

'Come on,' said Mike. 'Don't you want Delancey brought down? He screwed you around the last time, he almost split you and Nathan up –'

'Sometimes I wish he had,' said Scott. He couldn't believe that he'd said that!

Mike carried on, ignoring the outburst. 'He sold Leigh into slavery and had my brother murdered. The man is pure poison, Scott: he has to be stopped.'

'You don't understand, Mike: it's become an obsession. And anything that doesn't fit into it is pushed to one side. Friends, lovers . . .' He stopped when he realised that a third person was standing with them. He was in his late twenties, with very short curly hair. He was over six feet tall, although not as tall as Mike – very few people were – and very powerfully built. He had a round, friendly face.

'Mike! Didn't expect to see you here,' he said warmly in a thick Scottish accent. 'I thought you were still in Birmingham.'

'Jimmy,' said Mike, giving the other man a warm hug. 'How great to see you. I've been down here for a couple of months.'

'Who's your friend?' Jimmy asked, looking at Scott.

'Sorry – Jimmy, Scott, Scott, Jimmy. Jimmy's an old mate of mine from college. Scott's a new mate of mine.'

Jimmy raised an eyebrow. 'I see.'

'No, nothing like that.'

'That's good,' said Jimmy, smiling. 'Perhaps he'd like to be a new mate of mine too.'

Scott smiled. What was it Mike had said? Be careful what you wish for?

★

Nathan stood on the balcony of the apartment, a large tumbler of whisky in front of him. Dawn was just beginning to break over Gran Canaria, and, under normal circumstances, Nathan would have found it a spectacular sight, as the reds and purples of the rising sun spilt across the sky and reflected off the sea.

But not this morning. This morning, Nathan was having to come to terms with the knowledge that the Elective was nothing more than a carefully contrived scam.

He had really believed the Director when he had asked Nathan and Scott to root out any lingering corruption in the Elective. But now it seemed as if the Director was as guilty as Delancey had been. Nathan had devoted all of his time and effort into this task, proud to have been asked to help, proud that the Director had recognised his talents.

But it had all been an illusion. It meant nothing. Nothing at all.

And that was the point at which Nathan suddenly realised exactly what he had to do. It was the only possible solution.

By three o'clock in the morning, only a few people were left in the Crossed Swords. Leigh had decided to go home with his new friend – apparently he was a psychologist from Penge – leaving Scott and Mike with Jimmy. But time was getting on, and they would soon have to leave the club.

Scott just didn't know what he was going to do next. Jimmy was a really great guy to talk to, and the evening had simply flown by. So what now? Jimmy had already made it clear that he wanted Scott to come back to his flat in Vauxhall, but Scott wasn't sure. There was something about Jimmy, something special, that suggested that it wouldn't just be a one night stand.

And, given the current state of his relationship with Nathan, was sex with Jimmy really a very wise idea?

'Right – I'm off.' Mike had just come back from retrieving his coat from the downstairs cloakroom, and was pulling the black Schott jacket on. 'I'll give you a ring tomorrow,' he said to Scott. 'And Jimmy – great to see you.'

'And you, mate. Keep in touch.' With that, Mike was heading out, leaving Scott, Jimmy . . . and a decision to be made.

Do this and it's all over between you and Nathan, came the little voice.

But it might as well be over, said another conflicting opinion. *I'm young: I can't wait for ever while the brave and fearless Nathan Dexter rights all the wrongs in the world. I want to enjoy myself.*

It was at that point that Scott realised that he had already made his decision.

He loved Nathan, that was true. But there was nowhere to go in the relationship. It was time to move on and enjoy life, life away from the Elective, away from the Royal Enclosure, away from the uncertainty of not knowing where the hell his boyfriend was, or who he was with.

'I'll just get my coat,' said Scott. 'Is that invitation still open?'

'Thank you for coming so soon,' said Nathan to Ian Burke, the Elective accountant.

They were standing in the apartment lounge, a leather briefcase on the table in front of them. A very special briefcase: it contained the Director's Codes, and the heavy lock was a clear indication of its importance. And, very soon, the contents would belong to Nathan.

Ian was dressed far less casually than the jeans and T-shirt of the previous night: he was wearing smart white trousers and an open-necked silk shirt. He was actually quite attractive, Nathan thought: he was a little shorter than Nathan, with dark hair in a French crop, and a goatee beard.

If it weren't for what he represented, I could quite fancy him, Nathan thought lightly.

Lightly. That was exactly the right word. For months, the weight of the Elective had been on top of him, pressing the life from him, making him lose sight of what was important. Now that he was no longer worried about the Elective, his values were changing, going back to how they had once been: he was a journalist, not a fearless crusader. His life didn't consist of anonymous sex in darkrooms and saunas, it meant spending time with Scott, going out for meals with friends. All that would be his again – his life would go on.

And, ironically, it would be the man who had started all of this, Adrian Delancey, who would finish it, once and for all.

'I admit that I'm a bit puzzled – I would have thought that the restaurant would be a bit more civilised,' said Ian.

That's as maybe, thought Nathan, but that's also exactly what Delancey would have wanted. This way, Delancey had been caught on the hop, unsure of exactly what Nathan was planning. Which was exactly the way that Nathan wanted it.

'I need to get back to London a bit quicker than I thought,' Nathan lied. Or was it a lie? He needed to see Scott, he needed to apologise for ignoring him, for taking him for granted.

He needed Scott's forgiveness.

'Anyway, I presume that the briefcase contains what I've come all this way for?'

Ian nodded. 'I retrieved it from the bank about half an hour ago. I still don't know what you want them for, though.'

And you're not going to know, thought Nathan. Not until it's too late for anyone to do anything about it. 'You'll see. If this works out, the Elective won't ever have to worry about Adrian Delancey again.' He glanced at Ian as he said the accursed name, but there wasn't even a flicker of recognition.

You're almost as good a liar as your boss, thought Nathan. After this, hopefully he'll be able to find you a job in the Syndicate. Right – time to get rid of Ian and start the ball rolling.

'Anyway, I need to pack,' said Nathan abruptly. 'You can see yourself out, can't you?' That's it, Nathan, dismiss him like the two-faced liar that he is.

As soon as the door closed, Nathan picked up the briefcase and carefully entered his own code into the lock, the twenty-character code that had been assigned to him when he had taken the role as Deputy Comptroller. The letter from the Director had made it clear that only Nathan's code would open it: any other would flood the briefcase with acid and destroy the contents. All very *Mission: Impossible*, but Nathan didn't care – he had them!

With a click, the briefcase opened, and Nathan peered inside. It contained a thick sheaf of papers, and a cursory glance showed them to be exactly what he had expected: the names and addresses of all of the holding companies that created the financial backbone of the Elective. If they fell into the wrong hands, they could wreak unimaginable damage. Quite probably, they could destroy the Elective utterly.

With an evil grin on his face, Nathan sat back in the sofa and waited for the next stage of his plan to fall into place. Thirty seconds later, the phone rang.

'Phil – thanks for getting back to me. They've got the address? Excellent . . .'

Jimmy's flat was about ten minutes' walk from Vauxhall tube station. As they made their way there, Scott was still wondering whether he was doing the right thing. This wasn't just a one-night stand: it represented the start of the rest of his life – a life without Nathan. Then he glanced at Jimmy, and knew that he *was* doing the right thing: the big Scotsman was gorgeous. Scott couldn't wait to undress him, to kiss him, to take his cock in his mouth while Jimmy did the same to him.

'Here we go,' said Jimmy. They had reached an old Victorian terrace house. Jimmy unlocked the door and walked in.

The flat was on the first floor: two bedrooms, a living room, and an impressive view of the Thames. Jimmy ushered Scott into the living room and offered him a drink.

Five minutes later, they were sitting together on the sofa,

two cans of lager in front of them. Jimmy's arm was around Scott's shoulders – and it felt so natural, so right that it should be there.

'Thanks for coming back,' said Jimmy. 'For one moment I was afraid that you'd say no.'

Scott smiled. 'I almost did.'

'What changed your mind?'

Leaning over, Scott kissed Jimmy on the lips, his tongue seeking out Jimmy's. As he did so, he placed his hand on Jimmy's chest, stroking the big Scotsman's body, feeling the warmth of another human being close to him. Without saying another word, he began to undo the shirt buttons to reveal a lightly haired, muscular chest.

Jimmy did the same, unbuttoning Scott's shirt all the way down to his stomach. He eyed Scott's body with an impressed look on his face. 'Nice,' he muttered, before continuing to kiss him.

In one easy movement, Scott pulled Jimmy's shirt off, showing off his wide shoulders and muscular arms. Jimmy stood up, taking Scott's arms as he did so, pulling him to his feet.

'Come on,' he said. 'I can't wait any longer to get you into bed.' Hand in hand, they walked out of the living room.

'I'm afraid it's only a single bed,' Jimmy said apologetically.

'That's okay,' said Scott. 'I wasn't planning to get much sleep anyway.' He took off his own shirt. 'Do you like what you see?'

Jimmy nodded. 'You're one fit lad, aren't you?'

Scott gave an embarrassed grin. 'You're not so bad yourself.' With that, he embraced Jimmy, wrapping his arms around his broad body, feeling his hairy chest against his own. He kissed him again, more violently this time, almost as if he was terrified of letting him go. And, in many respects, that was exactly right: Jimmy represented a lot more than just a one night stand, even if they never saw one another again.

Scott's hands fell to Jimmy's waist as they sought out his belt; within moments, Scott had undone his jeans and was pulling them to the floor.

Jimmy wasn't wearing any underwear, and his impressively big cock was already erect. Scott grabbed it and gave it a gentle, slow wank. Jimmy smiled. 'You're great, you know that?' He undid Scott's jeans and let them fall to the floor. Then, urgently, he yanked Scott's boxers down.

Scott's cock was just as hard as Jimmy's; Jimmy fell to his knees and put his mouth around it, tasting it, tasting Scott. Scott thought about Nathan for a second: when was the last time he had felt as excited? His next words slipped out of his mouth without him even thinking.

'Fuck me, Jimmy. I want you to fuck me.'

Jimmy looked up at him. 'Are you sure? Is that what you want?'

Oh yes, thought Scott. At the moment, there isn't anything else in the world I want more than feeling you inside me, feeling your cock inside me. He sat down on the bed.

Jimmy needed no further persuasion. He grabbed a condom and urgently tore the packet open. As he rolled it over his stiff cock, he picked up a container of lubricant from the carpet and squeezed some of it into his hand.

'I want to be facing you when you do it,' said Scott. 'I want to see you face as you fuck me, as you shoot your load into my arse.'

The words seemed to excite Jimmy even more. He covered his own cock in lubricant before smearing it around Scott's ring, in Scott's ring. Scott gasped as Jimmy's finger penetrated him, not with pain, but with the anticipation of knowing that the next thing in his arse would be Jimmy's thick cock.

Jimmy lifted Scott's legs up slightly, so his arse was in the right position; Scott's ring was there, ready for Jimmy to take, ready for Jimmy to stick his big cock into.

Gently at first, Jimmy touched his cock to Scott's ring,

brushing against the fine hairs that surrounded it. Scott forced himself to relax, willing the muscles of his arse to ease so that he could take all of Jimmy inside of him.

For a brief moment, he felt the burning pain as first Jimmy's helmet, then his shaft, began to slide inside him, but that feeling soon passed as he felt Jimmy's cock begin to fill him up. Seconds later, he knew that Jimmy was completely inside him, and he could feel his helmet brushing against his prostate, sending a pulse of unbelievable pleasure through his entire body. He shuddered.

'You okay?' Jimmy asked. 'I'm not hurting you, am I?'

Scott shook his head. 'Anything but. Keep on going, Jimmy, please don't stop.'

Jimmy obliged. He pulled his cock from Scott's arse until Scott could only feel his helmet, sitting just inside his ring. Then Jimmy drove it all the way back in, and the feeling of contentment, of satisfaction, was overwhelming.

For long moments, Jimmy continued to drive himself into Scott, forcing his cock into Scott's arse where it filled Scott with a pleasure that he hadn't felt in ages. Scott's cock was so stiff, so sensitive, that he was convinced that he would come if he touched it.

Jimmy started to breath heavily as his rhythm built up. He slammed his cock into Scott faster and faster, and Scott knew that he was close, very close. But so was Scott – closer than he had realised.

With a cry that seemed to come from deep inside him, Scott came. He didn't even need to touch his cock: the thick white come shot from his throbbing helmet, spraying over his chest, leaving strings of white over the thick body hair. Another cry, another spurt of come – Scott couldn't remember an orgasm anything like this before.

But it got better: with an equally loud yell, Jimmy reached his own climax, and his cock exploded in Scott's arse. As Jimmy pumped his come into Scott, Scott's orgasm not only continued but intensified, filling his entire body, consuming him with a feeling of unimaginable joy and ecstasy. Finally, the feelings subsided, ebbing away until there was nothing but a tingling, and a sense of total and utter satisfaction. Scott flopped back on to the bed as Jimmy pulled his now limp cock from his arse.

'That was . . .' Scott shook his head. 'Words can't describe it.'

Jimmy gave a wicked grin.

'You ain't seen nothing yet,' he said mischievously. 'Just you wait and see.'

And Scott knew that that was exactly what he wanted to do.

The taxi pulled up outside the apartment block. It was still very early in the morning, and there were few people around to see Nathan Dexter get out, say a few words to the taxi driver, and then make his way to the foyer of the block.

The lift reached the third floor quite quickly. Nathan got out and looked for the apartment that Phil had told him about. Good old Mr Diamond: nothing happened on the Canarian gay scene that Phil couldn't find out about. Not even mysterious travellers from London with large amounts of money, renting apartments in the finest apartment block in Playa del Ingles.

Finding the door he wanted, Nathan rang the bell and waited. It was possibly the longest wait of his entire life. From this moment on, nothing would ever be the same again.

He tensed as he heard the bolt being drawn. Suddenly, the door was open, and he was finally face to face with the one person who had consumed so much of his life in the last year.

Adrian Delancey, once Comptroller of the Elective, now mastermind of the shadowy Syndicate.

To his credit, the shock on Delancey's face lasted only a fraction of a second before he regained his composure and broke into a warm, insincere smile.

'Nathan! Do come in. I should have expected you,' he said, almost as if he were greeting an old friend, rather than someone who had sworn to bring him down. He turned his back on Nathan and walked into the apartment. Nathan followed, impressed by the décor – the apartment was as luxurious as the one that he was staying in. Another indication that the Syndicate was as well off as the Elective.

Nathan entered the lounge, with its thick cream carpet, leather sofa and well-stocked drinks cabinet. 'Didn't your pet accountant warn you?' he asked sarcastically.

Delancey was at the drinks cabinet, holding a bottle of Jameson's. There was a pause. Then: 'Ian? He did say something about you changing the appointment time. But I told him, if Nathan Dexter wants to see you at the crack of dawn, he must have a very good reason for it. Drink?'

Nathan shook his head. It would have choked him. 'I did have a very good reason. This.' He threw the briefcase at Delancey, who expertly caught it. 'There you go: the Director's Codes.'

This time, the shock was clear on Delancey's face. 'What?'

Nathan allowed himself to relish the expression on his arch-enemy's face. 'The Director's Codes. It's what you wanted, isn't it? Well, there you go. There they are.'

'I don't understand,' said Delancey, pouring himself a large whiskey. 'You *work* for the Elective. I know you're not stupid – I know you know what these codes would do in the wrong hands.'

'Such as yours? Of course I do. With those names and addresses, you can use the Syndicate to cripple the financial backbone of the Elective. Eventually, you can destroy it. That's what you want, isn't it?'

Delancey shook his head, obviously unable to understand. 'I'm sorry, Nathan – you've lost me. Why do *you* want to destroy the Elective?'

'It's corrupt. At least your Syndicate is quite honest about its intentions – it exists to make money. The Elective claims to exist to help gay people, but I've seen precious little sign of that since I became a part of it. All I've seen is excess, sybaritic luxury, everything on tap for those at the top of the hierarchy. The corruption didn't end with you, Delancey, it started with you and then carried on all the way to the top. I've figured out what happened, you know. And I will have that drink after all.'

'So, what have you figured out?' asked Delancey as he poured Nathan's drink. 'Enlighten me.' He handed the tumbler to Nathan.

'The Director was in on your slave trade, wasn't he? When it all blew up in your face, he had to publicly disassociate himself from you to save himself, and the best way of doing that was by pretending to punish you.' Nathan was on a roll now, confronting Delancey with the evidence that he had amassed, showing the erstwhile Comptroller that he had met his match. 'You had to take the blame, didn't you? So you needed revenge – hence the Syndicate.' Nathan sipped at his drink. 'You want to bring the whole thing crashing down, don't you?'

Delancey smiled. 'Clever boy. Kirk meant what he said, you know: there's a job in the Syndicate for you. All you have to do is ask.'

'Leave Kirk out of this, Delancey,' said Nathan coldly. 'I'm helping you, but that doesn't mean I like you.'

Adrian smiled his predatory smile. 'Of all the adversaries that I've had over the years, you've been the most worthy. I always wanted you on my side.' He raised his glass. 'Cheers, Nathan. I can assure you that you won't regret this.'

Nathan downed his whiskey in one gulp. What was it he had said to Kirk? When you sup with the devil, you need a long spoon. He felt physically ill: the sooner all of this was behind him, the sooner he was back with Scott, the better. But there were still questions, gaps in his story that he needed to fill. And there was no better time than now, was there?

'There's just one thing that puzzles me. If you and Ian are such good friends – Marco and I saw you last night in the Yumbo Centre – why couldn't he just give you the Codes?'

'Ah – there you betray your lack of knowledge concerning the Elective,' Delancey said smugly. 'Ian could never have released them by himself, unless the Director was dead – and sadly he isn't.' Delancey gave a bitter sneer. 'They needed the Director's release code to allow him to take them from the vault in Gran Canaria, and the briefcase needed your code to open it. Your code was sent here by the one part of the Elective network that I haven't been able to crack yet.'

Nathan frowned. 'What about Andrew Burroughs? I'd assumed that he was on your payroll now.' If only he knew whether Scott and Mike had been successful on their trip to Manchester.

'He is now,' Delancey replied. 'But not soon enough for me to take advantage of him. I needed you to enter the code – and I see you have.'

'It's all yours, Adrian,' he said, using his Christian name for the first – and hopefully last – time.

'And what do you want me to do with it?'

Nathan's voice was emotionless as he answered. 'Do what you damned well like.'

Delancey gave Nathan a respectful nod. 'Be assured that I will, Nathan. And thank you – don't forget the job offer.'

Nathan didn't say another word. He walked out of the apartment, leaving behind the schemes and machinations of Adrian Delancey, leaving behind the Elective.

For ever.

The taxi reached the airport in record time, the driver living up to the reputation of all Spanish taxi drivers. The Canarian countryside flashed past as the car sped along the motorway to

Las Palmas, but Nathan saw none of it. All he could think of was that he was free. Free of the Elective, free of his vendetta against Adrian Delancey. They could destroy themselves for all he cared: and he hoped to God that they would.

Nathan had decided not to bother going back to the apartment: everything that he'd brought with him had belonged to Marco, and somehow he doubted that Marco would appreciate what Nathan had done.

But eventually he would; eventually he would realise that Nathan had done the only thing possible.

He had set them all free.

And, as the taxi drew into the airport, Nathan knew that that was all that mattered.

Scott glanced at his watch, and was shocked to see how late it was. Fair enough, he and Jimmy hadn't gone to sleep until it had been nearly dawn, but it was almost midday. Scott had a lot of things to do, but sitting in Jimmy's flat in Vauxhall drinking coffee wasn't one of them.

Not yet.

He stood up. 'I'm going to have to go, I'm afraid.'

Jimmy pouted. 'That's a shame.' He pulled Scott over to him and gave him a hug. 'Perhaps you'll stay longer next time?'

Next time? This was supposed to have been a one night stand. But Scott knew that the decision was out of his hands. He had known that the moment he had agreed to go back with Jimmy.

The future was no longer Nathan, the Elective, and those empty nights while Nathan flew across the world sorting out everyone else's problems while neglecting his own.

The future was now Scott's. Scott's to shape as he wanted.

Whether that future included Jimmy or not was still to be decided. All he did know was that it didn't include Nathan.

★

The plane began its descent into Gatwick. Nathan stared out of the window, watching the English countryside beneath them, but saw nothing. His mind was elsewhere, trying to weigh up what he was going to do now.

It was obvious that he would have to lie low for a while. The Elective wouldn't take kindly to what he had done, and he felt certain that even if they didn't put two and two together immediately and work out that he had given Delancey the codes, it wouldn't be long before the finger of suspicion pointed in his direction.

But that didn't matter. All that mattered was that he and Scott were now free to get on with their lives, free of the Elective's control. And that freedom was worth any risk.

'You look happy,' said James, dragging a large suitcase out of the bedroom. Their flight back to London took off in a couple of hours, and James had to confess that he would have liked to have seen a bit more of Gran Canaria. Oh well: he was sure that his master would bring him back here one day. James had been a good little slave for his master, doing everything that he asked him to do, including sorting out a courier to send that little package back to Britain.

Delancey grinned, a satisfied smile that James hadn't seen before. His master was definitely pleased with himself.

'Happy?' said Delancey. 'Happy doesn't even come close, James.' He nodded towards the briefcase on the sofa. 'I've won. From this point on, the Elective is no more. *I* am the future.'

James dropped the suitcase next to the others and repressed a frown. Sometimes his master frightened him.

But he was James's master. And that was all that counted.

Nathan got out of the taxi and walked up the driveway to his house, feeling oddly invigorated. He couldn't wait to see Scott's face when he told him that it was all over. But he felt sure that he would be pleased: Nathan couldn't wait to take him in his arms, hug him, undress him, suck his big cock and taste his spunk in his mouth. He wanted everything to be back to normal, back to how it had been when they had first met.

And now there was no reason why it shouldn't be.

Opening the door, he stepped into his house . . . and was immediately struck by a feeling that something just wasn't right. There was a sense of wrongness about the place, as if something was missing . . . He looked around, but couldn't see anything. It was just an instinctive thing, a gut feeling. But what was it?

'Nathan?'

Nathan turned to see Scott standing behind him. Holding a suitcase. Nathan frowned. 'Going somewhere?' That was his first thought: Scott had decided to take himself off on holiday. Nathan was always rushing off, so why shouldn't Scott? Still, it didn't matter now. They could go together.

'I'm leaving,' Scott said baldly.

'I can see that . . .' Then Nathan realised what Scott meant, could see the expression on his face. 'Leaving? Leaving here? Leaving *me*?'

Scott nodded. 'I'm sorry, but I need to get a life back.' The words were quiet, but the force behind them hit Nathan in the stomach like a pile-driver.

'Don't go,' he said softly. 'Not now. Please.'

Scott shrugged, tears in his eyes. 'I'm sorry,' he repeated. 'But I have to go, Nathan. Please don't try to stop me.'

Nathan shook his head, his own eyes moist. This just couldn't be happening! But no, he wouldn't stop Scott. Perhaps when Scott calmed down, they could talk about it, sort it out.

Who was he kidding? For too long, Nathan had been ignoring his instincts, and look where that had got him. Kirk, Delancey . . . all of them able to get one over on him because he had ignored his famous journalistic instinct.

This time he knew that Scott meant it: when he walked out

of that door, that would be it. He would never walk through it again.

'Goodbye, Nathan. Thanks for . . . well, thanks for coming into my life.' With that, Scott walked out of the house and out of Nathan's life.

Nathan sank to the floor, trying to take it all in. Was this the freedom that his betrayal of the Elective had bought? The freedom to be alone?

Then he noticed a package on the floor in front of him. It had been couriered here, according to the sticker on the jiffy bag, but there were no other clues as to its origin. Puzzled, he opened it, only to be even more mystified. There was no note, nothing. Nothing apart from a video cassette.

A few moments later, Nathan had shoved the tape into the VCR, intrigued as to what was so important that it had to be couriered to him.

'Good afternoon, Nathan. I hope you had a pleasant flight back to Britain.'

There was no mistaking the person on the tape. There, on the TV, was Adrian Delancey, sitting in what appeared to be the apartment in Gran Canaria. What the hell was all this about?

'I just wanted to thank you for helping me. Oh – and to explain a couple of points that I might have forgotten to mention when you were so kind to drop in this morning.'

Nathan had a sudden sinking feeling in the pit of his stomach. His instincts again, telling him that there was something terribly, terribly wrong. Delancey continued.

'While I have the greatest regard for your deductive skills, I'm afraid that you've been slightly misled.

'True, I have no love for the esteemed Director of the Elective – but simply because he was in my way. The slave trade was just the first stage of a plan that would have culminated in my assuming the mantle of power in the Elective. But thanks to you, that Australian deputy of mine, and the Director, my plans were cut short. Thankfully I had a backup plan, but you've all been a most unwelcome inconvenience.

'The Syndicate is the future, Nathan. The Elective, with its outdated ideals and morals, has no place in the world we are forging.

'And, thanks to you, I now have the means to control the Elective. Those Codes will ensure the Elective's submission.' He gave an evil smile. 'Its submission – or its destruction.' With that, he reached forward, presumably to switch off the camcorder, before suddenly stopping.

'Oh, and Nathan . . . I'm not a selfish man. I shall make sure that the Elective is fully aware of the debt of thanks that I owe you. Goodbye, my friend.' The screen faded into interference.

For long seconds, Nathan just sat there, watching the squirming patterns on the screen, trying to figure out the situation that he had unwittingly stumbled into.

What have I done? he asked himself. *I've lost everything: Scott, Marco's friendship, the Elective . . . everything. What the hell am I going to do now?*

Because how unwitting had he actually been? He had made the decision to destroy the Elective, trusting his instincts. Instincts which, for once, had proved to be completely wrong. Far from defeating Adrian Delancey, he had handed him the means of destroying the only organisation which could have stood a chance of standing against him.

The fight drained from him, Nathan stood up and walked over to the back window, and stared out at his garden, still dead from winter, dreary in the dim February light. In a month or two, though, it would all start growing again, it would all come back . . .

As would he.

A steely determination began to resolve within him, as he realised that wallowing in defeat was exactly what Adrian Delancey wanted. Okay, so things looked bad for Nathan –

PAUL C. ALEXANDER

very bad. But Nathan wasn't without resources of his own.
Brave and fearless Nathan Dexter would fight back.

And this time he would win.

Up till now, he had stayed on this side of a very thin
dividing line between what was right and what was wrong.
But now there was no doubt in his mind. The only way to
fight back was to stop Adrian Delancey once and for all, and if
that meant breaking the final moral restraint – then so be it.

Epilogue

Nathan sipped his beer, not sure whether it was his fifth or sixth pint. He didn't care: nothing really mattered any more. Not now.

The Royal Enclosure of the Brave Trader was quiet that evening – the only other person there was Little John, savouring his bottle of Becks. But Nathan wasn't in the mood for conversation. All he wanted to do was to sit there and let the beer take effect, let it wash the memories away.

It wasn't working.

'How are you doing?' came a familiar voice. Nathan looked up to see Mike Bury standing there, a look of concern on his face.

'How do you think?' he snapped, before taking a deep drink from his pint. 'I fuck everything up, let that bastard beat me, and lose my boyfriend into the bargain. I feel absolutely ecstatic.' And very very sorry for yourself, came the chiding inner voice. Get a grip on yourself. Nathan knew that it was good advice, but he simply refused to accept it. All he wanted to do was to wallow. Wallow and drink.

Mike pulled up a stool, and Nathan watched him as he did

so. The similarities between Mike and his late twin brother were fading with time: Mike's hair was a slightly different colour and style; he had a full beard of stubble, rather than John's goatee; his smile was easier, less forced . . . All in all, he was better looking than his brother. But now wasn't the time for things like that. Now was a time to get away, to run . . . Even if it meant escaping through the bottom of a bottle for an evening.

'I got a phone call from Leigh,' Mike said quietly. 'Marco's back in the country.'

Nathan raised an eyebrow. 'Let me guess – he's not very happy.'

'That's putting it mildly,' said Mike, shrugging. 'He wants to see you.' He looked at his watch. 'I reckon you've got about ten minutes before he turns up here.'

'Who sent you?' said Nathan. Mike couldn't be doing this out of the goodness of his heart, warning Nathan purely because it was the right thing to do. Nobody did anything out of the goodness of their hearts any more – another lesson learnt the hard way. 'Was it Leigh?'

Mike shook his head. 'Nope. If you must know, Leigh actually told me to keep out of it. I gather he's not exactly your number one fan at the moment either.'

Nathan looked into his pint and considered his future. Fighting back at Delancey was one thing, but fighting back at people whom he had once considered to be his friends . . . This was one occasion when discretion really was the better part of valour. Draining his drink in one, he grabbed his leather jacket from under a nearby ledge and threw it on.

'I suppose I could always go to the Europa Arms.'

'Next place they're going to look.'

'Crossed Swords?' Another shake of the head.

'Haven't seen the Collective since it was refitted –'

'That's where Leigh's going. Says it's where you first met, and that it's poetic justice.'

Nathan sighed. That's the problem with being so predictable, he thought ruefully. Everyone knows where you're likely to be.

'So, have you got a better idea?' he asked.

Mike grinned, but it was almost an embarrassed grin. 'Well . . . I've got some beers in the fridge. That's if you don't mind coming all the way back to Forest Gate?' His voice was low, and Nathan guessed that he was being discreet – if a member of the Royal Enclosure overheard, Marco or Leigh would be able to track him down immediately.

Nathan laughed. 'I don't really have much choice at the moment, do I?'

'Oh, cheers,' said Mike with mock hurt, and Nathan suddenly realised what was happening. Mike was trying to pick him up!

For a moment, Nathan hesitated. Did he really want to make his life even more complicated? But he did fancy Mike, and he did need all the friends he could get at the moment . . .

'Why not?' But Nathan was well aware that eyes would be watching – eyes and mouths which could tell tales. 'I'll tell you what: I'll meet you in the Midpoint in about twenty minutes.' With that, he finished off his pint and said his goodbyes, before leaving the Brave Trader.

Mike looked at his watch: he was about ten minutes late for his rendezvous with Nathan, having been virtually forced to have a drink with Leigh and Marco before making his excuses . . . and giving Nathan an alibi.

The Midpoint was near Charing Cross, but getting there had proved to be problematic: the streets were teeming with tourists, and even his height had been insufficient to give Mike much of an advantage. He was hot and flustered when he finally reached the Midpoint and pushed open the door. Nathan was sitting in the corner with a half-empty glass of Coke in front of him.

221

Nathan stood as Mike walked over to him. 'We'd better look sharp,' he said. 'I don't normally come in here, but if they're in the neighbourhood . . .'

Mike smiled. He liked Nathan. He liked Nathan a lot. Not only did he fancy him, but there was a sense of nobility about him. Seeing him so down, so defeated, was tearing at Mike.

'Come on, then. Forest Gate awaits.'

Nathan paid for the taxi, suddenly aware that, from now on, money would be an issue. No more Lear jets, no more Elective limousines . . . From now on, he was on his own. As the taxi drove off, he stared into the night, wondering what he was going to do next, but a voice suddenly reminded him that, in the short term at least, the future was quite plainly mapped out.

'Are you going to stand there all night?' said Mike.

Following Mike into the house, Nathan momentarily wondered whether he was doing the right thing. But doing the right thing hadn't done him a whole lot of good recently, had it?

'Coffee?' Mike threw off his jacket and walked into the kitchen. As he started filling the kettle, Nathan asked about the house.

'This gay couple I know. They're hardly ever here, though, so I get the run of the whole place most of the time. Great house, though. Even got its own dungeon.'

'Dungeon?' repeated Nathan. 'Sounds . . . interesting.'

'Want to have a look while we wait for the kettle to boil?'

'Why not.' It had been a while since Nathan had seen an honest to goodness dungeon in someone's house, and he was intrigued.

Mike opened a door under the stairs and flicked the light switch. 'After you,' he said.

Nathan reached the bottom of the stairs and looked around in the dim light from the single bulb. And was impressed. The walls were unpainted brickwork, the floor was concrete. To his left was what looked like an old work bench, but it held a very different set of tools. A row of dildos lay on top, all of different sizes and textures. Four or five sets of tangled hand-cuffs were next to them, as well as a couple of little brown bottles of poppers.

But the centrepiece of the room was suspended from the ceiling: the sling.

Four thick metal chains supported the sling, bracketed to the ceiling. The sling itself was thick black leather and, as Nathan approached it, the smell was overpowering. Overpowering and erotic. Standing there in the dungeon, his senses assaulted by the smell of leather, of sweat, of sex, Nathan felt his cock begin to stir in his jeans. Suddenly, Mike's arms were around him, holding him, hugging him. Nathan felt the breath catch in his throat: he hadn't realised how alone, how helpless he had felt.

'What do you think?' whispered Mike into his ear, his hot breath on Nathan's cheek, the smell of his body making Nathan even harder.

'I wouldn't mind trying it out,' he said, almost before he'd even thought the words.

'Easily arranged.' Mike started to take Nathan's clothes off, with a gentleness that belied the urgency that Nathan felt. All he wanted was to be taken by Mike, to feel Mike inside him, feel Mike taking complete control of him. Nathan just wanted to abandon all of his responsibilities, to give it all up and let Mike be his master.

Within moments, Nathan was standing there naked, his thick cock almost vertical against his stomach. And, from Mike's smile, he obviously liked what he saw.

'Get up there,' Mike barked. 'Go on.'

Nathan didn't hesitate. From this moment on, Mike was his master. He would do exactly what Mike asked him to do – or suffer the punishment that would result. He pulled himself onto the sling and lay back on it, grabbing the support chains to steady himself. He moved his legs apart, hoping that Mike would get the message. He wanted Mike inside him, he wanted Mike's cock sliding in and out of his arse, pumping away until he filled him with his come.

Mike took off his clothes and threw them in the corner. He stood there, naked, and Nathan admired his tall, solid body. Yes, it reminded him of Mike's late brother, but he could see Mike in his own right now, as his own person. And he knew he wanted to see – and feel – much much more.

But Mike had no intention of staying naked for long. It took him about a minute to pull on the leather body harness that was lying next to the work bench, fastening the straps and tightening them so that his body was secured in studded black leather. Nathan couldn't believe how horny Mike looked, standing over him, his face hard, his expression fixed, his body constrained by the harness.

'You want me to fuck you, don't you, boy?'

Nathan nodded eagerly. Perhaps too eagerly, given Mike's response.

'I'm not going to.'

Before Nathan could be too disappointed, Mike strode over to the work bench and picked up one of the dildos. A large one.

'But *this* is.' He approached Nathan with the dildo, eight inches of black latex, and a bottle of lubricant. Without another word, he squeezed some of the white lube onto his fingers and smeared it around Nathan's ring. Nathan gasped, both with the cold of the lubricant and the sensation of Mike's fingers, touching his hole, entering his hole.

'If you can take all of this, you'll get a reward,' said Mike. 'If not, I'm going to punish you.'

Nathan felt the helmet of the dildo touch his ring, and he relaxed as much as he could. But the pain that shot through him as the latex cock began to enter him was almost too much, a burning, tearing pain that made him feel as if he was being ripped in two. But to protest, to cry out, would be to invite punishment, so Nathan gritted his teeth and tried to relax even more. Suddenly he felt the dildo brush his prostate and he groaned as the pain was blotted out by a wave of pleasure which ran through him and made him shudder.

'Good boy,' said Mike, pushing it further, harder, until Nathan knew that his whole arse was filled by Mike's dildo. He squeezed his muscles around it, forcing his prostate against it and relishing the warm, glorious feeling that overcame him.

'Now I'm going to fuck you, boy,' Mike threatened. 'Fuck you like the dog that you are.'

As good as his word, Mike withdrew the dildo before slamming it back into Nathan, making Nathan groan. Again he pulled it out, only to force it into Nathan's arse, harder and faster each time, building up a rhythm that sent wave after wave of pleasure through Nathan, pushing him further and further towards his orgasm.

Nathan desperately wanted to grab his cock and wank himself in time to the hard strokes of the dildo, but knew that that was not allowed. He would come when Mike let him come, and no sooner.

He watched as Mike fucked him with one hand and wanked himself with the other, breathing in short hard gasps, his forehead gleaming with sweat. Watching his master pleasuring both Nathan and himself was the final straw, the thing guaranteed to push Nathan to the edge. Without touching his cock, without touching himself in any way, Nathan came, his cock shooting thick white gouts of come over his stomach and chest, pools of hot come that mingled with his thick chest hair.

Seeing him there, lying on the sling, his body coated in sweat and come, obviously proved to be too much for Mike as well: with a cry of triumph, he came over Nathan, his own load mixing with Nathan's as he shot again and again.

Finally drained, Mike leant back on the work bench, a satisfied grin on his face.

'That was . . . wow,' was all he could say.

225

Nathan smiled. For one moment, everything in the world had been forgotten. It had just been him and Mike – nothing more, because they hadn't needed anything more.

Just each other.

With growing realisation, Nathan suddenly understood. He didn't need to face this on his own. He didn't need to take on Delancey without friends or allies.

Now he had one: Mike.

And together ... together there was nothing that they couldn't do.

IDOL NEW BOOKS

Also published:

THE KING'S MEN
Christian Fall

Ned Medcombe, spoilt son of an Oxfordshire landowner, has always remembered his first love: the beautiful, golden-haired Lewis. But seventeenth-century England forbids such a love and Ned is content to indulge his domineering passions with the willing members of the local community, including the submissive parish cleric. Until the Civil War changes his world, and he is forced to pursue his desires as a soldier in Cromwell's army – while his long-lost lover fights as one of the King's men.

ISBN 0 352 33207 7

THE VELVET WEB
Christopher Summerisle

The year is 1889. Daniel McGaw arrives at Calverdale, a centre of academic excellence buried deep in the English countryside. But this is like no other college. As Daniel explores, he discovers secret passages in the grounds and forbidden texts in the library. The young male students, isolated from the outside world, share a darkly bizarre brotherhood based on the most extreme forms of erotic expression. It isn't long before Daniel is initiated into the rites that bind together the youths of Calverdale in a web of desire.

ISBN 0 352 33208 5

CHAINS OF DECEIT
Paul C. Alexander

Journalist Nathan Dexter's life is turned around when he meets a young student called Scott – someone who offers him the relationship for which he's been searching. Then Nathan's best friend goes missing, and Nathan uncovers evidence that he has become the victim of a slavery ring which is rumoured to be operating out of London's leather scene. To rescue their friend and expose the perverted slave trade, Nathan and Scott must go undercover, risking detection and betrayal at every turn.

ISBN 0 352 33206 9

HALL OF MIRRORS
Robert Black

Tom Jarrett operates the Big Wheel at Gamlin's Fair. When young runaway Jason Bradley tries to rob him, events are set in motion which draw the two together in a tangled web of mutual mistrust and growing fascination. Each carries a burden of old guilt and tragic unspoken history; each is running from something. But the fair is a place of magic and mystery where normal rules don't apply, and Jason is soon on a journey of self-discovery, unbridled sexuality and growing love.

ISBN 0 352 33209 3

THE SLAVE TRADE
James Masters

Barely eighteen and innocent of the desires of men, Marc is the sole survivor of a noble British family. When his home village falls to the invading Romans, he is forced to flee for his life. He first finds sanctuary with Karl, a barbarian from far-off Germanica, whose words seem kind but whose eyes conceal a dark and brooding menace. And then they are captured by Gaius, a general in Caesar's all-conquering army, in whose camp they learn the true meaning – and pleasures – of slavery.

ISBN 0 352 33228 X

DARK RIDER
Jack Gordon

While the rulers of a remote Scottish island play bizarre games of sexual dominance with the Argentinian Angelo, his friend Robert – consumed with jealous longing for his coffee-skinned companion – assuages his desires with the willing locals.

ISBN 0 352 33243 3

CONQUISTADOR
Jeff Hunter

It is the dying days of the Aztec empire. Axaten and Quetzel are members of the Stable, servants of the Sun Prince chosen for their bravery and beauty. But it is not just an honour and a duty to join this society, it is also the ultimate sexual achievement. Until the arrival of Juan, a young Spanish conquistador, sets the men of the Stable on an adventure of bondage, lust and deception.

ISBN 0 352 33244 1

WE NEED YOUR HELP . . .

to plan the future of Idol books –

Yours are the only opinions that matter. Idol is a new and exciting venture: the first British series of books devoted to homoerotic fiction for men.

We're going to do our best to provide the sexiest, best-written books you can buy. And we'd like you to help in these early stages. Tell us what you want to read. There's a freepost address for your filled-in questionnaires, so you won't even need to buy a stamp.

THE IDOL QUESTIONNAIRE

SECTION ONE: ABOUT YOU

1.1   Sex (*we presume you are male, but just in case*)
      Are you?
      Male   ☐
      Female   ☐

1.2   **Age**
      under 21   ☐   21–30   ☐
      31–40   ☐   41–50   ☐
      51–60   ☐   over 60   ☐

1.3   At what age did you leave full-time education?
      still in education ☐   16 or younger   ☐
      17–19   ☐   20 or older   ☐

1.4   Occupation _____

1.5   Annual household income _____

1.6 We are perfectly happy for you to remain anonymous; but if you would
     like us to send you a free booklist of Idol books, please insert your name
     and address

     _____

     _____

     _____

     _____

SECTION TWO: ABOUT BUYING IDOL BOOKS

2.1 Where did you get this copy of *Code of Submission*?
     Bought at chain book shop   ☐
     Bought at independent book shop   ☐
     Bought at supermarket   ☐
     Bought at book exchange or used book shop   ☐
     I borrowed it/found it   ☐
     My partner bought it   ☐

2.2 How did you find out about Idol books?
     I saw them in a shop   ☐
     I saw them advertised in a magazine   ☐
     I read about them in _____
     Other _____

2.3 Please tick the following statements you agree with:
     I would be less embarrassed about buying Idol
     books if the cover pictures were less explicit   ☐
     I think that in general the pictures on Idol
     books are about right   ☐
     I think Idol cover pictures should be as
     explicit as possible   ☐

2.4 Would you read an Idol book in a public place – on a train for instance?
     Yes   ☐   No   ☐

SECTION THREE: ABOUT THIS IDOL BOOK

3.1 Do you think the sex content in this book is:
     Too much   ☐   About right   ☐
     Not enough   ☐

3.2 Do you think the writing style in this book is:
Too unreal/escapist ☐ About right ☐
Too down to earth ☐

3.3 Do you think the story in this book is:
Too complicated ☐ About right ☐
Too boring/simple ☐

3.4 Do you think the cover of this book is:
Too explicit ☐ About right ☐
Not explicit enough ☐

Here's a space for any other comments:

SECTION FOUR: ABOUT OTHER IDOL BOOKS

4.1 How many Idol books have you read?

4.2 If more than one, which one did you prefer?

4.3 Why?

SECTION FIVE: ABOUT YOUR IDEAL EROTIC NOVEL

We want to publish the books you want to read – so this is your chance to tell us exactly what your ideal erotic novel would be like.

5.1 Using a scale of 1 to 5 (1 = no interest at all, 5 = your ideal), please rate the following possible settings for an erotic novel:

Roman / Ancient World ☐
Medieval / barbarian / sword 'n' sorcery ☐
Renaissance / Elizabethan / Restoration ☐
Victorian / Edwardian ☐
1920s & 1930s ☐
Present day ☐
Future / Science Fiction ☐

5.2 Using the same scale of 1 to 5, please rate the following themes you may find in an erotic novel:

Bondage / fetishism ☐
Romantic love ☐
SM / corporal punishment ☐
Bisexuality ☐
Group sex ☐
Watersports ☐
Rent / sex for money ☐

5.3 Using the same scale of 1 to 5, please rate the following styles in which an erotic novel could be written:

Gritty realism, down to earth ☐
Set in real life but ignoring its more unpleasant aspects ☐
Escapist fantasy, but just about believable ☐
Complete escapism, totally unrealistic ☐

5.4 In a book that features power differentials or sexual initiation, would you prefer the writing to be from the viewpoint of the dominant / experienced or submissive / inexperienced characters:

Dominant / Experienced ☐
Submissive / Inexperienced ☐
Both ☐

5.5 We'd like to include characters close to your ideal lover. What characteristics would your ideal lover have? Tick as many as you want:

Dominant	☐	Caring	☐
Slim	☐	Rugged	☐
Extroverted	☐	Romantic	☐
Bisexual	☐	Old	☐
Working Class	☐	Intellectual	☐
Introverted	☐	Professional	☐
Submissive	☐	Pervy	☐
Cruel	☐	Ordinary	☐
Young	☐	Muscular	☐
Naïve	☐		

Anything else? _____

5.6 Is there one particular setting or subject matter that your ideal erotic novel would contain:

_____

5.7 As you'll have seen, we include safe-sex guidelines in every book. However, while our policy is always to show safe sex in stories with contemporary settings, we don't insist on safe-sex practices in stories with historical settings because it would be anachronistic. What, if anything, would you change about this policy?

_____

_____

SECTION SIX: LAST WORDS

6.1 What do you like best about Idol books?

_____

6.2 What do you most dislike about Idol books?

_____

6.3 In what way, if any, would you like to change Idol covers?

_____

6.4 Here's a space for any other comments:

_____

_____

_____

_____

Thanks for completing this questionnaire. Now either tear it out, or photocopy it, then put it in an envelope and send it to:

Idol
FREEPOST
London
W10 5BR

You don't need a stamp if you're in the UK, but you'll need one if you're posting from overseas.